VIOLENCE

VIOLENCE

Festus Iyayi

Longman

Longman Group UK Limited,
Longman House, Burnt Mill, Harlow,
Essex CM20 2JE,
England

Longman Nigeria
P.M.B. 21036,
52 Oba Akran Avenue,
Ikeja, Lagos, Nigeria

and Associated Companies and
representatives throughout the world

First published in Longman Drumbeat 1979
First published in Longman African Classics 1987
Second impression 1990

ISBN 0-582-00240-0

Produced by Longman Group (FE) Ltd
Printed in Hong Kong

DEDICATION

This book is for

Charles Odigie Iyayi
who passed to the great beyond
just before the break of dawn
leaving behind unveiled pyramids

Chapter 1

It was a Sunday morning. The rain was falling. Idemudia raised his head on his hands and looked out through the window. He was so disgusted by what he saw that he fell back on their eight-spring iron bed with a groan.

'Open the window wider so that we can hear what time it is.'

He and his wife, Adisa, were tenants in one of the low mud but zinced houses along Owode Street. Adisa, who had been sweeping the badly cemented floor of the room, dropped the broom and stretched her hand across the table which stood against the window. The window screeched on its hinges as it went wider. Adisa bent down to pick up the broom. Then she resumed her sweeping. The broom was so short that she had to stoop substantially to sweep clean.

Soon, the notes of a radiogram sounding the hour came through the window from a neighbouring building. Idemudia listened intently until the voice said, 'The time now is ten o'clock.'

He whistled. 'Ten o'clock!'

But he didn't get up from the bed. Placing his hands behind his head and staring at the roof, he listened intently to the church songs coming from the radio.

They were hymns about bloody Calvary, about the heaviness of the cross, about the strength of the spirit and the weakness of the flesh.

Adisa continued to sweep, while the skies continued to weep.

Outside, the flood built up steadily and gradually. Owode Street, like its father, Ekenwan Road, was always over-flooded any time the rain fell. Two days before, two houses had collapsed on the street. A small child had been trapped in one of the buildings under the fallen mud walls. Fortunately, rescuers, including Idemudia, had dug the child out in time. For the people who lived in the mud houses on Owode Street, there was now another major preoccupation: which house would be the next to fall?

Idemudia shook himself free of this thought. If his house fell, he knew he would lose nothing except perhaps his own life. He wouldn't lose much property. He hadn't any to lose.

He knelt down on the bed and made a short prayer to God.

'You should be praying in the church, not here,' Adisa told him icily.

'Anywhere you can pray is a church,' Idemudia flung back. 'I am hungry. I want something to eat.' He fell back on the bed with a groan. The bed shrieked.

Adisa regarded him coldly. 'When you bring the money,' she hissed, 'there will be something to eat.'

Idemudia moved to the edge of the bed and turned on his stomach. He began drawing unseen circles on the badly cemented floor.

'I want to bring in the money,' he said defensively.

'Then why don't you bring it in?' his wife demanded.

'I try hard enough,' Idemudia insisted. 'It's not my fault.'

Adisa laughed. There was scorn in her voice. 'So you try hard enough? I can see it!'

'But you see me going out each day! Do you think I go to Iyaro and First East Circular on an empty stomach for the mere fun of it?'

He frowned. He was angry.

Adisa leaned against the door. She lifted the chewing stick which had acted as a sort of wedge on her tongue away from her teeth.

Her voice was bitter now, downright sarcastic. 'You go out each day and return each day,' she said contemptuously. 'With what? Is the coming back any better than the going away? Look at me! I am getting leaner and thinner and yet when I married you God knows I was fatter ...'

Idemudia sprang up from the bed and threw her a black look. 'God knows that you were fatter than a bar of key soap,' he flashed back. 'But stop it! Stop it, or you'll regret it!'

Adisa didn't look as if she had anything she would ever regret. She laughed.

Idemudia sat on the edge of the bed, his head bent low. 'God knows I try,' he cried out. 'What else can a man do that I haven't done?'

Adisa did not answer. She continued to lean against the door, the chewing stick in one hand, the broom in the other. The sun, momentarily breaking through the rain and coming through the window, caught her face in a crossfire. Her usually fair face glowed and the sweat from the morning's sweeping glistened on her like pearls.

Her long, jet black hair was now held in place with hairpins. Her lips were dark, decided and firm. Her nose was pointed, long, like a Fulani's. Her eyes were black and deep, like the quiet water of a deep and darkly moving stream. Her breasts were big and tight as they had been many years ago. They heaved now against her chest as she stood leaning against the door, her full round lips pressed against the door's hinges, the blue curtains slightly caught back by the curving elegance of her hands. Her fair legs were long and straight with two dimples behind each knee. Now they were thrust slightly apart, her face dreamy, her sparkling eyes drinking in the dark incense of the morning sun.

Idemudia looked at her and he thought of his own mother. He remembered the last time he had seen her nearly three and a half years ago. He swallowed hard, turned his eyes away from the door, lay on his side and let himself be preoccupied with thoughts about his mother.

It had been three and a half years ago. He had been home, away from the town, frustrated and angry because there had been no job, no matter how hard he had looked for one. 'It is the work of our enemies', his mother had written. 'Come home and we will go to the native doctor.'

So he had gone home because there was nothing else he could do.

'They want a goat,' she informed him on her return. 'They want a goat, they also want a cock and a tortoise. I can provide the cock and the tortoise. Your father must provide the goat.'

'All these things will need money,' he had reminded his mother. 'A goat costs at least twenty naira and if I had had that three years ago, perhaps I could have completed my secondary school education.'

'But it's a job you want now,' his mother said, her face sad.

'Oh yes,' Idemudia replied. 'It is a job and twenty naira will help me with some people. I even had to borrow money to come here.'

'Never mind about that,' his mother consoled him. 'When you get the job, we shall pay off all our debts. We shall yet show our enemies that we are stronger. But go and meet your father. He has to get a goat ready in two days' time.'

Idemudia had smiled cynically. It wasn't easy to meet his father for anything, particularly when a cold animosity existed between father and son.

When he had been driven away from school because of school fees three years before, he had found his father uncompromising.

'I have no money,' his father had said after neglecting to return his greeting.

'But that may mean that I won't be going back to school again!' he cried, his heart nearly bursting. His father's face remained unemotional.

'I have no money,' he repeated. 'You can ask your mother to pay your fees from now on.'

Idemudia frowned. Six months earlier, his father had married a new wife, his third.

'My mother has no money,' Idemudia had told his father.

'Then you'll have to go to school and bring your box back. I have no more money. I can't pay any more school fees.'

Idemudia had gone back to his mother heartbroken and in tears.

'How can I stop going to school!' he had cried.

In the morning at about seven o'clock, they had heard a knock on the door. One of his half-brothers had gone to open it. And then there had been excited voices. Idemudia had got up from sleep to find his uncle in their parlour.

'The tax collectors and policemen are in the village,' his uncle explained. 'They are arresting anybody who has not paid his tax.'

'What shall we do?' his father asked.

Their uncle had not taken long to reply.

'I have no money,' he said bitterly. 'I am taking to the bush.'

Both his father and his uncle had then hastily departed and jumped into the bush behind their house.

Later on at about ten o'clock, the policemen and tax collectors had arrived.

'We want your father,' they demanded.

'He went to the farm a long time ago,' Idemudia replied.

The shortest and most thick-set among them, who was also the police officer, removed his glasses.

'I see,' he sniffed. 'Ran away when he heard we were coming? But we are more than prepared for all of you now. You will take us to his farm!'

Idemudia shrugged his shoulders. 'You can wait here until he returns,' he said. 'But I can't take you to any farm.'

'You can't do what?' the short and thickset policeman demanded.

'I say I can't take you to the farm. I am here and not at school because I was driven away for not paying school fees. If he had any money he would have paid my school fees.'

The short man paced about the room. Finally in a harsh voice he ordered one of his constables to seize Idemudia.

'Either you show us his farm or we will hold you surety for your father,' the man said.

An argument had immediately ensued between his mother and the tax collectors.

In those days, policemen were terrors in the villages. Nobody knew exactly what their authority was and therefore what part of it could be challenged. They acted on behalf of the government, not on behalf of the people.

And so, Idemudia had been seized. They took him to Ubiaja where he spent three nights in the cell. After the third day he was released, according to the officer, 'for want of evidence.'

And so he had returned home. But returning home

6

gave him no peace. He was surprised to find his mother's face swollen, her limbs broken and one of her teeth broken. Shocked, he immediately asked what had happened.

'It's your father,' his mother explained. 'He wanted to kill me because I asked him to go to Ubiaja so they could release you. He hit me on the face! He used my own pestle on me! He ...'

She broke down into tears ...

And so, three years later, when his mother asked him to go to his father with the request for a goat he had not been enthusiastic.

But he had gone all the same.

His father had received him coldly. 'So it's a goat she wants now,' he said.

'She doesn't want it,' he explained patiently. 'She was told to get it on my account.'

'But where do I get a goat from?' he frowned.

Idemudia kept quiet. Finally his father stood up, and readjusted his loincloth. 'I don't think I can get any goat,' he said.

'She says it is for two days' hence.'

His father walked to the door and leaned against it.

'I don't think I can get any goat,' he repeated. 'Let your mother go and find one. Later we can settle the account.'

Annoyed, Idemudia had gone back to his mother. His mother too had been annoyed.

'When it is something that concerns me or my children, he never has any money,' she complained. 'Anyway I will wait until tomorrow morning and then I am going to meet him.'

It had been six o'clock in the morning when Idemudia's sleep was rudely interrupted. He heard the hurry of feet, screams, harsh blows and more feet.

Very quickly, he got into his trousers and rushed

to the backyard, where all the noise was coming from.

There in the early morning light, he found his mother in the mud and his father pounding away at her. Her whole face was muddy and twisted with pain. She just lay there writhing and struggling, unable to fight back, unable to defend herself, helplessly taking all the brutal punishment that his father was giving her.

Idemudia had rushed up to his father. But for one blinding flash of reason, he might easily have committed patricide.

He rushed up to his father and stood between him and his mother. Surprised and angry at the sudden intrusion, his father made as if to brush him aside. But Idemudia gripped the hands of his father. There ensued a brief struggle. His father couldn't loosen his hands, try as hard as he could.

Idemudia's teeth were set. 'Don't touch her again!' he warned. 'Don't strike her again! You have already nearly killed her and this is the second time on my account. Just don't try it again!' he cried, breathing harshly.

The other doors in the compound were flung open. His father's two other wives came out. Idemudia was bitter against all of them.

'You all shut your doors when you heard him trying to kill my mother,' he accused them bitterly. 'None of you came out to stop the fight!'

He released his father's hands. 'But I am saying it now that as long as I am alive, nobody is going to kill my mother. Nobody!'

There was muted anger on his father's face like clotted black blood. 'You will pay for this!' he threatened his son. 'You will pay for this with your life!'

He had gone into the house and reappeared.

'Your mother is leaving my house at once. And she can take all her children with her. I am going out now for some time but by the time I come back, I do not want to find any of you here.'

Idemudia had bitten his lip, as he helped his mother up out of the mud. Her lower lip was cut and bleeding. On her forehead there was a long ugly gash from which blood gushed out. Her clothes were torn, her hair in complete disarray. Her eyes too were swollen.

And she was crying ... silently.

His heart was nothing but bitterness and hatred. And as he sat by his mother on the mud bed, he promised himself that if his father did come back to threaten them, then that would be the last straw.

His younger brothers and sisters crowded around, crying.

And in the compound, the two women began talking loudly in parables.

'If my child has ever spoken any harsh word to the mother of any other child, then may the rising sun with all her arrows dip for me as from now. If however my child has never spoken any rude word to the mother of any of his brothers then may this rising sun ...'

Idemudia had ignored both women.

In the late afternoon, people had begun crowding into the compound. The news had already gone round the whole village. Idemudia had known of course that while some of the women came to sympathise, others came to spite.

It was dark when his mother regained more control of her scattered emotions. And she began to pack up her things one by one.

'Darkness must not find us here,' she told her son. 'We must go. We must leave.' And she cried while her children gathered around her.

Idemudia had watched his mother gathering her things and he had sworn never to set foot in that house again. His mother had packed up and trekked the long distance to her parents in a village nearly seven miles away.

Idemudia and the rest of her children had accompanied her. They had crossed the little dark stream, the forests and the thick bushes. They had all herded together. And his mind had grown bitter. He had sworn that he would pay his father back in his own coin. And because of his mother, he had sworn never to beat his wife, never to beat a woman for that matter.

He lay on the bed now, his face to the wall and thought about his past life. Since those three years and six months, he had not been able to see his mother. He had been unable to visit her because he had no money. Adisa had been sent to him from home by his mother and she had visited home only three times. On her last visit, she had left their first and only son with his mother, because they found it increasingly difficult to take care of the child, their own child.

He had heard too about his father. He had married another wife. He wished him luck. Then only a few months ago, an urgent appeal had been sent to him to come home because his father had been on the point of death.

Idemudia had laughed bitterly. He wished his father had actually died. In the event, he didn't go home and neither did his father die. He had recovered. And yet he was his father's eldest son.

Idemudia turned on the bed. His wife was sitting on the edge of the bed now. He regarded the nape of her neck with affection. If only he had the means to make her happy, instead of beating her ... He closed his eyes. He didn't want to think about it. The only thing he could think of now was that he was hungry and that instead of understanding him, Adisa was sneering at him.

Chapter 2

Idemudia got up from the bed. And meticulously he began to search in both his pairs of trousers, for any hidden money. He found none. Next he searched the pockets of his shirts. He found nothing.

His face was serious and deadly set, forbidding. Adisa watched him with some amusement. 'You are looking for manna from heaven,' she chided him.

Idemudia did not answer her but continued to search his shorts and pants. In all these too, he had left and forgotten nothing, so he found nothing. Disappointed, he sat again on the bed beside his wife, not because he wanted to but because there was nowhere else to sit in the room, apart from the chair on which Adisa had placed a bowl.

He had to do something. His stomach churned, turning and gnawing upon itself.

Worse still, he found Adisa's attitude increasingly unbearable. He wanted understanding, not scorn, from her. He remembered that when she had come to him three years ago she had been understanding, never sneering or scornful. Why couldn't she have remained that way?

'There is no need to smile or laugh like that,' he told her now curtly.

Adisa turned her face sideways to him. In profile, her face was beautiful, her nose elegant, her eyes shining defiantly.

'How should I smile?' she demanded. 'I am hungry. You should have known that when you started talking about yourself. Or perhaps you want to beat me again!'

Idemudia did not answer her but began putting on his trousers. Next, he seized a shirt and flung it over his shoulders. Adisa who had been silently regarding him now faced him.

'Where are you off to?' she demanded.

'Out,' Idemudia answered. 'I am going out.'

Very swiftly Adisa crossed the room and stood against the door. 'You are not going anywhere,' she threatened. 'You are not leaving me here to go outside to eat in your friends' places.'

Idemudia was exasperated but he held his anger in check. He knelt down to buckle his sandals. In between he looked up at her.

'Why don't you ask what I am going out for?' he asked.

'I am asking you nothing,' Adisa flung back. 'All I know is that you are not going anywhere.'

Idemudia finished buckling his sandals and stood up. He could of course easily throw her out of the doorway, but instead he turned his back on her and looked out of the window. Even one glance outside killed his desire to go out. The whole street was immersed in flood. The sun had vanished from the morning now. The rain had increased from a little shower to a downpour. However, he had to go out. He couldn't stay indoors doing nothing. They could gain nothing simply by looking at each other. He turned back to Adisa.

'I want to go out,' he said, firmly now.

Adisa said nothing.

'I want to go out,' he repeated and took one step forward.

Adisa remained rooted to the doorway, her face set.

Idemudia took another step forward and stood face to face with his wife.

'Leave the door!' he warned her.

'I am not leaving it,' Adisa replied firmly.

'I say leave the door unless you want to cry!' Idemudia further threatened.

'Listen to him! Listen to him!' Adisa scoffed. 'Unless I want to cry! You try anything! You try anything and we shall see. Have I not cried before? What is new in tears that I have not known? You want to beat me? Then go ahead.' Her voice rose.

Idemudia seized her by the arm and dragged her into the room away from the door. Meanwhile Adisa with her free hand knotted up in her fist all the flap of Idemudia's trousers.

'You will kill me today! You will kill me today!' Adisa screamed. 'If it's my meat that you want, you will have it.'

They became locked in a fierce struggle, Idemudia trying to break her grip and she trying by all means to retain it. They panted and they sweated, struggled and cursed.

In a corner of the room the cooking pots stood empty. The kerosene was finished in the kerosene stove. There was no food in the house. And both were hungry . . .

Finally, the superior strength of Idemudia began to tell. He got Adisa in a kneeling position and with a savage jerk ripped her hand away from his trousers. But then he was infuriated and maddened when he saw the buttons and zip of his trousers coming away with her hand.

'You bastard!' he cursed. 'You fool!' And he raised his hand and struck her violently on the side of her face.

Adisa staggered sideways, dazed and then stared in hatred at him and then as he raised his hand to strike her again, she threw herself on the floor and began to scream wildly. Very slowly, the blood welled from the side of her nose and trickled down the corner of her mouth to her chin.

Idemudia stepped over her and went outside. Then he looked at his pair of trousers and again he swore loudly because he knew he couldn't go out, the way he was, with his trousers ripped open in the front. He came back into the room breathing harshly.

'You will pay for this,' he warned her. 'You will pay for this pair of trousers you have torn.' He hovered menacingly over her but seeing the blood on her face he stopped. He removed the pair of trousers he was wearing and put on another pair that was patched on its seat.

Adisa got up from the floor. 'You are not going out,' she cried. Her voice was sharp and filled with hatred. 'You are not leaving this room. If you go out, I am going out, too. I am going to find some means to feed myself.'

Idemudia looked at her and suddenly he began to laugh. 'You are going to find some means to feed yourself?'

'Yes, and why not?' Adisa replied defiantly. 'Or perhaps you think you are the only man in the world?' Her eyes shone with scorn.

'So, you are going to find another man?' Idemudia said, and flexed his muscles so hard they twitched. 'You let another man come near you and I'll kill you,' he said fiercely, and his face was contorted with his anger. 'I'll find out and I'll kill you. I'll tear that thing which you think you've got out of you and I'll throw it to the dogs outside.'

'Ha! Ha! Ha!' Adisa laughed. 'You think you will kill me? You think you will tear me apart? You will kill yourself first before you can lay hands on me.'

Idemudia regarded her and his voice was so cold and so flat and so dangerous, that Adisa took a step back, away from him, terrified.

'You heard me,' he said through clenched teeth. 'I'll find out. I'll find out, and I'll kill you. Make no mistake about it. You think you are attractive enough to use your body and you say to me things which a woman never says to her husband. But you try it and that will be your end.'

Idemudia went out of the room and crossing the common passage came to the verandah outside. The rain was still pouring and the flood outside reminded him of the deluge.

The whole vast area was flooded. Idemudia could not tell where the street was nor where the gutter was. And if he entered the water, he had no doubt that his pair of sandals would suffer.

He stood there, his arms folded across his chest and regarded the sky. It was black and wild. The rumblings of thunder and flashes of lightning coupled with the pouring rain made the sky forbidding, unfriendly.

But he had to go out, he had to go and borrow some money, if only one naira so that he and his wife could eat! If only one naira! But who would lend him the money? He didn't know. Friends were few indeed. Nobody would lend him money knowing full well that he hadn't the means to pay back.

He became weak from the pain of thinking. He had been standing, leaning against the wall. Now he sat down on the wooden bench that was outside, his head thrown back against the wall. From that position he became vaguely aware of his surroundings. He caught glimpses of the taxis wading in the water, of the private cars, some of them big Citroen and Mercedes Benz cars also slushing past in the water. There were no pedestrians. The flood and the sky were so forbidding.

He was perspiring and sweating profusely now. Where was he to go? The wind howled, the rains poured, the lightning flashed and the thunder rumbled and grumbled. Idemudia sat on that bench, his head thrown back, trying to devise a means of feeding Adisa and himself. As always, he hated himself for having beaten her. Why did he have to beat her as his father

16

had always beaten his mother? Why couldn't he re-
strain himself? But surely what Adisa had said to him
was unpardonable? How could she threaten him the
way she had done? That she would go to another man?
He would kill her if she did it. He would strangle her,
he would tear her apart ... I mustn't think about it,
he said to himself. I should think about the food. Food
and money. Money! Money. Christ, money!

He struggled up from the bench, unsteadily. It was,
he realised, wishful, sitting on that bench, just thinking. He had to go out into the rain.

Just as he was about to go into the rain, a Mercedes
Benz car coming from Owode Street skidded off the
flooded street and ran into the gutter. Idemudia
watched the car trying to get off. The engine only
made more noise. The hand of a woman lowered the
window and beckoned to Idemudia.

Idemudia hesitated. He was angry. 'When they are
in trouble, they remember us,' he thought bitterly.

However, he entered the pouring rain and went towards the car. He went over to the driver of the car,
a large black man in a lace *agbada.*

'Put the car in reverse,' Idemudia told him and went
to the front of the car so as to push it from there.

Then he applied all the strength left in his weak,
hungry body. The car wouldn't move. Idemudia came
back to the man in the lace agbada.

'Put the car in first gear,' he suggested.

Again the man complied. Idemudia went behind the
car and began to push. The man revved up the engine.
It whined and croaked loudly. Then it slid forward
slowly and then it spurted forward with such a sudden
force that both the flood and the mud were sent flying.
Idemudia was propelled forward by the onward rush
of the car and with great difficulty he regained his
balance.

17

A few yards away, the car stopped. The woman again beckoned to Idemudia.

'Thank you very much,' she said. 'My name is Queen and my husband owns the Freedom Motel. We are looking for people to help us unload some cement.'

Idemudia thought for a while. 'How many people?' he asked.

'About three or four people,' the woman answered, fiddling with the purse on her lap.

'How soon do you want them, madam?' Idemudia asked, immediately realising that here was his chance to earn some money.

'Well, as soon as I come back, say in thirty minutes' time. There are about five hundred bags of cement and the rain might spoil them.'

'I'll get the people before you come back,' Idemudia promised and tried to wipe away the trickle of water running down his nose from his hair. He was thoroughly soaked.

'I hope you know the Freedom Motel,' the woman said.

'Oh yes, madam, I do,' Idemudia replied and stepped back as the car began to draw away.

Nearly an hour later, Idemudia and three other friends of his stood at the entrance of the Freedom Motel. Two hefty waiters were busy emptying unfinished meals into the large dustbin.

'What do they do with that?' Osaro asked.

'I think they sell it to the poultries and also to pig farms,' Patrick answered.

As Idemudia watched the unfinished jollof rice, *dodo*, meat and beans being emptied into the dustbin, the sweat broke out on his forehead. Very quickly, he turned his eyes away, biting his lips sharply.

The three big trailers filled with cement bags and covered with large tarpaulin sheets stood outside the motel, away from the entrance.

'Where do we empty the cement into?' Omoifo asked.

'The woman said she was coming to show us the place,' Idemudia answered, looking at the wet ground.

One of the two waiters who had been emptying the food into the dustbin called to them from the shelter of the verandah of the motel.

'The cement bags are to go into that shed there,' he pointed.

'Where?' Idemudia asked, looking closely at the man and noticing that the waiter was fat and plump, unlike himself, nor any of his friends.

The waiter pointed again. 'I heard madam discussing it.'

'We should wait,' Osaro pointed out.

'We will,' Patrick agreed.

'And by the way,' Omoifo asked, 'Has the woman told you how much she is going to pay?'

Idemudia shook his head. 'She only said she needed three or four people immediately and I ran to call you.'

'You should have asked her how much she was going to pay.'

'I had no time.'

'Anyway it makes no difference,' Omoifo said.

The four men herded themselves together under the little shed meant for the security guards. There, the rain drove at them only from the side, their heads were protected.

They stood there silently and waited, each man thinking his own thoughts. Idemudia wondered again about what Adisa had said to him. His mind felt like ice as he remembered her words. How could she have uttered those words? He shook his head. He didn't know.

'So the pigs and hens are going to eat all that,' Osaro hissed.

Patrick laughed. 'I thought you had forgotten about that dustbin.'

Osaro's face was serious and his voice was bitter. 'How can I forget?' he asked. 'I am hungry. I haven't eaten since morning.'

'I have had nothing to eat too,' Idemudia said, and tried to forget Adisa.

'It's so unfair,' Osaro added. 'One man has enough to eat, in fact so much that he throws some away. Yet here we are, hungry, with nothing to eat.'

'Well, all fingers are not equal. Everything is God's work,' Patrick said.

'*Kai*, it's not God's work, it's man-made,' Omoifo disagreed.

Their conversation was broken up by the arrival of Queen. This time she came back in a Peugeot 504 car, and as soon as the car rolled up to the gates, a girl came out of the Freedom Motel, and ran towards the car with an umbrella.

'The rain is terrible,' Queen said to the girl, taking the umbrella from her.

'Yes, Ma,' the girl said and then she darted away to the Freedom Motel.

Queen came to the shed and seeing Idemudia she stopped.

'I see you are here,' she said and pointed to the three big long trailers. 'That's where the cement is. I want the bags taken to the shed over there.'

Idemudia followed her pointing fingers.

'But the rain might spoil the cement, madam,' Patrick said.

Queen wanted to cut the conversation short at all costs. Her brocade dress was gradually being marked by the rain.

'I know,' she said. 'But the trailers have to start going back to Lagos this evening.'

'And you said there were only five hundred bags of cement,' Idemudia reminded her.

Queen laughed. 'I meant in each trailer.'

'Then how much are you going to pay us?' Osaro asked.

'Two naira each.'

Omoifo whistled. 'Two naira to offload fifteen hundred bags of cement! No. No, madam.'

'Then how much do you want?'

'At least ten naira each,' Patrick said.

Queen stared at Patrick and drew up her black leather handbag. 'I'll pay you five naira each, nothing more. If you don't want it, you can go away,' and she began to walk away.

Idemudia and his friends stood in the rain while they debated whether or not to accept the five naira. In the end they decided they were going to and moved with one accord to the nearest trailer.

Chapter 3

At the éntrance to the motel, Queen waited and watched as the four men debated whether or not to accept her terms. If they refused, she would obviously have to offer them more than five naira each. Then she saw them going towards the trailer. Satisfied, she went into the motel and sought out her husband. One of the waiters informed her that Obofun had not yet returned from the City. Annoyed, she climbed the stairs to their living room. It was a luxurious place and she sank into a large sofa. Then she removed her headtie. The wig came away with the headtie. She set it on a stool near her and called for Richard.

Richard was the houseboy upstairs and he had been with them for many years. Richard came to the sitting room, barefoot. He always had to leave his slippers at the entrance to the sitting room. He kept the house, he cleaned the rug in the sitting room, cleaned the other rooms and washed the floors. Richard was approaching thirty now and he was unmarried.

'I want some whisky,' Queen told him. 'Bring the bottle and a glass.'

Richard went out and came back with the whisky and glass. Queen removed the headtie and the wig from the stool and placed them near her on the sofa so that Richard could set the drink and glass in their place.

Richard did so and was about to go out when Queen stopped him. 'Where is Lilian?' she asked.

Richard put his hands meekly by his sides. 'I do not know, madam,' he said.

'When did she go out?'

'I don't know, madam.'

'Okay, you can go,' Queen said dismissing him. But she wondered where Lilian could have gone. Lilian was one of her three daughters. She was a day student at Ideha College.

Queen poured out the drink for herself. She had managed to get this cement from the factory, and cement now cost upwards of six naira per bag. When six naira was multiplied by one thousand five hundred, the figure was staggering. Just to think! The things a woman could do!

She already owned two modern storey buildings in New Benin. One of the houses she had let out to the University at nine thousand naira a year and the University had paid rent for two years in advance. The things a woman could do!

For Queen had a pair of neat legs, long and straight. Her backside was a landslide, her breasts heaved like a bunch of ripe oranges on an overweighted branch. Her oval face ended in a small chin, her shifty eyes were half concealed by bushy and jet black eyelashes. Queen had a husky voice, as if she suffered from a sore throat.

But men forgot about her voice when they looked at her hips, the neat pair of legs, the breasts heaving to go, the ... Queen was a woman to look at and once looked at, never easily forgotten.

At the moment when her husband was trying to expand the Freedom Motel, she was setting up her own hotel along Sakpoba Road. Also, she was building another house at Ugbowo. She had been reliably informed that the future of the city lay there and she was determined to get a foothold there before it became too late.

Queen sipped her whisky and thought about that house at Ugbowo. The contractor building the house was a thief, she decided. How else could a four-bedroom house cost twenty thousand naira?

The contractor had spoken dejectedly about the cost of building materials.

'It's gone up fourfold,' he had informed Queen.

Queen had thought for some time and then told the man, 'I can't pay as much as twenty thousand naira! I think we can modify the original design. We can remove the second staircase that ought to be outside.'

The man had shaken his head adamantly. 'In that case we must get the approval of the government.'

Queen had been annoyed. 'Who is the government?' she had cried angrily. 'The government is made up of people, and every man in this country has a price.'

The contractor had shrugged his shoulders. 'Okay,' he had conceded. 'The second staircase goes but that doesn't reduce any costs. At most it knocks off a few hundred naira.'

Queen was annoyed now as she remembered the conversation. 'The bastard!' she cursed.

Of course she had gone to another contractor. After looking at the design, the man had quoted twenty-five thousand naira.

She had there and then decided that she would build all her houses herself in the future. The more she had thought about it, the more strongly the idea had appealed to her, and when she finally won the contract to build low-cost houses for the government, her mind was made up. She registered her company as Queens Nig. Ltd. and employed an engineer. This engineer was now supervising the building of the low-cost houses although she had left the building of her own house to the first contractor. There wasn't much she was losing anyway. After all, the money she was using to build the house came from the mobilisation fee she had been paid on the low-cost houses.

She stood up and took the glass of whisky with her

to the balcony. She wanted to see how the men were offloading the cement. She noticed that the rain had abated a little.

She could also see the men carrying the bags of cement to the shed inside the compound. In about three or four hours she guessed that the offloading would be completed. She would then be paying them twenty naira! She licked her lips and smiled. But then she knew that had it not been for the rain and the fact that the trailers had to go back that same night for more cement, she would have paid still less for unloading all the bags of cement. She saw Idemudia carry a bag of cement on his back and then move towards the shed. Surely, she thought, it should be possible to make use of that man more often. Instead of going to Iyaro or to First East Circular and be mobbed by those dirty struggling labourers, she could always tell Idemudia that she needed so many men and Idemudia could always help her out.

'Mummy!'

Queen turned round to see Lilian standing in the doorway.

'Where have you been?' she demanded of her daughter.

Lilian held a notebook under her arm. 'I went out to copy some exercises with my friends,' she defended herself and brandished the notebook as an exhibit.

Queen turned back to the balcony.

'There are some men downstairs,' Lilian told her mother.

Queen turned round again, 'Yes?'

'They want to see you.'

'Who are they?'

Lilian shook her head. 'I don't know them.'

'Has Esie come back?'

'I don't know, Ma.'

Esie was Queen's second son. He also attended a school in the city and was in Form Four. He had been a boarder but after persistently warning him for fighting, the principal of the school had finally decided that Esie must become a day student. Obofun had gone to the principal to contest the decision but after being shown the file on his son, he had returned home with a stern warning for Esie. However, he made sure that one of his drivers took Esie and Lilian to and from school each day.

Queen followed her daughter into the sitting room. 'Tell Richard to take that bottle out of here,' she said to her daughter, handing her at the same time the glass of whisky which she had already emptied.

Lilian took the glass while her mother went down stairs. But Lilian didn't call Richard to take the bottle of whisky away. She took the bottle herself and went into her mother's bedroom. Once inside the room, she unscrewed the cork of the bottle and poured herself a drink. Instead of sipping the drink, she tossed the whole glassful down her throat. The whisky was so harsh on her throat and so hot in her chest as it travelled down that she began to cough violently. Her eyes filled with tears.

There were many people in the large modern restaurant. The music was playing and it was mellow. People were eating and drinking and so the forks clattered, and the conversation was muted by the food and the drink.

At the far corner of the restaurant, two men sat over a large bottle of whisky. Both of them wore French suits.

'That's her coming,' whispered the man in the blue French suit. The other man turned round automatically,

'She is a beautiful woman,' admitted Dala, the second man, whose suit was grey.

Iriso, the first man, agreed immediately. 'Very sexy!'

Dala lightly slapped the other man on the back. 'Aren't you ashamed to say that about another man's wife?'

'Why should I be?' the other man immediately countered.

'Hm,' Dala breathed. 'You should be careful. It is rumoured that Obofun doesn''t care but he may not like such hot passes at his wife, right under his nose and in his own house.'

Iriso laughed. 'You just watch. I told you I came here for business. You just watch.'

Iriso was the superintenent of the Food Production Department in the Ministry of Agriculture. He had promised Queen quite a lot. She could have meat, eggs, milk, fish and so many other things. But they hadn't agreed on price.

After seeking them out and recognising them, Queen came and sat by them.

'Well?' she asked instead of greeting them, the whisky heavy on her breath.

Dala and Iriso exchanged quick glances. Queen noticed the exchange and was irritated.

'Is anything wrong?' she demanded.

Iriso laughed to cover up some of his embarrassment. For an answer, he patted Queen's outstretched long fingers on the table. Queen withdrew her fingers as a snail is withdrawn into its shell.

'I promised you I would find out,' he said. 'And I did. You can have anything you want.'

The irritation immediately vanished from Queen's voice. She was setting up a hotel of her own along Sakpoba Road. It was almost ready but she hadn't started using it. She wanted to be sure that the materials and customers would come in steadily before she officially opened the hotel. And on the material side, Iriso was of tremendous importance.

'That's very good,' Queen said lightheartedly. 'Very, very good indeed. I am so happy to hear that.'

Iriso coughed. He was coming to the difficult and the most important part of the bargain.

'It's risky,' he said carefully.

Queen looked sharply at him. The corners of her lips were dipped in the fountain of a smile. 'There is nothing that isn't risky,' she replied. 'Even sitting here is.'

Iriso laughed. 'There are different kinds of risks,' he reminded her.

Queen had an answer ready. 'I am going to pay you,' she said.

Iriso's laughter diminished to a smile. 'How much?' he asked.

'Oh well,' Queen replied, 'I haven't seen anything yet. But it will all depend on you.'

Iriso frowned. How could it depend on him? 'How?' he asked.

Queen looked sideways and significantly at Dala. 'We can go upstairs to the sitting room and discuss it,' she suggested. 'Your friend can wait for us here.'

Iriso pinched Dala on the shoulder. 'I won't be long,' he promised, and walked after Queen who was already half-way across the hall.

Dala was left alone to his thoughts. He decided it would be better thinking with a bottle of beer, instead of all the whisky he had been drinking, so he ordered a bottle of beer. And yet when they brought it, he left it untouched. He remembered that drinking the beer after the whisky might not help his thinking in the long run. If anything, he could get a headache as a prize. So he concentrated on the whisky.

Five minutes passed, then it was ten. Still Iriso did not return. He was irritated and would have gone home but it was still raining and Iriso had the keys to the car. So he waited, impatiently tapping his feet on the floor and gulping down the whisky. 'What are they haggling about?' he thought darkly.

After almost fifteen minutes had gone by and Iriso still did not emerge, Dala saw Obofun himself crossing the hall of the restaurant. Dala knew Obofun very well. At one time they had both worked in the Ministry of Works and Transport. Then it was rumoured that Obofun had been loaned some money by the Ministry with which to build a personal house. According to the rumour Obofun had built the house but instead of living in it, had let it back to the Ministry at an extraordinarily high price. Some put the figure at twenty thousand naira a year. Obofun, who neither confirmed nor condemned the rumours, soon moved over to the Ministry of Lands and Housing. That was many years ago. Dala waved to Obofun now. 'How are you?' he called.

Instead of answering, Obofun walked to Dala's table and shook hands with him warmly. 'Honestly, Dala! I can't imagine you drinking alone!' he said, surprised.

Dala laughed. 'Ah Obofun! Why can't you imagine that a man can be alone once in a while?'

Obofun roared with laughter. 'Of course I can. I can. Why not? Only not men like you. You have never been alone, at least as far as I can remember.'

He was going to offer Dala a drink on the motel when he noticed a large bottle of whisky, still one quarter full.

'Well, how is the work?' he asked.

Dala spread out his hands on the table. 'It's bad,' he complained. 'Nothing ever goes well except in the private sector.'

Obofun immediately disagreed. 'It can't be true!'

'Then why did you quit?' Dala asked.

Obofun smiled, 'Because you stayed on,' he said, and both men laughed.

'Actually I did have company,' Dala now admitted. 'Only he is a man and not a woman.'

Obofun immediately seized upon this. 'Then I wasn't wrong,' he said. 'Dala never goes alone. Have a drink on the house any time you want,' he offered. 'I'll inform the waiters.'

Dala thanked him. And then Obofun moved to another table where two women and one man were sitting, before finally disappearing from the restaurant. Dala stared nervously at his wristwatch. At least twenty minutes had passed. He waited another five minutes before Iriso appeared. But to Dala, those last five minutes and the whole period of waiting seemed an eternity. He couldn't keep the anger out of his voice or his face.

'What have you been doing?' he asked angrily.

'I am very sorry,' Iriso apologised.

Dala was not satisfied. He had already emptied the one quarter contents left in the whisky bottle and now he stood up, swaying lightly. He had made up his mind that he would always go in his own car any time he went out in the future.

Iriso sensed that Dala was angry. So he said,. 'It wasn't my fault. I wanted to leave earlier. I kept reminding her that you were waiting.'

Dala did not answer but walked unsteadily across the restaurant to the exit. The rain was still pouring and by the time they got to Iriso's car, both men were wet.

'She is a cunning devil,' Iriso said as he started the car.

Dala made no reply but inwardly grumbled deeply. Both his reason and the alcohol struggled inside him. Dala was used to consuming large quantities of liquor. But today he was unbalanced emotionally and that made a difference.

'I thought we were going to her sitting-room as she had said, but she led me straight to her bedroom!' said Iriso.

At this Dala was stirred. He became interested although he also felt some jealousy. 'Then what happened?' he asked.

Iriso wore a subdued look on his face. 'I am in trouble,' he complained. 'We went into her bedroom and she started telling me that she would want a regular supply of peak milk, beef, eggs and other things. I told her there was nothing wrong with that except that she had to pay for it. She said nothing for a long time. As I told you I have met her quite a few times before and it was also through her husband. But this time I was quite unprepared for what happened.'

Iriso blasted his horn at a taxi which suddenly appeared in front from nowhere on the major road. He cursed and turned his headlamps full on the taxi.

Dala waited for him to continue. Iriso, however, took his silence for drunkenness.

'Are you asleep?' he asked.

Dala lifted his head from the seat. 'Of course not,' he replied. 'I am listening.'

Iriso took a piece of cloth and wiped the front glass to clear it of the mist. Then, sitting back more contentedly behind the steering wheel, he continued his narrative.

'Well, I didn't tell you but they have a door which leads directly to the bedroom. That way you don't have to go through the sitting-room. She said she didn't want us to go there, I mean to the sitting-room, because she didn't want any distraction. I remember that the last time I was there, her children fought around us. There was such an uproar, such a commotion! As I was saying, instead of telling me exactly how much she would be prepared to pay, she came out with it and said that there were different kinds of payments. Then she said she liked me, stood up from the bed on which she had been sitting and invited me to help her undo the zip of her dress.

'She was going to change her dress, she said. She expected some important visitors. You can trust me of course. I helped her get off her dress and that was the beginning of the end. I couldn't help it. Very soon I was on top of her, and promising her to bring all the things she wanted for nothing. Then she pushed me away. Didn't I know she was a married woman, she asked. Anyway, she had to see all the things first before she actually paid me in kind.'

Iriso breathed hard. The passion was still hot and heavy on him.

'So nothing eventually happened?' Dala prompted.

Iriso agreed sadly. 'Nothing. She didn't let me go any further. Of course I struggled with her but she is an experienced woman. She gets only what she wants. So she said. When I looked at her legs, at her breasts all heaving to go and then her scanty blue pants with all the dark hair showing between her legs, I just couldn't be angry.'

Dala managed to laugh in spite of the fact that his eyes were already beginning to play tricks on him. 'You should have asked me before you went in there with her,' he laughed. 'We've all heard about Queen in the Ministry. She uses her body to get what she wants but she doesn't give herself until she has got whatever it is firmly in her grasp. No wonder she is richer than Obofun.'

'How did I know that that was going to happen?' Iriso asked.

'I saw Obofun go upstairs just about five minutes before you came out,' Dala remembered. 'Did he not catch you on top of his wife?'

Iriso breathed heavily. 'How come? We were already in the sitting-room when Obofun came upstairs. He is so unbearably loquacious. As soon as he came in, he started telling me how faithful and honest and loyal his wife was. "The only one in the world!" he boasted. Of course I laughed in his face.'

'Just like Obofun,' Dala exclaimed. 'That's what he used to say even in the Ministry! Well, what happened then?'

Iriso sped the big Volvo car along Mission Road. 'I have arranged to supply her with some of the things tomorrow morning and then I will be meeting her later on in the afternoon at her house.'

'And I can bet you that Obofun will be away on business,' Dala added after a minute's thought.

'Oh well,' said Iriso, 'That is their headache. All I know is that I have an appointment with Queen tomorrow.'

Chapter 4

For more than four hours, the four men laboured to clear the cement. Osaro and Patrick stayed on top of the trailer from where they handed down the bags of cement to Idemudia and Omoifo who then carried them either on their heads or on their backs to the shed, more than ten metres away. At the beginning they shouted as they worked.

'Oshobe! Eh!'

'Oshobe! Eh!'

'Now! One, two, three ...'

But gradually, their shouting died out. They became silent as they worked into the evening and as the hours passed, they became worn out. The men on the ground dragged their feet. The men on the trailer leaned against the uncleared cement bags, tired out, exhausted. And they were all hungry. Their backs ached, their stomachs ached, their heads ached also. But the work had to go on because they were hungry and because they needed the money to buy the food.

They didn't even look at each other now. They breathed in thin long, sharp gasps as the hunger gnawed at their stomachs and tore at their hearts, almost making them dizzy. They worked mechanically but resolutely, stubbornly, determined not to give up. And at the back of each man's mind was the money. Five naira. Nothing much, but enough, each man knew, to dull the sharp pain of their hunger.

And like any war, the work came to an end. The men looked at each other now. They did not smile but the light was back in their eyes as they stood, slumped against the wall of the little shed that housed the guards and waited for the guards to come out.

'I think somebody ought to go inside the motel,' Osaro said at last, breaking the silence.

'We should wait,' Patrick said. 'Perhaps one of the guards will come.'

'But where could they have gone to?' Omoifo asked.

Idemudia shrugged his shoulders. 'Nobody knows. But I think Osaro is right, Somebody ought to go into the motel.'

'Then you go,' Patrick said.

'Yes, I will go.'

Idemudia went into the restaurant and immediately, he drew the attention of many of the customers sitting inside. A waiter instantly approached him.

'What do you want?' he demanded.

A pool of water began to form around Idemudia where he was standing. His torn shirt was stripped from his chest and it hung loosely around his waist.

'We want madam,' Idemudia replied, eyeing the fat waiter.

'Then wait outside!' the waiter ordered.

Idemudia stood for a moment undecided and then went outside the door and then beckoned to his friends to join him at the entrance to the motel.

They had to wait another twenty minutes before Queen arrived, the loose ends of her long dress gathered in her left hand.

'So you have finished,' she said eyeing the men.

The four men stood around her with hard expressions on their faces. Looking at them Queen shuddered and involuntarily she drew back a little in the motel's entrance.

'We want our money,' Idemudia told her. 'The work is done.'

Queen tried to look across and above the men at the shed. 'Let somebody turn on the outside lights!' she called. The lights were turned on. She could see the cement bags piled high up, like groundnut pyramids.

'How many are there?' she asked.

Osaro bit his fingernails. The nails were dirty and smelled strongly of cement. 'We didn't count them, madam,' he said.

'Then I'll better count them first before paying you!' Queen said.

Idemudia moved away from his place near the wall and came to stand directly in front of Queen.

'It is not necessary to count them, madam,' he said in an exasperated voice. 'We took out of the trailers all there was to be taken out.'

Queen peered at the cement bags stacked high in the shed. 'But how can I be sure they are complete?'

Nobody answered her.

'You can come back tomorrow afternoon,' she said finally. 'By that time I will have counted them.'

'Madam, we want our money!' Osaro said tersely.

'I have said you must come back tomorrow.'

'We want our money now!' Idemudia said angrily, and at the same time moved to block the entrance into the motel.

One of the guards who had been standing behind them now walked up. In a loud voice, he threatened 'Madam has said you should go away.'

The four men ignored him. 'We want our money, madam. We cannot come back tomorrow.' Their voices were bitter.

Queen shrugged her shoulders. 'Okay then, wait,' she said carelessly and pushed past Idemudia into the motel. Three waiters came out now and stood at the door.

'Where are the other security men?' Idemudia heard voices asking inside the restaurant.

'They should be outside too,' other voices answered.

36

The four men waited outside for another five minutes. Then surprisingly Queen reappeared.

'I have brought your money,' she announced benevolently. 'I know where one of you lives, so if there's anything wrong my husband will find him.'

She gave Idemudia the twenty naira after counting the four five-naira notes three times.

Idemudia took the money from her and after they had gone some way away from the motel, he gave five naira to each of his three friends.

'We should be very grateful to you,' Osaro said as he accepted the money. 'You don't know how much this money means to me.'

'Ah, there is no need to be,' Idemudia said. 'You would have done exactly the same for me.'

His mind went to Adisa. What was she doing? What had she done throughout the whole day? Somehow he was worried and ashamed of himself now. After beating his wife, he had kept her in hunger for a whole day! And this had been neither the first nor the second time. What if the news got home to their village, to her parents?

He parted company with his friends at the Ekewan junction. Then he walked slowly back to his house. He climbed the three steps wearily. His legs felt as if they didn't belong to him. His hands were heavy. His jaws trembled, making his teeth chatter noisily. He had a terrible headache and his whole body was hot. The door to his room was closed. Was Adisa asleep? Or had she gone out to carry out her threat? He turned the door's handle, then drew the door towards him. It yawned with age and rust as it opened. He stepped into the semi-darkness of the room, and looked about intently.

There was nobody there. Adisa wasn't asleep as he had imagined. Then she had gone out. He sat down wearily on their single wooden chair and dropped his sandals on the floor. He had been holding them in his hands from the Freedom Motel.

Where had Adisa gone to? Had she really gone out to carry out her threat? Or had she run away from him? He stood up uneasily and stretching out his hands he felt the wall for the switch and turned the light on. He saw that Adisa's clothes were still in the room. The cooking utensils and the plates were also there. If she had left him, surely she would have taken her things? He nodded his head slowly. Yes, most women took these things when they left their husbands. So, where had she gone to? To her aunt's place? Most probably, he told himself. But perhaps she had gone to find a man? Did she know any man? Had she met any man through her aunt? He told himself he would kill her for it if she did. Yes, he would kill her, strangle her, murder her.

He took out the wet and crumpled five naira note and now sitting on the bed, he smoothed it across his knee. Five naira! Money! When had he ever had money? When had he ever been free from hunger, from want? He shook his head, and standing up walked to the table and placed the money on it. He felt immensely weak now. His head ached and his stomach churned over itself. It must be the hunger, he thought, and went back to the bed and sat on it.

But then, he felt dizzy. What is happening to me, he asked himself. I mustn't collapse. He shook his head vigorously and then immediately regretted it as the hammers in his head beat viciously against his brain. He held his head with both hands and noticed that his hands shook and trembled.

Biting his lips, he struggled up and took off his clothes and then suddenly, without warning, he collapsed and fell across the bed. He was unconscious for a long time and when he came back, it was pitch dark in the room. He sensed that he was lying across the bed so he dragged up his feet to the bed and tried to remember. But he couldn't because the ache was back in his head and his body was hot, like a glowing piece of coal.

He cried and screamed on the bed. He choked and struggled fiercely. Yet he didn't sweat. He said things he couldn't understand. He moaned and cried from the pain that tormented him. From this corridor of pain, he slipped back into a half-sleep, a half-sleep that was nothing but moans and cries because his imagination was feverish.

He struggled helplessly. And Adisa did not come.

He opened and shut his mouth a hundred times and somewhere in his half-consciousness, thoughts of death and dying gripped the half-light of his soul. Was he dying? He didn't know. All he knew was that he was struggling with himself on the narrow bed, that his body was on fire and his imagination with it.

Somewhere in between this passionate struggle against death, Idemudia heard a low scream, feet panicked and then a white candle threw out its halo of yellow light and Adisa was standing, bending over him, her eyes frightened, confused. She drew back from the bed and mechanically she went back to the light's switch and turned it off and on until she knew that the bulb must have burnt itself out. She went back to the bed and for the first time observed that Idemudia's clothes were in a heap, on the ground. But she couldn't understand what was happening. Had he got himself drunk? No, that was impossible because he had never got drunk.

She was shocked to see that he was stark naked, But what had happened? Again, for the second time, she went away from the bed, and placing the candle on the floor, she went to the door which she had left open and closed it. What was he muttering?

Then again, she approached the bed. Gingerly, she stretched out her hand to feel his forehead. But like a bolt, she drew her hand away. What had she touched? She stood for a moment, uneasily, dazed. Her hand went back, this time to be really sure. Then she cried out as she realised that Idemudia was sick and that his forehead was hotter than a blacksmith's fire.

She held her head and then very slowly she sat on the bed beside him. What was she going to do? What could she do when she hadn't one kobo? Her eyes were arrested by the crumpled heap of clothes on the floor. Idemudia was muttering something to himself. 'Five naira!' What about five naira? Idemudia's hands groped about the air. 'Five naira,' he repeated again and again.

She stood up and picked up the candle and raising it above the table, she saw it. The green note lay damp on the table. She placed the candle on the table now and looking out she saw that the rain was still falling. But what did they say should be done in such a situation? Cover him up with clothes? Yes. Cover him up with clothes. She packed all her wrappas and carrying them over, spread them over him.

What should she do next? She had to get help. Mama Jimoh was there. She rushed out of the room and began to knock on the door of her neighbours.

'Who is that? I say who is there?' She could hear Mama Jimoh asking.

'It's me! It's me! Adisa. Please open the door!' Her voice was urgent.

'Who?' the suspicious voice of Mama Jimoh called back through the closed door.

'It's me! Adisa! My husband is dying!'

Mama Jimoh flung her door open. Her movements took on the note of alarm.

'Idemudia dying? From what?' she asked incredulously, tying the wrappa more securely around her waist. Her husband hovered in the doorway.

'What is wrong with him?' he asked.

Adisa's hands were crossed over her breast. 'I don't know,' she poured out in tears instead of in words.

They crowded after her into the room. Idemudia lay still, breathing heavily. Papa Jimoh, a small dry man in his mid-thirties, took command. He was a driver in the Sugar Company.

'He must be rushed to the hospital,' he said, after feeling and quickly withdrawing his hand from Idemudia's forehead. 'He is so hot!' he exclaimed. 'It must be malaria!'

'Ah, if it is malaria, then it will go,' Mama Jimoh said placatingly. 'It isn't dangerous.'

'But how do I get him to the hospital?' Adisa cried.

'There may be no taxi at this time of night,' Papa Jimoh said, 'But who knows? You go out to the roadside and wait. We will wait here. Hurry.'

'Yes, you had better go there,' Mama Jimoh agreed. 'We must hurry.'

Adisa snatched up the money on the table and hurried out of the house. She held her hands to her breasts as she hurried, breathing quickly.

'Oh God!' she prayed. 'Please let a taxi come. Please!' The night was dark and cold and as she stood at the Ekenwan Road junction, her heart hammered within her. What would she do if he died? 'Oh no!' she cried. 'He must not die. He must live. Please God, send a taxi, send help!'

She waited for a long time and then she saw a car coming rapidly. She moved forward, into the road, and began to wave frantically. But it was all in vain. In a flash, the car was past her, the tail lights glowing red and warm in the black night.

She went forward along the road. She had to get to the Ring Road and wait there. Yes, there. That was the busy place. She could get a taxi there. She would get a taxi there. She ran, she walked, she stumbled, but always she hurried.

She came to the empty Ring Road and her heart sank. What was she to do? Go back to Idemudia? 'No. I can't,' she said to herself. 'I can't.' She would go to the hospital instead, directly. They would be able to prescribe something for her. She hurried towards the hospital, and panting and out of breath, she finally arrived at the gates of the hospital.

She paced up and down the corridor as she waited to be allowed to see the doctor. She was angered at the leisurely way the nurses moved about. Couldn't they see she needed help urgently? Couldn't they see?

The doctor was a very young man. He looked tired and angry.

'Yes, woman? What is it?' he asked curtly.

'It's my husband ...', Adisa began.

'Yes, your husband. Where is he?' the nurse asked.

'At home.'

'At home?' the doctor asked.

'Yes. He is dying. He needs help, urgently. Please help!'

'What is wrong with him?'

'His body is hot. He keeps talking to himself, he ...'

'Some fever,' the doctor murmured to himself. 'But madam, there's nothing I can do. I can't prescribe anything unless I see him. I can't do anything unless you bring him here.'

'But we tried. Please, doctor!'

'What about the ambulance?' the doctor turned to the nurse.

'Oh, the driver has gone home,' the nurse said. 'We don't know where he lives. Look, woman, why don't you look for a taxi or go to a chemist?'

'I have looked for a taxi,' Adisa pleaded. 'There are no taxis.'

'Then you'd better go to a chemist,' the nurse said again.

'But how can I go to a chemist? Doctor, please.'

The doctor shrugged his shoulders. 'Look, woman, we are sorry. I can't prescribe anything for your husband unless I see him, and even if I could the pharmacy is closed and most probably you won't even get the drugs here. Do as the nurse says. Go to a chemist.'

Adisa stood up shakily, her lips trembling. How could she go back without some drugs? The thought frightened her and very slowly, the tears came.

She left the hospital grounds very slowly, disappointed and bitter. Surely Mama Jimoh would be waiting and Idemudia would be waiting. She couldn't go back without some drugs. She went up Ikpoba Road, past the Bank and the petrol station, before she saw a chemist's shop on the other side of the road. Would the chemists open the shop at this time of night? she asked herself. Everywhere was so quiet. There were no other people on the street.

But she needed the drugs. Hurriedly, she crossed to the other side of the road, climbed up to the chemist's shop and with a deliberate effort began to pound on the door. She didn't care if she woke up the whole street. She was desperate now. Then she heard voices inside the shop – and then suddenly a man appeared from the side of the house and he held an iron rod in his hand.

'What is it, woman?' he demanded, approaching cautiously, looking round him all the time.

Adisa threw up her hands helplessly. 'It's my husband,' she cried. 'He is dying. I need some medicine.'

'What is wrong with him?' the man asked, and he

stood by her side now and looked over her shoulder carefully.

'His body is hot. Hotter than fire, and he keeps on talking to himself,' Adisa said.

'Looks like high fever,' the man grunted. He called to somebody else and then another man emerged from the other side of the house. In his hand he held a big cutlass.

'You'd better come this way,' the man with the cutlass said. 'It is late and normally we do not attend to customers at this hour, but if it is a matter of life and death, we are prepared to help you.'

They entered the house through a side door and then they were inside the chemist's shop. The man with the cutlass leaned his weapon against the wall.

'I'll give you some aspirin to bring down his temperature. He'll also need some novalgin and then of course one or two antibiotics, something like crystalline penicillin. He should be all right after taking them.'

'Oh thank you, sir,' Adisa said gratefully.

'Here,' the man said to Adisa, and handed her the drugs. 'He should take the drugs straightaway. One of each of these, and four of those, and er, it's only four naira eighty kobo.'

'Oh!' Adisa exclaimed, disappointed. She couldn't possibly spend all the five naira on the drugs!

'Well, don't you have enough money?' the man asked.

'I was ...' Adisa stammered.

'I see,' the man said quickly. 'I'll give you the basic ones then but you must get the other as soon as you can. Ninety kobo only.'

Adisa thanked him again and again.

'It's all right,' the man said, and proceeded to return the other drugs to the shelves. 'Remember, first time, four tablets. After that, two tablets every four hours.

That means,' and he glanced at the clock hanging from the wall, 'he should be given another two at six o'clock. You can see it is nearly two o'clock now.'

Adisa thanked him again and again and then very quickly she went out of the shop through the side door and now, she was again on the streets, alone, the night cold and quiet, her heart beating wildly.

Papa Jimoh and his wife were still standing beside the bed when she got home.

'At last,' Papa Jimoh said. 'Have you found a taxi?'

Adisa shook her head. 'I had to go to the hospital and then to a chemist. I have brought some drugs.'

'Very well then,' Mama Jimoh said. 'We will go to sleep but should you need any further help, wake us up. Papa Jimoh sleeps lightly.'

Adisa thanked them and after they had gone, she bolted the door and dragged up the wooden chair to the bedside and roused Idemudia.

'You have to take some of these tablets,' she said to him and looked at his face. Idemudia's eyes fluttered momentarily and closed again. She saw that he had emaciated considerably even in that short time. She couldn't believe it. He was like a big tree which a gigantic storm had toyed with. The trunk and the branches remained but the leaves were gone. The storm had carried them away. Seeing him so weak and fragile, Adisa cried, now.

Idemudia held out his hand mechanically. His hand shook as he took the tablets and placed them in his mouth, one after the other. After drinking them down with the water she gave to him, he fell back on the bed, not still knowing exactly where he was. It was all like a bad dream. The yellow light from the candle looked so very unreal. Everything floated before him like shadows and he simply felt himself a part of these shadows, light, dark, floating and unreal.

The tongues of fire burned inside him, making his head feverish, his body hot, his imagination riotous and confused. Now, he would call on the name of his mother and then he would go blank while his head was tossed about on the bed by the white winds that blew inside him.

Adisa sat on the chair and watched the struggle. 'And to think that this is the same man who struck me this morning and even threatened to kill me!' she thought. 'Surely, I can never leave him now. My aunt was mad to think that even if I could, I would. I do not want to be like my aunt. No! I will never be like her.

'What kind of life can a woman live with so many men in her life? It isn't that I blame my aunt for living the way she does. God knows how she has suffered. God knows that her husband was a cruel man who not only regularly beat my aunt after drinking himself silly, but borrowed money in her name. Wasn't that shameful?' she asked herself. 'A man borrowing money in his wife's name and then, to crown it all, running away from her. And he has never come back. My aunt had to find the money for the rent, for feeding and for clothing the children and herself. Who can blame her if she chose to live the way she now does?

'And who can blame her if she talks the way she now does?'

'No man is worth suffering for,' her aunt had said that evening. 'You sacrifice everything for them and what do you get in return? Nothing but beating and desertion. You get nothing but blood and tears. And are our men cruel! Adisa, look at you who are married no more than three years. What have you got to show for those three years? Nothing but ingratitude and beating. Our men test their manhood by their ability to beat their wives, not by their ability to protect their wives and provide for their children. You are still a beautiful woman, Adisa. And if you had lived as long as I have, you would know that now is the time to abandon your man. Leave him before he makes you produce more children. You must leave him.'

'But, Auntie,' Adisa said, 'How could I leave him?'

'Oh my God!' her aunt cried. 'Oh my God! What rubbish! How could you leave him! You pack your things and you go out. That is how to leave him. You pack your clothes and your pots and you leave him to rot in his own vomit before he poisons you with it. Or do you want me to go with you?'

'No, Auntie. It isn't that. Where would I go?'

'Where? You come here until you are able to take a room somewhere else. Oh, Adisa, you are a beautiful young girl still and you will see how the men will run after you. That husband of yours is a fool. You must leave him!'

She shook her head. 'No, Auntie,' she said. 'I cannot leave him. I couldn't stay in a room all by myself, and I would die if the hands of other men were to touch me. Honestly, I couldn't bear it. I would die!'

'Adisa! Don't be a fool!'

'But Auntie . . .'

'How do you know you will die when you haven't even tried? Ah yes. I thought so myself when my husband left me. I thought I couldn't bear to have another man touch me. But I soon found out I could when the children cried and coughed each night and when the landlord came each morning and threatened to throw us out. After I had heard my children coughing and crying and after knowing that they coughed and cried because there had been nothing to eat, I knew that there wasn't anything I couldn't do or bear to see that they didn't cry nor cough. Oh yes, I know what you may be thinking now, Adisa,' and she had looked at Adisa knowingly. 'You think now that if my

47

husband had remained, then perhaps things would have been different. But you are wrong, you see. Things would never have been different. The children had always coughed and cried even when their father was here. And not only had they cried, but I, also. But now it is very different. I do not cry any more, and at least, the children are alive. The only thing I ever really regret is that I allowed myself to think and believe that there was no other alternative to staying with a man who cared neither about you nor about your children.'

'But, Auntie!' Adisa cried. 'Idemudia is different. He beats me all right. I have tasted my own blood and my own tears but you see, somehow, I . . . I cannot hold him responsible. He tries, only he never succeeds.'

'You are a fool,' her aunt said angrily. 'Never in my life have I heard so much rubbish.'

'But it is true.'

'Oh yes. It is true that he will destroy you gradually and that by the time you realise it, it will be too late. If you ever want to be happy, you must leave him.'

'No, Auntie, I cannot.'

'Then you must stay there until he kills you.'

Adisa fell silent and her mind went back to Idemudia's face when in reaction to her bluff in the morning, he had threatened to kill her.

Then her aunt had broken into her thoughts and said, 'Since you do not want to leave him, what do you want?'

Adisa shrugged her shoulders and then stood up. 'Aunt Yasha,' she said, 'It's only money that we want. Just any amount of money.'

'Oh, I see,' her aunt said thoughtfully. 'And who doesn't want money? Why, the world would be all right if everybody had money. God knows I have no money. The money I make from my trade I always spend on feeding and providing for the children.'

She looked now at her husband and her aunt's words rang in her head. 'You must leave him! Leave him! No man is worth suffering for. Leave him!'

'No! No! No!' she cried to herself aloud now, and stood up suddenly and held her head in her hands.

Idemudia stirred on the bed and his eyes that were wild went over the room and again he felt himself a shadow, floating, suspended, and he moaned. For more than twenty-four hours he hadn't eaten anything. His mouth was bitter now – more bitter than gall. And the fire inside him raged on.

He cried out loud now. 'Mother! Oh my mother! Oh! Adisa! Adisa! Oh my mother! Mother! Eh! Ah! Eo!'

Adisa heard her name called and she stood rooted to the ground, stupefied.

'Eo! My mother! Um! Adisa!'

Then she looked now at her husband and very slowly and wearily, she sat back on the chair and placed her hand on his forehead. She shook her head from side to side as she withdrew her hand. His forehead was still very hot.

She stood up and went to the table and took the small khaki envelopes and then she drew some water from the pot with a glass and came back and sat by his side on the bed.

She opened the small khaki envelope and took out two of the small white tablets.

'You need some more tablets,' she said to him, her hand trembling. 'Take some more tablets.'

She reached for his hand, which also trembled, and placed the tablets in his hands. Again, Idemudia forced the tablets down his throat with the water, and everything was bitter and sour in his mouth. Adisa sat in the chair, afraid to close her eyes, afraid to think of what her aunt had said. No, never. She could never leave her husband. It was impossible! How could she leave her husband and take a room in the city where other men would come to her? Even if her husband had not called her bluff, she told herself that she could never do it. Not on her life. She dozed off.

The cocks were already crowing when she woke up in the chair. She glanced furtively at her husband and relieved, saw that he was asleep. She stood up, exhausted, undecided, not knowing what to do or think of first. Surely they ought to eat something. She would make some pap for both of them. Idemudia could easily keep the pap down. Yes, that was the best thing. Decided, she hurried outside. She knew a woman who sold the starch she wanted for the pap. And as soon as she had bought the starch, she hurried back into the house. She needed hot water. But Christ! She had forgotten that there was no kerosene. She took out the kerosene bottle and went outside again. Then she came back and made the fire, and in another thirty minutes the pap was made and it steamed. There was no sugar. Ought she to buy some? It was so expensive! One cube of sugar for one kobo! Wasn't that how they sold it now? Idemudia had complained about the bitterness in his mouth. Perhaps it was best to buy a few cubes of sugar. And again she went outside.

At last ready, she sat on the edge of the bed and proceeded to feed him with the pap. As she held Idemudia's head on her lap, she swore that she would never go back to her aunt's place, come what may. She might quarrel with her husband and they could say vile things to each other but she didn't want anybody to put ideas into her head. What her aunt had said frightened her. But then, they did need money. Where would they get the money from? Oh, if only she could start a trade! That was the answer — a trade! But again, how would she get the money? And what could she sell anyway? She shook her head. She didn't know.

The spoon rattled in between Idemudia's teeth. Sick and exhausted, Idemudia was like a child, helpless. His eyes were watery, a defeated look in them. He was silent as she forced the pap down his throat. And again, she could not help thinking how only yesterday morning, he had forced her to the floor with the mere superiority of his strength. Now, he was helpless. 'Helpless!' she cried in her heart.

What was she going to do? What if he died? No, she mustn't think of death. Mama Jimoh had said it was only malaria, that he would recover. But as she sat near him, she doubted it. How could Idemudia recover when his body was so hot, when he could not even take in the pap?

At that moment Idemudia coughed. The pap he had been drinking came out of his mouth and nose and flew in all directions and as he choked, Adisa cried out in terror and misery, 'Oh God! Oh my God! I do not want to be like my aunt! Oh God, please. Please save him!'

The spoon slipped from her fingers and crashed to the floor, as her hands and whole body began to tremble violently.

Chapter 5

She heard rapid tapping on the door and stared vacantly in front of her. Then she heard Mama Jimoh calling, 'Adisa! Adisa!'

She stood up slowly and crossing the room opened the door.

Mama Jimoh removed the chewing stick from her mouth, as she stepped into the room.

'How did he sleep?' she asked.

Adisa went back to the chair by Idemudia's bed and sat down wearily.

'He didn't sleep!' she said. 'I thought he was going to die!'

Mama Jimoh frowned. 'We must take him to the hospital. Let the doctors there look after him properly.'

Adisa was not sure. 'How?' she asked.

'I have told Papa Jimoh,' the other woman said. 'He will bring his van round. You can then accompany them to the hospital. The University Hospital is better.'

At about seven o'clock in the morning, Papa Jimoh brought the van round. 'You better get him dressed while I get ready,' he told Adisa.

Idemudia felt very weak. He opened his eyes briefly and then closed them again. 'Where am I?' he asked, in a voice that seemed so far away.

'You are going to the hospital,' Adisa told him, placing her hand over his forehead. 'Papa Jimoh is taking us there.'

She struggled to get his trousers on him. Idemudia sensed that he was being dressed. He wasn't himself any more. The hunger and that hot fire in his blood had reduced him to nothing more than a child. He was helpless now and he detested himself for it. He had to pull himself together. He had to fight off this over-whelming weakness that made him gasp for his breath. He struggled up from the bed and attempted to stand on his feet. He swayed so dangerously on his feet that Adisa and Papa Jimoh had to support him. Then they led him to the van, one on each side of him and Mama Jimoh bringing up the rear. They led him outside and as they were about to enter the car, Idemudia's feet wobbled. He slumped against his supports, and bore down heavily on them. They struggled to get him into the van and once there, he shivered and moaned, the whole agonising fever coming back in successive waves.

Even at that early hour, the University Hospital was crowded. It was a pitiable sight. So many people were sick and in need of the doctor. The long benches were full. The porch outside was filled by patients who were able to stand. Some of the waiting patients coughed violently. Mothers who carried sick children moved agitatedly. The faces that waited there were grim, serious and preoccupied with worry.

Papa Jimoh and Adisa led Idemudia into the ward at once. Other patients made way. Once inside they sat him on a chair and drew the attention of a nurse.

'What is wrong with him?' the nurse asked, cards in her hand. Adisa tried to explain.

'Has he been registered yet?'

Adisa shook her head.

'It's one naira, ten kobo,' the nurse said. 'The counter is outside.' Adisa held back her tears. She had only a few coins. She had forgotten to bring more money.

'I think I must be going,' Papa Jimoh announced. 'If I am late for work, I will be fired. Nobody listens. I am fired and they employ another.'

He moved away from the chair. Adisa looked helplessly after him. 'Don't be worried!' he called back on reaching the exit. 'He will be okay.'

Adisa could no longer hold back the tears. 'I didn't bring any money,' she pleaded with the nurse. 'And I can't leave him here to go for it!' she cried. The nurse regarded her sympathetically. 'Bring him this way then,' she told Adisa. 'I think he needs admission. But don't be afraid. He will be all right.'

Another disappointment awaited her at the doctor's consulting room. There was no bed available in the male wards. 'The patient must go to the Ogbe Hospital,' the doctor said.

Adisa watched the doctor as he wrote out the prescription and signed it. She took the slip of paper from him and stood there, disappointed. The doctor looked up sharply at her. 'You've heard, madam. There's no bed in this hospital. I know he needs admission. However, we will treat him here before you take him away. Follow the nurse.'

Adisa stood rooted to the floor. How was she to get him back to the Ogbe Hospital? The nurse roused her.

'Come this way.'

As soon as they left the consulting room, the doctor removed his glasses and placed them on the table. He was a young man of about twenty-seven. Spreading his hands across the table he looked at the Staff Nurse who stood beside him.

'I hate sending these people to the Ogbe Hospital,' he said, his voice sad and serious.

'But it's not your fault,' the nurse said to him.

'All the same, I feel very badly about it. This was the seventh case in a single night! And some of them are really terrible. I feel each time as if I am sending them to their death.'

'Come on, doctor!' the nurse rebuked him. 'You don't have to feel like that at all.'

They both fell silent. The doctor put on his glasses again but his mind went back to the dark tunnel of the numberless sick, their abject poverty and from that to the helplessness of their position. He couldn't understand why in the midst of so much disease, the government concentrated on building hotels instead of hospitals. He simply couldn't understand.

The nurse had finished giving Idemudia the third injection in a series. She now took some cotton wool and began to wipe the blood away.

'You shouldn't be too worried,' she reassured Adisa. But she knew that the injection was not to effect a permanent cure, but only to relieve the pain of suffering temporarily.

Adisa led Idemudia outside. He was so weak and so fragile-looking that again she wondered in her mind if she were not on the way to losing her husband to death. The reassuring words of the nurse died away in her mind, and in their place came the voice of her aunt: 'You will take up a room of your own in the city and the men will come running after you. You are still young and beautiful.' She shuddered.

Idemudia followed his wife silently. His eyes were half shut. Inwardly he was asking himself what was happening to him. Why couldn't he walk firmly? He must walk firmly. He mustn't stagger or waver. His mind must be clear. He had to picture, visualise, things as they were. He fought the disease as he followed his wife. He kept telling himself that he had to be strong. He had to get another job soon. The money he had brought some time ago would soon be gone and again they would be plunged into despairing hunger. He must ... He grew dizzy. His mind lost track of events, the thread of consciousness on which he had stumbled along, grew thinner. He staggered and fell heavily on Adisa.

Two men walking behind Adisa saw Idemudia collapsing. One of them rushed up and seized Idemudia by the waist.

'What is wrong with him?' he asked Adisa after they had both carried him to a bench by the side of the gates. Adisa shook her head.

'I do not know,' she said, weeping again now.

'It must be the disease,' one of the men said. He spat on the grass and then went away.

The crowd gathered there regarded them. Their eyes followed them.

Getting a taxi posed a big problem. No taxi wanted to go to the Ogbe Hospital for only twenty kobo. Eventually, however, she secured one.

The Ogbe Hospital was an even bigger market of patients than the University Hospital. There were haggard and distraught faces everywhere. Worry had eaten deep into the faces of the majority of them. Wrinkles and cracks were in abundance. It was evident that these were people who had been engaged by life in a terrible and fierce struggle and that they had come out of each bout worse and still more badly battered.

Children cried, women wept, everywhere there was a great urgency and paradoxically little activity: a hopelessness and helplessness that invoked the onlooker to tears. It was simply a wonder why, so much the worse for wear, these people still struggled and aspired to keep their lean flames of lives going. There seemed to be no point in seeking recourse from death, the abundant evidence of life about was distressing and frustrating enough. And yet, even as the women wept and the children cried and the men sat or stood about with stony watery eyes, coughing and spitting and occasionally going to the fence to urinate, there was in each pair of eyes a stubborn determination not to let go of life no matter how filthy and degrading it was.

On the other side of the fence was Sapele Road. The traffic moved on it in an endless confused stream, horns biting and barking, voices cursing, tyres screeching. These were the Volvos and the Mercedes Benz cars and the taxis and the motorcyclists and the truck pushers and the beggars and the insane. Everywhere life was one heated and confused argument, leading nowhere.

A bus came screaming into the hospital yard. The nurses came out now, their eyes angry and defiant. A man jumped out of the front of the bus shouting:

'Accident! Accident! Accident!'

The back doors of the bus were flung open. Inside the bus and on the seats, two men lay unconscious. One of them bled profusely from the nose, mouth and ears. The nurses crossed their hands over their breasts, and watched.

'Where from?' one of them asked.

The man who had jumped down from the bus shook his head.

'I don't know. I was told to bring them here from the University Hospital.'

Two hospital attendants arrived and then they began moving the men onto the two stretchers that they had wheeled up.

'Better move them to the OP Ward!' one of the nurses called to the attendants and now, all of a sudden, there was genuine panic, a flurry of footsteps.

'Why did they have to bring them from the University Hospital?' one of the nurses asked the man who had come with the bus.

'I guess there were no beds.'

Then the man looked round quickly, drew the nurse aside and whispered in her ear.

'What!' the nurse exclaimed.

The man fell into step beside her as they followed behind the rapidly moving mobile beds.

'Oh yes,' the man said in low voice beside her. 'The doctor there looked at both of them and said their condition was bad. Next he phoned and asked for advice. He was told to get them off as quickly as possible. They didn't want any more deaths there. Besides, the other man who brought in the two accident victims disappeared during the original confusion. So you can understand.'

The nurse was very bitter. 'You don't turn patients away because nobody will be responsible for settling the expenses!'

'But it has happened!'

'It's terrible.'

There's nothing you can do about it. It happens every day.'

They passed by Idemudia and Adisa who were sitting on a bench close to the entrance of the consulting room. Adisa was shocked at the sight of so much blood. She half rose and then sank back to her seat again. People crowded all round. It appeared that one of the accident victims had come round. He was groaning and moaning.

'Eo! Eo! Aai!'

The murmuring along the whole verandah died down. The groaning was so pathetic that the gathered people were forced momentarily to forget about their own troubles. There, Adisa recognised, was a tragedy far more urgent than her own. The consequences might be the same but she saw in the bare bodies of the accident victims, in their blood and unconscious groans and tears something much more pathetic than even her own sleepless night and the destructive fever that was eating deep into her husband.

She swallowed hard. Ther throat became dry. Life was so terrible, so horrible. She was afraid.

The green curtain fell over the door of the consulting room. The painful humming around the consulting room resumed. Children began to cry. Mothers paced to and fro. Lean old men held around their waists and led by their hands stood or sat about. Their faces were dry, their eyes hollow. Here were diseases. Many people were so sick! Adisa observed all this and she shuddered and held more tightly to Idemudia's hand, wondering when the whole nightmare would end.

The two accident victims were rushed out again. This time they were covered up with white sheets, like the dead. The doctor came out behind them, hovered around the entrance, his face grim and then he went back into the consulting room. Then a nurse came out and said in a loud voice, 'Next!'

Adisa went inside, half dragging Idemudia with her. His eyes were, again, half closed. He was vaguely conscious of his surroundings. He was weak and exhausted from hunger and disease.

'What is wrong with him?' the nurse in attendance asked. Adisa brought out the slip of paper she had been given at the University Hospital.

The nurse took it and examined it. She frowned.

'How many more of their cases are we going to treat?' she asked angrily.

'What?'

'They have been referred here from the University Hospital because there are no beds there.'

'Let me see.'

The doctor, a young man of about twenty-nine, took the slip of paper and examined it.

'We have no beds here either,' he complained.

'Why, he can share a bed or sleep on the floor,' the nurse suggested.

'Too many people are already sharing beds or sleeping on the floor.'

'What then do we do?'

'The Senior Service Ward is almost empty.'

'But you can't send him there,' the nurse said sharply.

The doctor looked from Idemudia to Adisa. He noticed that she was a beautiful woman. 'If only she had gone to school!' he thought sadly.

Aloud he asked, 'Can you bring a mattress from home?'

Adisa nodded vaguely. That would reduce her to sleeping on bare iron springs. Or perhaps ... No, she didn't want to think about her aunt's place.

'Where are you going to put him? In the corridor?' the nurse asked.

The young doctor thought for a while. 'I guess he can share a bed with that patient from Asaba. Get him over to that bed there.' He pointed to the bed that stood in a corner and against the wall of the consulting room.

Adisa and the nurse helped Idemudia to the bed, then laid him flat out.

'How long has he been sick?'

'One day.'

'Only one day?'

'Yes. I was in here during the night,' Adisa explained. 'But the doctor would not help me, because I did not bring him with me. So I went to a chemist instead.'

'What did the chemist give you?' the doctor asked.

Adisa took out the small khaki envelope and passed it to the nurse, who took it and passed it to the doctor. The doctor took it and examined its contents, mumbled, and continued with his examination.

'He is very weak.' The doctor felt around Idemudia's

ribs, chest and lungs. 'When did he last eat?' He straightened up.

'He hasn't eaten for . . .' Adisa began, and kept quiet.

The doctor looked at her shrewdly and then averting his face, chewed on the upper part of his pen.

Adisa remained silent. How could she explain that they hadn't anything to eat for two days? That Idemudia had fallen sick while she was away?

The doctor looked at her now and his voice was moist and his eyes clouded.

'The first thing is to get him something to eat,' he said to the nurse and then he went over and sat on his chair. He began to write out a prescription. 'Most of the drugs you need are not here,' the doctor said, and his voice was full of resentment. 'You must go to Everyman's Chemists in New Benin to get them.'

Adisa nodded dumbly. Everyman's Chemists! Where was the money going to come from?

The doctor was speaking again. 'You must hurry because he has lost a lot of strength. Get some milk, sugar and a tin of Ovaltine. Nurse, please 'phone to the male medical ward. Let them prepare that bed. He will have to share it with that other patient. And while she is gone to look for the drugs, let them quickly get him something to eat.'

He handed over the slip of paper to Adisa. They helped Idemudia out of the bed. Another nurse appeared.

'Is that the patient?' she asked. She was a small woman with a disproportionately large nose.

The first nurse, a taller and slender woman, nodded. 'You can accompany her,' she said to Adisa and Idemudia.

They followed the small woman out of the room. Adisa's brain was full of questions. Where was she going to get all the money for the drugs? Then there would be the hospital fees? And how was she going to buy the beverages? How? How? How? In her heart, she cursed Idemudia for falling sick. He had brought home only five naira and now his illness had already cost her a lot of worry. 'Where am I to get all this money?' she cried to herself.

She stumbled against a stone and nearly lost her balance.

'You better be more careful,' the nurse said to her. 'This place is filled with so many stones.'

Adisa could hear the loud voice of the first nurse from the other side crying 'Next!'

'Oh God! Oh my God!' she cried in her heart. 'What have we done? Why are we so unlucky?'

Chapter 6

Adisa was scarcely able to stand on her feet when she got home. She took a spoon and a plate and wrapping them in a piece of paper, placed them on the bed beside her. She smiled cynically to herself. How was she going to buy the beverages when she herself was starving? Where was she going to get the money from? She took the prescription and looked at it. The drugs would cost money. Drugs were expensive. A pity that the dispensary attendant had confirmed that the dispensary didn't have any of the drugs. So she must buy them. And then the hospital bills would come. Had the nurse not told her it would cost them more than three naira and seventy-five kobo for each day that her husband would spend at the hospital?

● She flung the thin slip of paper on the bed beside her and dropped her head in her hands. It was impossible to believe that all this could have happened to them within the space of a single day and night. And she hadn't slept. Since yesterday morning when she had picked up the broom to sweep the floor to the present time, it had been nothing but troubles and worries.

Her eyes went back to the slip of paper on the bed. Again, her mind went to how she was going to get enough money to buy the drugs. How much would the drugs cost? When would Idemudia recover? How soon! And what was she going to do? For God's sake, what was she going to do?

She heard some feet outside and listened. Perhaps that was Mama Jimoh. But Mama Jimoh would have gone to the market and if she had returned, she wondered why so early.

A knock sounded on her door. Surprised, she looked up and answered in a small voice, 'Yes?'

The knocking continued, and she was about to stand up when she saw two hands parting the blue curtains. Then a man's head and shoulders appeared in the room.

'Madam!'

Adisa did not answer but stared at him.

'Madam!' the man said again. 'My Oga wants to see Idemudia!'

Adisa stood up wearily and went to the door. 'Which Oga?'

'He is outside,' the man said.

Adisa followed the man outside. He wasn't wearing a shirt and his back glistened with the sweat. Outside the house, Obofun waited. He wore a grey French suit, and although he smiled when Adisa appeared, his face was hard.

'I want to see Idemudia,' he announced, not bothering to return Adisa's greeting.

Adisa adjusted her loincloth. 'My husband is in the hospital.'

Obofun drew a sharp breath. 'I see. From the hospital he goes to prison!'

Adisa frowned. She could not understand. 'What has my husband got to do with you?'

Obofun regarded Adisa, from head to toe. He could see that she was tall and slenderly built, and that she was beautiful. He liked her at once, particularly the pathetic look on her face. Surely, if he could ... But he was here on business. He thrust his hands deep into his pockets. 'Your husband and some of his friends have robbed my wife of one hundred and fifty bags of cement.'

Adisa's frown burrowed deeper into her haggard face. 'How?'

'Last night they helped in offloading bags of cement from three trailers. This morning we discovered that one hundred and fifty bags of the cement were missing.'

Adisa looked Obofun full in the face. Her deep black eyes penetrated his angrily. 'Do you want to search our house?' she asked.

Obofun laughed. 'You don't expect a thief to keep what he has stolen under his bed!'

'My husband is not a thief!'

'He has stolen our bags of cement!'

'We may be poor but we have never stolen!' Adisa said, the anger showing in her voice and in her face. Then she took a step backwards. 'You can go and call all the police you like,' she said defiantly. 'My husband did not steal any bags of cement. Throughout last night he was sick. Mama Jimoh and Papa Jimoh can testify to that. When then could he have stolen the cement?'

Obofun took that one in like a knife in his heart. It was quite possible that somebody else might have stolen the bags of cement. The police would definitely want to know whether Idemudia had been caught red-handed stealing the cement. To them Idemudia would only be a suspect, not a thief. And perhaps ... the realisation struck him like a blow. What if the trailer drivers had removed the bags of cement on the way? After all, the bags had not been counted before being off-loaded. The futility of his mission struck home to him and he began abusing himself for following his wife's words without properly checking to see if they were actually true.

However, in his next question, there was nothing to indicate that he had realised he had been beaten.

'Which hospital is he in?' he demanded.

Adisa hesitated.

'I want to know which hospital he is in,' Obofun repeated.

Adisa shrugged her shoulders. If this man was going to bring the police, she didn't want them to get at Idemudia. She kept quiet.

Obofun stood there awkwardly for another few seconds. Then in a threatening voice he said, 'We shall definitely find out where your husband is and when we do both of you will be sorry.' Inside him, however, he was unhappy. He knew he was merely threatening, making a fool of himself. The best thing would have been to apologise and go away. But he didn't apologise. He turned away and went down the stairs to his white car which was parked outside the house.

Adisa watched him go. Then the man who had first come to knock on her door also left and continued on foot after the car, down the street, towards the Freedom Motel.

'What sort of trouble is this?' Adisa asked herself as she went slowly back to their room. Now, she understood where Idemudia had caught the fever. So he had been off-loading heavy bags of cement the whole day under that heavy rain! And without food! And what had her aunt said? That she should leave Idemudia. No, she could never. She knew how hard Idemudia tried. It wasn't his fault if they remained poor. She entered their room. Her eyes went again to the slip of paper on the bed. She must go out now to the chemists' shop. 'Everyman's Chemists,' the doctor had advised her.

'You will get all the drugs you want there,' the dispensary attendant had told her.

She picked up the change from the five naira note from the table. She must go to the shop. She put the plate and the spoon that she had wrapped up under her arm, and after locking her door, she put both the key and the wrap into the black handbag she always carried, a handbag she had carried now for almost three years.

Outside, the weather was dull, moody. She knew it would soon begin to rain and quite heavily. She stood there and watched the people hurrying along Owode Street, to get home before the rain came pouring down. And she? She had to go to New Benin to this Everyman's Chemists. That was a long way away from Ekewan Road. The ten kobo coins felt hard in her hand. How could she spend any money on taking a taxi? A whole ten kobo! If only she could walk it. If only she wasn't so tired, so weak and exhausted. And now, this man Obofun. What could he gain by putting Idemudia into trouble? She knew in her heart that Idemudia would never steal. They were poor and ate anything next to grass. Last Christmas, she had bought and prepared a chicken that had died from an illness. She had specially looked for it because there had been no money. Idemudia hadn't gone to steal then. No, she said to herself. This man was only trying to put them into trouble. And she was worried. She didn't want any police, she didn't want any dealings with them. Their troubles never ended. Once they got into a man's house, it was difficult to get them out. And they hadn't any money with which to bribe anybody. As she stood outside, looking at the dark, threatening skies, the woman who lived in the next house came out and, seeing Adisa, approached her.

'I hear your husband is ill,' she said sympathetically.

Adisa avoided the other woman's eyes. 'Yes,' she confirmed in a weak voice. 'He is in the hospital now, in the Ogbe Hospital.'

'What is wrong with him?' the other woman asked.

'Well, Mama Jimoh thinks it's only malaria, but I don't know.'

They were both silent for a while, then the other woman said, 'My husband died last year,' and there was sadness in her voice.

'He was ill?'

'Yes, for over two months. We couldn't go to hospital. So we used native medicine. But he died and now I have five children to look after alone.'

Another short pause ensued. Each woman thought her own thoughts. Then the other woman said again, 'It's going to rain again. It never stops raining.'

'Yes.'

'It's our house. We are afraid it might collapse. The roof already leaks badly. There is no man to mend it. My husband's brother is away. He has never lived here. Their mother is here with me. She too is sick now.'

Then another pause engulfed them, deeply, briefly. It was the other woman who again broke the silence.

'You are going out?'

Adisa nodded. 'I am going to the chemist's. My husband needs drugs. There aren't any in the hospital. So I have to go out to buy them.'

'They are expensive.'

'They are expensive.'

'Anyway, you better start going before the rain begins to fall. Nowadays, people just die from no causes at all. I hope and pray that your husband gets better. Don't worry. Good luck and goodbye.'

She went back to her low mud house, thatched with old leaves that were gradually giving out to the weather.

Very slowly, Adisa climbed down the steps. The soil was wet and red with the recent rain and as she walked along the road, her slippers threw up the mud on her

dress. But she didn't care. She went slowly towards the
junction where Owode Street met with Ekenwan
Road. The gutters were filled with heavy red water in
which the frogs croaked hoarsely in the night. There
were also the flies, and because the flood was fresh, the
mosquitoes flew about, disturbed. There were the
innumerable pools of water on the twisting, untarred
and uneven road.

In front of the houses along the street, people sat and
watched the weather. Men and women, all jobless, sat
on the long wooden benches, their backs against the
rough mud walls. The children were mostly naked,
and they were thin and had sores on their legs, from
which they frequently drove the flies. Most of the
people who walked along the streets were barefooted
and as the cars passed, some of them Mercedes Benz
cars, they splashed the red muddy water on the people
but drove on, carelessly, secure inside.

Adisa walked along the edge of the road to avoid
the cars and the red water that they splashed.

The horn of a car sounded behind her, and as she
scrambled still further to the side of the road, the car
went past her slowly and she saw that it was the same
man who had accused her husband of stealing his
cement who was driving the car. She looked thoughtfully after the car, and then to her surprise, the car
drew to the side of the road near the road junction and
stopped. Adisa stopped where she was and waited.
Again, surprised and apprehensive, she saw the car
reversing back towards her. Then the car was level
with her and the man rolled down the glass by her
side.

Adisa looked at the man and frowned.

'Madam!' Obofun called.

Adisa bent down towards the window of the car.
What did the man want now?

Obofun leaned over from the driver's seat on the other side of the car.

'Where are you going to?' he asked Adisa.

Again, Adisa was surprised. But . . . Was he trailing her so that he could discover where Idemudia was? Adisa thought it over quickly.

'I am not going anywhere ' she said.

'Don't worry about that,' Obofun replied, and smiled. 'If you are still thinking in terms of your husband, forget it. We have found out that it was the drivers' fault. So come on. Don't be afraid. I'll drop you wherever you are going. It will start raining soon.'

Adisa hesitated and as Obofun unlatched the door, the first showers of the rain came pelting down.

Reluctantly, Adisa opened the door wider and sat down in the passenger seat. Now that she was in the car, she again, for some unknown reason, became apprehensive. She didn't know what to think or what exactly was happening to her. She sat woodenly while Obofun started the car, and engaging the gears, moved off.

'And so, where are you going?' he asked now.

'To New Benin,' Adisa answered mechanically, afraid to think.

'To the market?'

Adisa nodded.

'But that is so far away,' Obofun said as he drove slowly along the road. 'You could have gone there instead,' he said and he pointed with his right hand to Oba Market.

Adisa did not answer.

'What does your husband do generally?' Obofun asked.

Adisa took some time to answer. 'He has no job.'

'And you?'

'What can I do?' Adisa asked.

'Well, something. Is your husband not educated?'

Adisa brushed her face with her hand and did not answer immediately. The rain had increased to such an extent that Obofun was forced to slow down even more now. The wipers hummed, wiping the screen backwards and forwards. The drops of rain were large and many. In a way, Adisa was glad now that she had accepted the lift. She could see some cyclists still riding in the rain and they were drenched to the marrow. So also were the few pedestrians who were about, defying the downpour. The majority of people stood under the cover of open shops and in front of houses along the street. They stood and watched the rain, their faces grim and set.

'My husband is well, er, educated,' Adisa said at last. 'Government Class Four,' not understanding why he should ask her.

'Why, that's something,' Obofun admitted. 'And you?'

Adisa did not want to think about herself at that moment. She would rather have discussed something else. She didn't want to remember the pain of withdrawing from school when she was already in Class Two in the secondary modern school. And all because her father had died.

In the villages, most people died in middle age, between the ages of thirty-five and forty years. They were cut down swiftly, mercilessly and without warning. As the women took over the farms the men had farmed, village life became harder still and malnutrition and disease increased.

A young man still growing had enough strength to fight off the disease. An ageing man succumbed ultimately to it. It was rare to find people who survived the age of fifty and even when they did, they were invariably killed by time a few years later. Time fattened the men as cows were fattened and then killed them off in the prime of their lives. Time was the hard labour on the land, the malnutrition, the diseases, the ignorance, the poverty. Time was the hunger, the hopelessness, the defeated but stubborn look in the eyes of the people. Time was the cruelty and the bitterness into which these people were born and in which they ultimately died.

Obofun looked at Adisa sideways. 'So you are educated,' he said.

'No,' Adisa replied, shaking her head sadly. 'I stopped in Secondary Modern Two.'

But Obofun whistled now, 'No wonder!' he exclaimed.

'Why, no wonder?' Adisa asked, and looked at him for the first time.

'I have been thinking that your language wouldn't be so perfect if you were not educated.'

Adisa was not taken in by the flattery. Her voice was bitter. 'Is a Secondary Modern Two any education?'

'It is! It is,' Obofun insisted. 'The majority of people in government positions today are people with Standard Six or less. That is the equivalent of the secondary modern school.'

Obofun himself had stopped going to school in Standard Four because the teachers had caned the pupils too much. But with the help of his father's money, things had come right for him in the world.

Obofun drove along Old Lagos Street, and turning right, he joined the traffic going to New Benin along Mission Road. The traffic lights at the junction were were not working and he had considerable difficulty working his way out of the confusion.

'You have not told me your name,' Obofun said to her now.

She looked at him again sideways, and a bell began to ring in her head. 'I'll find out and I'll kill you!' the bell rang. 'I'll find out!'

'Adisa,' she said simply.

'Adisa? Why that's a beautiful name,' Obofun said, and the big paraffin lamp that was his smile glowed.

The bells began to ring louder in Adisa's mind now. And in between the ringing of the bells, Adisa could see her aunt's face and hear her voice saying, 'You are still young and beautiful and many men will come running after you. Ah, you think you would die to have another man touch you? You are wrong. There are other alternatives to marriage. You can take a room ...' And then another bell began to ring and it shrilled, 'I'll find out! I'll kill you!'

'Are you not interested in working?' Obofun was asking.

Adisa shook her head, curiously.

'Wouldn't you like to work?' Obofun asked again.

'Work?' she asked surprised but apprehensive.

'Yes, work,' Obofun repeated.

Adisa laughed a little bitterly. 'My husband has been looking for a job for over three years. He has found none. There are no jobs anywhere.'

'Perhaps he hasn't looked hard enough,' Obofun said.

'Do you mean that a man has to look for work all his life to look hard enough?'

'Well, perhaps he hasn't looked in the right places then.'

'He has looked everywhere.'

'But you too could look for work,' Obofun insisted.

'You really expect me to succeed where my husband has failed?'

'Well, you could trade, sell things.'

'Ah, we have thought about that,' Adisa said sadly. 'But there is no money.'

Obofun thought for a while. 'I have things you could sell for me.'

Adisa looked at him sharply. 'Really?'

'Yes,' Obofun answered. 'Really.'

She wanted to say something but then the bell was back in her head, ringing loudly, and her heart began to beat wildly. She stared in front of her, afraid, and inside her head the voices debated fiercely, heatedly.

'You know I own the Freedom Motel? Obofun asked.

'Yes,' Adisa replied, and continued to stare ahead.

'I also own the Samson and Delilah on Airport Road. You could call on me there today. Ask for Obofun.'

Adisa did not answer.

'You could come in the evening. I am not usually there until seven o'clock,' Obofun said, glancing at her, his own heart beating rapidly.

But she still did not answer.

They continued in silence until they got to the junction with New Lagos Road. There again, there was confusion. A heavy lorry was in the middle of the junction and cars trying to circle round it ran into each other. There were curses, loud screechings of tyres and shouting. The traffic lights were not working.

'I will get out here,' Adisa said as soon as Obofun had got out of the confusion, and gathered her dress about her.

'Are you sure you are all right here?' Obofun drew the car to the side of the road.

'Oh yes, I am. Thank you very much,' she said, and quickly stepped out of the car.

'Well, don't forget to call on me,' Obofun called after her. 'I will be waiting for you.'

Adisa did not answer but ran for the opposite side of the market where the traders sold radio cassettes and cartridges at cheap prices.

Chapter 7

They put the drugs in a polythene bag because the rain was still pouring. She was already wet and so did not care about the rain. She wanted to get to the Ogbe Hospital, deliver the drugs and get the assurance that Idemudia would be well. But the hospital was so far away and she was so weak that she would have to take a taxi.

Taxis were scarce because of the rain. Then again there was the fuel shortage. Taxi drivers demanded twenty or forty kobo for a drop. And the drugs had cost her as much as two naira and seventy kobo. The big wall clock in the chemist's shop read seven minutes past eleven. She had to hurry to the hospital.

She stepped onto the roadside. The taxis passed by her, their windows closed up tight. She waved her hand, cried 'Twenty kobo', but in the slush and noise of the rain, the taxi drivers drove by, scarcely paying attention to her.

She waited five minutes, ten minutes. No taxi stopped. Disappointed, she began walking the long distance to the Ogbe Hospital. She hurried as fast as her feet would carry her. She hurried, she ran. She had to get to the hospital.

When at last she arrived, there were some patients lying in the corridor in front of the ward. The rain drove at them, but there was nowhere else for them to go. The ward itself was crowded, like a war camp. Most of the patients were sharing the narrow beds. Some slept on the floor between the beds. It was terrible the way the patients were kept, almost like criminals.

The patient with whom Idemudia shared a bed was

a small dry man, emaciated and with a cough that never seemed to end. When he wasn't coughing he was calling hysterically on Anuoha.

'Anuoha! Anu! Anuoha!' Then again the whooping cough, drawn out and dry, like a person choking from dust in his windpipe. One of the patients was crying. 'Toilet! I want the bucket! Toilet!' But to Adisa's surprise, none of the nurses who sat at their desk at the far end of the ward answered him. One of then even hissed. 'As if anybody here is called a toilet!' she said resentfully.

Adisa did not watch the moment develop to a crisis. She went over to the nurses.

'My husband is there,' she said.

The staff nurse looked up at her. 'And so what?'

Adisa looked back at them uneasily. 'I have brought the drugs.'

'Let me see.' A student nurse took the polythene bag from her, and passed it to the staff nurse.

'The man with whom my husband shares a bed coughs so much!'

'What do you want us to do?'

'Can't he ... ?' Adisa stammered.

'Listen to her!' the student nurse snapped. 'You are not even glad that he is not sleeping on the corridor.'

'I am glad.'

'Then what are you complaining about?'

Adisa fell silent.

'Generally we don't allow people into the wards ...'

'But he hasn't eaten.'

'Who told you he hasn't eaten?'

'Well ...'

'Look, woman. I have told you that we do not allow visitors into the ward at this time. You can come in the evening between the hours of two and six.'

'I am his wife.'

The two nurses laughed loudly. 'As if we have no husbands! You'd better leave. Go away and come back in the afternoon!'

Adisa moved towards Idemudia's bed. The dry man was coughing. Idemudia lay on his side, his back towards the other patient, unable to sleep. 'I'll be coming back. I have brought the drugs.'

Idemudia looked at the floor. He lay on his side. Because of the other patient, he couldn't turn any other way.

'Have you eaten anything?' Adisa bent down and opened the locker that stood beside the bed. There was nothing in it. She closed it and turned round to see the nurse standing in front of her.

Her voice was menacing, threatening. 'Were you not warned just now?' And then she hissed, 'These illiterates!'

Adisa turned round in anger. But she held her tongue. As she walked out of the ward, she could hear the dry emaciated man calling, 'Anuoha! Anu! Anuoha!'

Her heart sagged within her. God! She had told herself, promised herself, never to see anything of this kind again, and here it was happening all over again. No, this was her first real experience of a hospital. It was the other experience in a police station that reminded her so strongly of the hospital atmosphere. Yes, the police station had so much in common with this hospital. The same terrible cases, nervous people pacing to and fro, the same overcrowding, the same urgency, the same confusion, the same indifference from the officials.

Was it not only three weeks earlier when Mama Jimoh had come home weeping?

She could see Mama Jimoh now, crying, 'They have arrested him!'

It is nearly eight o'clock and she is in the compound pounding the yam under the moonlight. Then she rests the pestle against the side of the mortar and her hands fly to her breasts as she looks at the wild face of Mama Jimoh.

'Arrested whom?'

The large woman beats her hands against her chest. 'They have arrested Papa Jimoh. They have locked him up. They won't even let me see him! They...'

Adisa feels worried, anxious. But why should they lock him up? Her first thought is that Papa Jimoh has perhaps committed an offence on the highway, run into another vehicle or knocked somebody down. Idemudia is not at home.

'I must go back there! I must see him to find out what he has done!'

'Wait for me, Mama Jimoh,' Adisa offers. She rolls the pounded yam into a plate and covers it up. 'Idemudia should know where to find his food', she thinks, knowing that indeed Idemudia is lucky to have any food waiting for him.

Mama Jimoh paces about the compound. The chickens pecking at what crumbs of food there are on the ground scatter hastily in front of her.

'They should let us see him!'

'Come on, go inside and don't come out!' Adisa tells Mama Jimoh's three children, and she ties the wrappa more securely around her waist. 'Come, let's go.'

Mama Jimoh follows dumbly behind. Adisa is worried, greatly worried. Here is a tragedy, she thinks. What will happen if Papa Jimoh has indeed knocked somebody down? There are always so many careless cyclists and motorcyclists about.

She walks on in front. 'Don't worry,' she consoles Mama Jimoh. 'Papa Jimoh is a careful driver. It must be something else.'

Inwardly, however, she is afraid. She is not so sure. If there is any trouble, perhaps Papa Jimoh will go to prison. And that will be terrible. Unless he has enough money with which to bribe the police. She doubts this very much. Papa Jimoh may be richer, far richer than she and Idemudia. But he will not have that kind of money, enough to bribe the police. Not when the case is serious. So she hopes it is something else. If only for the sake of Mama Jimoh!

They arrive at the Police Station panting from the effort of hurried walking.

'I saw that man before,' Mama Jimoh whispers and points to a police officer with two red star-shaped stripes on his shoulders.

'What did he say?'

'He said my husband was a dangerous criminal. Couldn't be seen by anybody!' Mama Jimoh breaks down into tears again. Adisa looks at the large woman weeping, and the tears almost come to her own eyes.

Adisa moves towards the Corporal. He is a small man with a peculiar hairstyle. Now he is talking to another man across the high counter. 'It can't be done,' he says. 'Oh no, it can't be done.' He turns to the constable near him, to his right. 'Have you heard their request? They want to release on bail that man who helped that girl commit the abortion! Isn't that terrible? Heh? A young man getting himself into such a mess. He would have had the child. Now the girl, oh poor girl, is lying down in the hospital. Nobody knows whether or not she will survive. But I have never seen so much blood gush out of a single person! Not even during the war.' He removes his cap from the top of the counter and places it firmly on his head. Adisa moves nearer him.

'Oga Sir?'

The little man removes his cap again from his head

and puts it on the counter. 'Yes, madam.'

Adisa beckons to Mama Jimoh. 'A friend of ours,' she points to Mama Jimoh, 'Her husband has been arrested. We do not even know what he has done. We want to see him, please.'

The small corporal laughs. 'It can't be done,' he says. 'That man is a criminal. It's a serious case.'

To the police, of course, any case is a serious one. At least classified as such, it offers limitless opportunities for demanding and receiving bribes.

'Please sir.'

'Madam,' the small man laughs again, completely indifferent. 'There is no begging in the case. He was brought here by his employers.'

Mama Jimoh has come close. 'By his employers?'

'Didn't you know? He took out their car after working hours and was on his way from Agbor when he had an accident. But he didn't let anybody know. He took the car back in the night and parked it.'

Mama Jimoh frowns. 'My husband knows nobody at Agbor.'

'So? Madam, you people are wasting my time!' The man readjusts the cap on his head. The cap now clings to his head at a precarious angle. He turns his attention to the constable who is sitting to his right. 'Tell me ...'

Adisa and Mama Jimoh have to wait a few more minutes, then forseeing no help they walk out of the police building. Outside there are dozens of people pacing to and fro, talking in agitated voices. Two taxis screech to a halt, five men jump out, followed by three other women.

'Where is he? Where is he! He must pay for this!' One of the men has his head bandaged up. Obviously there has been a fight.

People rush to and fro, following close on the heels

of police constables and officers. Explanations are being offered, instances are being stressed; voices are weeping and crying, pleading innocence, begging to be allowed bail, begging to be allowed to send out messages. In the cell itself there is only one double-decker bed. And inside the twelve by ten feet room, some forty people are herded and hooded together, Papa Jimoh among them.

Adisa swears never to go back there. The place destroys her peace of mind; the mad rush, the averted faces, many of them pleading or weeping ... She is afraid. She has never been aware that anything like this exists.

Papa Jimoh is released two days later after spending three nights in the cell. Mama Jimoh, Idemudia and herself are there, almost at the moment of his release. Papa Jimoh is beaten down. His human pride is flat out, knocked down by this cruel bout with other human beings.

All along he protests his innocence.

'I didn't do it,' he protests. 'What type of trouble is this again?' He is subdued. And he talks on at random. 'I didn't do anything. I never took out the car. I left the key on the board, in the usual place.'

Mama Jimoh does not say anything. She is still clearly afraid. She does not know that the matter will end yet.

'Something must have happened,' Idemudia says, walking a little behind Papa Jimoh.

Papa Jimoh has grown even thinner from the two days and three nights of confinement. Like other inmates in the cell, he has urinated on the floor and passed faeces into a general bucket which had been kept under the double decker bed. He has not slept but stood against the wall of the cell throughout. It is impossible to sit on the floor what with the urine and the strong smell of faeces. He hasn't eaten anything too. Whenever he opened his mouth, the foul smell in the room rushed down his gullet and upturned his stomach in the most violent manner. He has therefore been unable to eat his share of the bread which his wife had brought to him.

It is the habit in the cell to share out whatever food any of them is brought. Then too they all have turns at sitting on the double-decker bed. Each day some of their members are taken out while others are brought in to replace them. The experience, the first of its kind in all of Papa Jimoh's thirty-five years of life, is a terrible and a most horrible one.

'How could I have taken out the car?' he says again and again. 'I parked it at five o'clock and left the key on the board. Throughout the evening I was at home. When could I have driven the car?'

Idemudia holds him back when they get to the traffic crossing. The bank stands on the right.

'You shouldn't worry. You have been released,' Idemudia reassures him.

'And what about my job?'

'Well, you are a driver.'

'Oh no. Not with this type of accident.'

'But you are innocent.'

'You should know. You were at home on that same day.'

The next morning, however, another driver comes to their compound. Adisa is out sweeping the long strip of corridor that runs in front but parallel to her door.

'Has anything else happened?' Papa Jimoh asks.

The driver shakes his head. 'No, nothing has happened.'

'Then what do they want me for?'

Mama Jimoh comes out of their bedroom and parlour then. 'No, you are not going anywhere. If they want to arrest you again, let the police come here. Papa Jimoh will stay at home.'

Papa Jimoh looks at the face of the other driver. 'Well?'

'You are quite innocent,' the other driver says. 'They have found the real driver who took . . .'

'What!'

'He took the keys. He didn't sign for them. He returned the car under the cover of darkness.'

'My God!'

'They have handed him over to the police.'

'And they locked you up!' Mama Jimoh cries and her voice is bitter. 'Now tell me where God's justice is. They locked you up for three days. In that police station. For nothing!'

'I think you should come along to see the Personnel Manager,' the other driver advises Papa Jimoh.

Adisa listens to the conversation and she is shocked and resentment is clear and sharp in her voice. 'But they should not have locked you up!' she cries.

A little later, Papa Jimoh accompanies the other driver. In the evening, he returns, his prison experiences forgotten. But the company does nothing to compensate him for the three nights he spends in the cell! Absolutely nothing.

Adisa tightened her lips. Yes, she had sworn never again to go to places that were overcrowded with frightened people pacing to and fro, crying . . . And yet here she was, barely three weeks after.

She swallowed hard. She must get home in time. She was hungry. She had a headache. Her stomach felt hot. There was sweat on her forehead. 'I'll go by Oba Market,' she told herself as she felt the change she had left.

Touching her pockets reminded her of the wetness of her dress. She shivered and tried to increase her pace. But no, she couldn't. Her feet simply dragged beneath her body.

Truck pushers and cyclists were out again on the road. The earth smelled strongly of the rain but the human flood could not be held back. It now flowed riotously again on the streets. She circled the Ring Road and went behind the bank, past the publishing house and arrived at the outskirts of the market. The market flowed with people and red water. The gutters separating the stalls were filled to the brim with filth and decay and what with the heavy rain, some of the dirt and filth and decay surrounded the stalls, the people and their wares. But people marched on them, even barefooted as they were. It was difficult to tell what the filth actually was, the people, their stalls and wares or the decay. All were so thoroughly mixed, so completely part of each other!

Adisa went past the stalls stacked with clothes, shoes. Then came the stalls stacked high with plates, cutlery, cookers and beverages. Adisa went past all these. She was impelled forward by the increasing hunger within her. She didn't stop until she came to the stalls that displayed various items of food. Here, she bought one bonga fish, three milk tins of garri, a bunch of bitter leaves and half a bottle of palm oil. She had some salt and pepper at home. She looked round now. What else did she need? No, she needed everything. She looked round to see what else the money she had could buy. There was nothing else.

All around her, people bargained in hard impersonal voices. Naira notes changed hands. Numbers of kobo were handed back. There was so much that could have been bought and yet there was little or no money. The majority of the people left the market, the disappointment clearly written in their eyes. The prices were up and soaring.

Adisa counted the money she had left. It was only thirty-five kobo. She bit her lips, and slowly made her way out of the market. The sky was still dark and hung low over her as she walked along Ekenwan Road towards her street. The taxis that passed by her splashed some of the red water on her. But she didn't care. She wanted to get home, prepare some food to eat and then have some sleep.

Mama Jimoh was out when she got home. Wearily, she opened the door. Their room looked different to her eyes. It looked as though a great fight had taken place there. She peeled off her clothes and sat on the bed. Her eyes clouded over. Her head grew heavy. She thought about Idemudia in the hospital. She had to go back there in the afternoon, she told herself. She also wondered about her son. What was he doing? Was he sick? And then her mind went to Obofun. What could Obofun do for her? Would she go? What if she did and Idemudia found out about it? Even if nothing had happened between them, Idemudia could kill her, that is if she took his threats seriously. Did Obofun want her because he found her attractive? She wasn't sure. She had to find out. Yes, she would go to see him in the evening and at seven o'clock. She would go to see him to find out how he could help her, and Idemudia would never find out. She rested her head on the pillow. Going to see Obofun did not mean that she was going to give herself to him. She would go to find out how Obofun could help them so that they wouldn't always be hungry, scratching the bottom of pots and racking their brains over how they were going to get their next meal.

Now, she told herself, she needed to rest a little to get rid of the headache that was gnawing at her. Yes, only a short rest. She lifted her legs to the bed, drew out a wrappa and covered up her body. Her wet clothes hung on the chair as it stood beside the bed. She would spread them out to dry after she had rested. And then she would eat. But she must rest first. She was so tired! Very gradually, her mind dulled and she slipped into a shallow, hungry sleep.

Chapter 8

There were at least a thousand eggs and as many tins of peak milk in the big jeep that drew up outside the Freedom Motel on Monday morning. The driver jumped out and ran for the swing doors. It was raining.

Queen went downstairs. She had sighted the jeep with the government number plates from her room upstairs and she had guessed correctly what was packed in it. In fact she knew. Iriso had promised that these things would arrive that morning but that the beef would arrive later.

The driver was standing at the receptionist's desk when she came downstairs.

'You are from Iriso?' she asked, matter of fact.

'Yes, madam,' the driver answered, looking at the long dress of the woman. It hung about her like a bridal dress. It was of a pale grey material and it darkly revealed what lay behind. He handed her an envelope.

Queen tore the envelope open and unfolded the letter that lay inside. She had had no formal education but because of the demands that her business interests made on her, she had come to educate herself, in an informal way. She went through the short note and mumbled to herself.

'Twenty cartons of milk containing almost two thousand tins of peak milk plus three thousand eggs.'

This definitely was something. She turned to the waiters. 'Take out four cartons of milk and count one thousand eggs.' She turned to the driver. 'One of them will accompany you to remove the rest of the milk and eggs to Sakponba Road. There is a place there called the ...' She thought for a while. She hadn't given the hotel any name yet.

The driver looked at her and then asked, 'Any message, madam?'

Queen nodded, 'Tell him I'll be waiting to see him. And thank him.'

She turned to one of the waiters. 'James, you will accompany the driver to the house on Sakponba Road. Now, unload the milk.'

James accompanied the driver out of the motel. She watched them running across the pebbles and grass to the jeep. She climbed upstairs and sat down in the sitting room. She thought over the whole deal.

'What does it matter?' she asked herself. 'Nothing,' she answered. 'I'll see him and then we'll go to Sakponba Road.' Men were so foolish, she thought. And so cheap! She would have paid no less than five hundred naira for the things Iriso had brought. And in fact it wasn't the money. Milk and eggs were difficult to get. That was the major problem.

Like the cement, for instance. The cement deal had gone off very well. She had been with the man only twice and the cement had come. And to think that the man had come to her many times before she had finally agreed! She had no doubt that he would come again. They always came back. Then she thought about the government contract and she was annoyed that she should have been given an ultimatum to complete the low-cost houses she was building. The workers were so lazy! But she needed many more. Hardworking and dedicated people who didn't want her money for nothing. 'Oh yes,' she told herself. 'Hardworking people like the men who offloaded my bags of cement. That man who brought his friends yesterday must be contacted again. They were so fast! A pity some bags went missing.' But then she thought she knew who the thieves were. 'The trailer drivers!' She would send for Idemudia and ask him to come at once. The man looked reliable.

She heard steps coming up the stairs. James appeared.

'We have finished, madam.'

'How many of the milk did you remove?'

'Four cartons.'

'And the eggs?'

'One thousand.'

'Good. Now accompany him to the house at Sakponba Road. Take the rest off there.'

'After that?'

'Come back here. What else? And be quick.'

James went downstairs. But Queen called him back. He appeared, visible only from the knees upwards.

'Do you remember the man who unloaded the bags of cement yesterday?'

James walked into the sitting room. 'Yes, madam.'

'When you come back, go and call him. I want to see him.'

'Okay, madam.'

'I hope you know where he lives?'

'Just before the junction. We are from the same town.'

'Good. Make sure he comes with you.'

Queen had already decided what to do with the eggs and the milk. She would make Obofun pay for the ones she left behind, while those that had been taken to Sakponba Road would be redistributed at higher prices and some of it kept at her hotel.

Again her mind went back to the government ultimatum. 'You must finish the house within the specified time,' the letter had warned her, 'or else you will be blacklisted.' She was not so much afraid of being blacklisted as having a job on her hands which she could never complete. She didn't want her efforts and her attention tied up in one place for too long. She decided she would employ more men and get the job done with.

A door to her left opened.

'Richard!'

The door snapped shut. There was no answer.

Queen called again, 'Who is there?'

A minute passed and Lilian appeared.

Queen was surprised. 'What, didn't you go to school?'

Lilian stood and faced her mother. 'No,' she answered without remorse.

'Why not?'

Lilian looked out of the sitting-room into the compound, outside. The sky was dark grey, on its face was the heavy shawl of the rain.

'Why not?' Queen asked again, anger in her voice. 'And you expect to pass like this?'

'I am not well, Ma.'

'You are not well? Who did you tell? What is wrong with you? Not well? Liar! Not well!'

Lilian fell silent. Queen stood up, then bent down again to put on her shoes. Without another word, she abandoned her daughter in the large sitting room and went down the stairs. She went into the store at the side of the restaurant. The four cartons of milk and the egg containers were there. She picked up one of the eggs. It was big and heavy. 'Very good,' she said to herself, 'Very good.'

She came out of the restaurant and went into the bar. A few men and women sat at various tables, drinking. One of the men waved to her. She waved back. But the hand persisted, beckoned to her. She went towards the table. Three men were seated there. She immediately recognised one of them. She smiled at them, circled their table and took the vacant chair by the side of the man.

'Long time no see,' the man said, staring her in the eyes.

'Why, Lami, it has been your fault, not mine.'

Lami laughed and introduced his friends.

'It wasn't my fault,' he laughed. 'It's business,' he said seriously. 'Business. It has involved me up to the neck. No way out.'

'You shouldn't complain then. You have done well.'

'Oh no, no, no. There is no doing well in business. One manages.'

He prodded Queen with his finger in her side. Queen stood up. 'I am busy now,' she excused herself. 'You know you are always welcome, Lami.'

'And my friends?'

Queen smiled broadly, 'Your friends included.'

She moved back into the restaurant. James had come back. His hair was wet and it shone from the hanging raindrops. He brushed the rain away from his face.

'We left the milk there,' he informed Queen.

'And the eggs?'

'The eggs too.'

'Your feet are wet,' Queen observed.

James looked down at his feet and acknowledged the fact.

'You are dirtying the hall. Go and remove your shoes. Then come back and wipe up the water.'

'Yes, madam,' James answered, and moved towards the back of the restaurant.

Queen paused for a second. She had so many things she wanted to do. She needed to take along quite a lot of money to the furniture makers. She also had to make arrangements for the signboard to be written and installed. She would discuss the name of the hotel with Iriso.

She heard a car stopping outside. She moved out of the restaurant into the passage where the receptionist's desk stood. She couldn't see far outside because of the rain. She cursed the rain; why would it never cease? Yesterday it had rained. Today it was raining again. She heard somebody stamping his feet on the cemented floor outside. Then Iriso appeared. He carried a black umbrella in his hand. The umbrella was folded and dipped downwards to let the water out. A quivering streamlet of water followed closely behind Iriso.

Queen advanced towards him and took his free left hand.

'You have come,' she said.

'You got the things I sent?'

'Oh yes. Thank you. Wait here. I will be down in a minute.'

Iriso stood against the receptionist's high desk. He had expected Queen to take him upstairs immediately. What did she mean by telling him to wait? He swallowed hard and looked down at the little pool of water forming at his feet. His own image was beginning to be reflected there. He watched his image grow larger as the pool widened. He watched fascinated. So even a drop of water could draw the reflection of a man! He had never noticed it before. He walked towards the entrance of the motel. In the small pools that formed on the cemented pavement, he could catch glimpses of the sky and the surrounding trees. He laughed to himself, happy in this discovery. The smallest pool of water could reflect even the vast orb of the sky! It was wonderful. Who could ever have thought that this was possible?

But then did not so many impossible things happen and quite frequently? Take his own milk and egg transaction, for instance. He shivered. He knew that if it were discovered, he would be in some difficulty. Not in too much difficulty anyway. After all his immediate boss had only the week before ...

A hand touched his shoulder. 'I am ready,' Queen said. She had changed from her long dress to a buba and wrappa. The materials were of lace. Iriso eyed her. What was Queen up to?

'Where are we going?' he asked, snapping the umbrella open so that it could accommodate both of them.

'To Sakponba Road,' Queen informed him. 'I have a house there I want to turn into a hotel.'

'Why a hotel?'

'What else?' Queen asked. 'It's the best business.' They came to Iriso's car. The Volvo glistened under the rain.

'We can use my car,' Iriso suggested.

'How do I come back?' She thought for a moment, her hand pressing against Iriso's side. 'Wait,' she said, and took the umbrella from Iriso. Iriso opened the door of the car and quickly got inside.

Queen went back to the house. She went up to the receptionist.

'Tell the driver to bring my car round to Sakponba Road. He knows the place.'

Then she walked back quickly to the other side of the car, wrenched the door open and got inside.

Iriso started the car. 'Are you always so well dressed and so beautiful?' he asked.

Queen laughed. 'Better watch where you are going.'

'I can see clearly enough.' He stretched out his left hand and placed it in Queen's lap.

Queen let him have his way for some time, then she pushed his hand away. 'You want them to pick up your car at the Motor Traffic Division?'

Iriso smiled pleasantly. 'Never. My mind is on the road.'

'And your hand is here. Do you drive with your mind?'

'Of course. The mind controls the hands.'

'But if you have no hands? Tell me, I want to set up this hotel. That's where we are going. I want a name for it.'

'You could use your name. The Queen's Hotel. But why do you want a hotel?'

'It's easy. I'll get all my eggs, meat and milk from you.'

'And if I quit like your husband did?'

'There always will be ways.'

'In any case you don't need a hotel. You could set up a shop. You don't need a hotel. You already have a hotel.'

'That one isn't mine. It's my husband's.'

'So what belongs to Obofun does not belong to you?'

'In a way, yes. But it doesn't mean I shouldn't struggle. Obofun encourages me. He tells me it is good.'

Iriso thought 'Shylocks', but he said nothing aloud.

'Are you going to help me with a name for the hotel?' she asked.

Iriso patted the back of his neck with his right hand. 'I have been thinking of names,' he said.

'Well, suggest one.'

'Let me see, let me see. What about the Inner Circle Hotel?'

Queen tested the name on her tongue. 'Isn't that too long?'

'Not longer than many others I know.'

'But you can suggest a second name.'

'I already have,' Iriso reminded her. 'The first one was Queen's Hotel. That's short but it doesn't seem to appeal to you. You can even turn it round. This way ...' Iriso slammed on his brakes hard. There was another car in front. He hadn't seen it in his talking and imagining the developments that were forthcoming. Queen was slightly thrown forward from her seat. She eyed Iriso.

'I told you to watch the road.'

'Ah, it's nothing. A bastard driver suddenly appearing. He would have had it. Mine is a Volvo. It wouldn't have felt the impact. And ... er, as I was saying, you can turn the name round. It becomes Hotel Queen.'

'I like that,' Queen admitted. 'Hotel Queen. But something again is missing. I think I prefer the other one, The Inner Circle.'

'Then take it.'

'I will. I will get a signwriter to put up a board there tomorrow.'

'So quick? What about the other things? People to work there and what-not? Have you thought about that?'

'Of course I have.'

'Where would you advise us to be coming to? The Freedom Motel or the Inner Circle?'

'Who do you mean?'

'I mean your present customers.'

'You can always pick your way out. I am not afraid of getting customers. Many, if not most, of our people are drunkards. And after drinking, they must eat, chew something. You can't eat and drink in a shop.'

'I guess you are right,' Iriso agreed. He circled the Ring Road. The traffic there always got on his nerves. Nobody seemed to know how to get on to the road. There were so many inlets and outlets into the ring that they involved all the users in a battle for the right of way. Iriso drove slowly and carefully.

'What part of Sakponba?' he asked Queen. 'Upper or Lower?'

'Not far from here. You turn off after the church.'

'What! So close to the church?'

Queen looked at Iriso. There was amusement in her eyes. 'So many people go to the church. Before they enter and after they come out, the majority of them are bound to call there, at my hotel.'

'And you are not afraid that God will go after you? You will be taking his congregation away. You will be making them drink.'

'God didn't say that people shouldn't drink. If you remember, the first work of Christ was to turn water into wine. It makes the congregation warmer, their donations more generous. I even expect the pastor to call here a few times.'

'Your Inner Circle will take over from the Church.'

Queen laughed. 'It's business. The Church also is business. Slow down. That house there, that uncompleted storey building. Decked already.'

'And painted too,' Iriso observed.

'That was done last week. The painters were thieves. They asked me to buy forty tins of paint. They ended up using only twenty-eight. At least so one of them told me after. But all the tins were empty when they came to check with me.'

Iriso swung the big car off the road and drew up beside the house Queen had indicated. The rain had degenerated to nothing more than a shower.

They climbed up the three steps to the front door. Queen took out a bunch of keys and opened the door. The room inside was dark. She found the switch and turned on the lights. It was a gigantic hall, and its walls were panelled with brown wood, the floor was tiled with red and black stones.

'This will be the restaurant,' Queen explained. 'The bar will be at the other side. Come.'

She led the way to a side door. They entered another large room. 'But I intend that they should always come into the restaurant from the bar. So I am making another door there.' She pointed.

'It's a good idea,' Iriso said.

'It is,' Queen agreed. 'The rooms are at the back. The manager and a few guests can always be housed there.' Again she led the way back into the restaurant and parted two curtains at the far side. She opened the door. Iriso came out to a passage. It was a passage to another building altogether but the doors to the rooms there ran parallel to the wall cutting off the restaurant. Queen opened the door nearest to her.

It was a large bedroom, already fitted out. Queen entered the room. Iriso followed closely behind her. The door slowly dragged back on its hinges and snapped shut.

'Well?'

Iriso turned Queen round so that she faced him. He put his arms round her. 'You are a wonderful woman,' he said.

'Me?' Queen pushed him away. 'Many do not think so.'

'Then they are blind.'

'Perhaps they are not. Perhaps they see correctly.'

'They do not,' Iriso replied. His voice was beginning to grow thick with desire. Once again he circled Queen and put his arms around her. Very slowly he edged her towards the bed and then pulled her down on himself.

'You think I am a prostitute,' Queen accused him. Iriso did not answer. He was busy loosening the wrappa and fondling her breasts.

'Speak out,' Queen told him. 'You think I am a prostitute. You think so in your heart but you will not say it. That is why you are silent. You are convinced, so you say nothing.'

Iriso was perspiring on the forehead. 'I would be foolish to think you are a harlot,' he said densely. 'You are not. You are just a woman, a beautiful woman, a wonderful woman.'

'You flatter me but I am not deceived. You think I am a cheap woman.'

Iriso cursed her in his heart. Why did she want the assurance from him? He had never even thought about it.

'You are not a cheap woman!' he said fiercely.

Queen laughed. 'I don't believe you.' She got herself free from Iriso.

'Where are you going?' Iriso asked, his voice parched with lust.

'I am going home,' Queen said quietly.

'Home? Why home?'

Queen laughed again. 'What kind of question is that? Why do I want to go home? I came from there. I belong there.'

Iriso sprang up from the bed. All the veins in his body stood out violently. He saw Queen's straight legs, her heavy breasts, her landslide backside and something in him went mad.

'You can't go! You can't go away,' he cried.

'Are you going to stop me?' Queen asked.

'And the milk, the eggs? After everything I supplied you! After all the risks, the expectations!'

'I am going to pay you!' Queen snapped back.

'I don't want any money.'

'So? What then do you want? I am going to pay you!'

'I don't want your money!' The words tore out of Iriso's voice savagely.

'So you don't want any money?'

'I don't want any money,' Iriso insisted.

'What then do you want?'

'You know what I want. You can't pretend not to know.' Iriso was again close to her and again he put his arms around her and dragged her to the bed.

'I am a married woman,' Queen pointed out, as she struggled with Iriso on the bed.

'It doesn't matter,' Iriso insisted.

'Can you imagine another man telling your wife that? Telling her it doesn't matter to commit adultery. What would you do?'

Again Iriso cursed her. His wife wouldn't want milk or eggs from any man anyway. So the question of adultery would never arise.

'It doesn't matter,' Iriso repeated, as he fumbled with the tips of Queen's breasts. But the brassiere was tight and it held. He couldn't get the hold he wanted.

Finally, Queen said, 'Let me get up.'

'Why?'

'Oh, I am tired of struggling. I will undress. By myself.' Iriso let her go. But he didn't believe her.

Queen got up from the bed and very slowly began to undress. First she removed her lace buba. Next, the lace wrappa went. On the bed, Iriso struggled with his tie. Then he kicked off his shoes before undoing the buttons of his trousers.

They slept together for an hour, then exhausted, both fell apart. Then he came back and pressed the flat of his stomach against the flat of her stomach, cupped one of her breasts in his hand and ran his other hand up and down her spine. There was no denying the fact. Queen was a great woman. She had beaten him each time, taken the victory from him before he was ready to give it.

'You are a lazy man, Queen said, not moving.

'I, a lazy man?'

'Yes, you tire so easily.'

'You wait until next time.'

'What makes you think there will be a next time?' She lifted her breasts from the bowl of his hand. 'You are hurting me. Don't press so. Hard, I mean.' She turned away from him and lay flat on her back.

'Why do you think this will happen again?' she asked.

Iriso looked at the ceiling. 'Won't there be a next time?'

'The bitch,' he thought. 'As if she is not going to need any more milk, eggs and meat. If she won't need any of these, she will need other things, and if a man supplies them, she is going to use her body to pay for them. Harlot!' He spat out towards the other side of the bed on the wall.

'What are you spitting on the wall for? Can't you keep your mouth dry after sleeping with a woman?' she said with scorn.

'Prostitute!' his mind fumed. Then he was angry with himself. Flinging away nearly five hundred naira so easily. Just for an hour's lovemaking. Oh that he could be vital again! But he was dead there. Dead and sore and there was nothing he could do about it. But there was no doubt about it, Queen knew how to make love to a man so that he would invariably want to come back for more. Suddenly he laughed. Queen had cried and moaned as only a virgin would. She had moaned in the heat of passion as a child would with high temperature. 'Very well practised,' he thought bitterly. 'Very well practised.'

Queen also was staring at the ceiling. 'What is wrong with this man?' she thought. 'Some of them talk their senses out, afterward, proud of their conquest. Their ego swells. They can even insult the woman, say those things they would never have said before the event. Of course they always come back. But they talk, unlike this dumb and sullen elephant.'

Aloud, she said, 'I am going home.'

She got up from the bed, drew her pants from under

the pillow. She straightened them out because they were crumpled. Then she put them on. Next she put on her brassiere, then went and stood in front of the mirror.

On the bed, Iriso remained sullen. 'Five hundred naira!' his mind cried. 'Three thousand eggs, two thousand tins of milk! Christ! What have I done? Given them away for nothing?' He cursed himself.

Aloud he said to Queen, 'When do I see you again?'

Queen turned away from the mirror. She didn't care much about Iriso now. But she said, 'I am always at the Freedom Motel.'

'Not like that,' Iriso flung back, salt in his voice. 'Like how then?'

Iriso tapped on the bed. 'Like this, here.'

Queen crossed over to the bedside and picked up her *buba* which lay on the ground. She struggled into it. Already angry, Iriso watched Queen's heavy buttocks, naked but for her pants. Perhaps it had been worth it, he began to think. This woman wasn't just the ordinary type of street woman. She was different.

'You have not answered me,' he said to Queen's back, and flung his hand to slap her on the buttocks.

Queen moved out of reach of his hands. Next she put on her white underskirt. Then she began to tie her *iro*, or wrappa, round herself.

'You won't see me here again,' Queen answered him at last.

Iriso still lay stark naked on the bed. 'What?'

'What will you want to see me for?'

'But this cannot be the end!'

Queen sat on the bed to put on her shoes. 'Why don't you get dressed? Don't you want to go home or to your place of work?' she scolded him.

Iriso spat again on the wall.

'Keep your mouth dry. This is not a toilet!' She was angry.

'Where else am I to spit? I am disgusted. Utterly disgusted.'

'With what?'

Iriso swallowed the saliva.'With you,' he said. 'With you. How can you say this is the end, when it is only the beginning? Won't you need more eggs or meat and milk? Are there no other things you will need? And er, I like you. Come to think of it, I really like you.'

Queen regarded him as he lay naked on the bed. She wanted to spit herself. But she checked herself. 'Get dressed,' she said earnestly. 'Get dressed and let's go. You know I have a lot of things to do. And if we are going to meet again like this,' she slapped the bed, 'then it won't be here. It will be at the Samson and Delilah.'

Iriso struggled up from the bed. 'What? Why there? Along Airport Road. Isn't it?'

'Yes, it belongs to my husband.'

'To your husband?'

'Yes, didn't you know?'

'I didn't. I can see that you are both out to capture the whole catering market in this city.'

'Get dressed! Get dressed! Let's go!'

Iriso put his feet on the floor. Pieces of toilet paper lay about the floor. 'Are you leaving these on the floor?' He pointed.

'Get dressed. Let's go. I am going to flush them as we go out.' She began to gather them up into a heap.

'Tell me more about this Samson and Delilah.'

'What do you want to know about it?'

'Anything. How many chalets are there?'

'Seventeen. The seventh and thirteenth are reserved for us and our guests.'

'That's excellent. Isn't it? But why did you have to do that?'

'We are always having visitors,' Queen said, 'and as

you know, they always think they can get accommodation, that we can always evict our customers, which isn't possible. So we left those two chalets vacant. They are never occupied by other customers.'

'But you and I are going to occupy it one day,' Iriso said.

'Shut up.'

'Won't we? And for how many days?' He was smiling.

'I said shut up.' 'Now he is going to talk,' she said to herself. 'He is going to brag, ugly cow.'

'And how many people have occupied it with you ever since?'

'Oh, all of you are just the same,' she said with disgust.

Iriso's chest heaved with laughter. His eyes watered and he used the back of his hand to wipe the water away.

'So when do we see each other again?' he asked seriously.

Queen was offended. 'Never,' she said. 'Never.'

'I was only joking.'

'You were not. Men often speak their minds out when they are drunk or when they have just slept with a woman. You were not joking. Hurry up. Let's go.'

'Honestly, I was only joking.'

'Swallow your jokes. Stop spitting them out as you have been doing with your saliva.'

She gathered up the toilet paper, went to the door leading to the bathroom, opened it and went in. Iriso could hear the water running.

'To hell with her,' he thought viciously. 'And I needn't bother anyway. When she wants the milk, she is going to contact me.'

Queen came out. 'Are you set?'

'Yes.'

She opened the door and Iriso went out. Then she turned off the lights and came out of the room herself. She was so composed that no one who saw her at that moment would ever have guessed what had transpired between her and Iriso.

They went into the restaurant and came out through the front door. Queen locked the doors. The rain had stopped and her driver sat in the car waiting, in the intense sunlight.

'We'll be seeing each other then,' Iriso said again.

'Oh yes. We'll be seeing each other. Goodbye.'

She watched Iriso get into his big yellow car. Then she came down the stairs and took the back of her car. It was a white car and she had only recently bought it.

'We are going to ABC Furniture,' she instructed her driver.

She took out her bag and opened it. Why, she had put in some money there? Five hundred naira. The money wasn't there. Her mind went to Iriso. No, he wouldn't touch her bag.

'Aluiya, turn back. We are going home.'

'Home, madam?'

'Yes, home. We are going home. You can take the next street. It brings us to Sapele Road.'

Had she forgotten to put the money in her handbag? Her mind went again to Iriso. Iriso didn't look like a person who would steal from a woman. But what if he had when she had gone into the toilet to flush those pieces of toilet paper? 'Remember,' she told herself, 'he wanted you to go and flush the toilet paper. Why?' She shrugged her shoulders. Iriso wouldn't be the first man to have stolen from her. Only he hadn't looked like a common thief.

Aluiya turned off Ekenwan Road and entered Owode Street. As they went past the house where Idemudia lived, she looked at the house and saw Adisa who was going out of the house at that moment. She told herself she would send for Idemudia as soon as she could. Perhaps James had already seen Idemudia and passed on her message to him, but she had to go back to the ABC Furniture immediately. 'I must complete all the arrangements for the rest of the furniture today,' she said to herself.

So, when they got to her compound, she didn't come out. Instead, she said to Aluiya, 'Go upstairs and ask Lilian to bring me the money in the left hand drawer of my dressing table.'

If the money wasn't there, then Iriso must have stolen it. Five hundred naira *and* herself for the milk and the eggs! That would be too expensive, she told herself.

The driver came out of the house. But instead of entering the car, he leaned in at the window. 'There is trouble upstairs, madam.'

Queen frowned. She wasn't prepared for any trouble.

'What type of trouble?' she asked, leaning forward from the back seat of the car.

'I don't know, madam, but Lilian is screaming.'

'What is wrong with her?'

Aluiya shook his head. 'Madam, I cannot say,' and he opened the door for her.

Chapter 9

The rays of the sun were strong upon Adisa's face. She had woken up from sleep to find that sunlight had taken the place of rain and her spirit had cheered a little. She was able to start a quick fire outside, prepare some bitterleaf soup and *eba*. The bonga fish came in handy. It sweetened the soup and by the time she had finished eating, her zest for life had returned.

She spread out her wet clothes outside, selected another dress and put it on. The one she now wore was old but she told herself that it was better than nothing, and headed for the hospital. The old man with the cough and a strange attachment for the name 'Anuoha' was asleep. So was Idemudia, but after some fifteen minutes Idemudia woke up as if by a strange reflex.

'So you are here,' he said, and he closed his eyes, briefly.

She nodded, 'I have only just come in. You were asleep.'

'Oh yes. I know.' He tried to sit up in bed so as to examine her more closely. But the effort was too much. He fell back.

'What did the doctors say?' Adisa asked, apprehension in her voice.

'The doctors have said nothing. But I heard the nurses saying I have pneumonia.'

'That's like malaria.'

'I think so. But I am not sure.'

'It's not worse anyway.'

'I heard the nurses say I was lucky to have been brought in when I was.'

They both fell silent.

'What have you been doing?' he asked, and eyed her.

'Sleeping.' She could not tell him about her evening's appointment with Obofun. It might never materialise, she thought, and even if it does . . .

'You have eaten?'

'Yes. Nothing much but at least something.'

He turned his face away and again they lapsed into silence. Women and children sat or stood by patients in the ward. The majority of the patients still shared beds, many more slept on the floor. It was like a pigsty, this ward, swarming with the sick, as pit toilets swarm with flies.

On the next bed, a patient was surrounded by his family and friends. The man had his head and hand bandaged. There were tears in the eyes of his wife.

'The police have arrested them,' the woman said through her tears.

'How many of them did they take?' the man with the bandaged head asked. There was pain in his eyes, red-hot pain from the effort of talking.

'Do not talk,' one of the standing sympathisers told him. 'All you can do now is listen. I will tell you the story as it happened afterwards.'

Adisa sat in silence and listened to the story. The events which the man narrated had taken place in a village not far away from the city. It appears a man, a wealthy one from the city, had gone to the village with armed men and attacked this family over a piece of land.

'He kept on claiming to the police that our father had sold the piece of land to him. He brought out papers with marks on them which he claimed were the thumb marks of our father.'

'Our father would have told us if he had sold the land!'

'Of course he would have done so. We would have

had a copy of the agreement. Our father never sold any land.'

'He never did.'

'This man is out to make trouble,' the woman added.

'And what will the police do?' another in their midst asked.

The man who had been talking was not sure. 'Nobody knows what the police will do. The men were arrested on the land, they were caught still destroying the cassava.'

'Surely that is enough to send them to prison?' the woman said.

'It is enough. More than enough, but I understand that the man making all this trouble is a rich man. You know how the police are.'

The woman bit her lip. 'A rich man,' she repeated without hope and with great bitterness.

'They say he has always taken land from people like that. But he will never take ours. We will die fighting on it.'

They all fell silent.

'How is the head?' the woman asked.

The patient moved his hand weakly. They had struck him on the head and hand with matchets.

'These troubles will never cease,' Adisa said to herself. She was angry at the man who had caused all the fighting, subconsciously. Idemudia had drifted again into sleep. She stood up from the edge of the bed and went towards the door.

Osaro was just hurrying into the ward. There was no smile on his face. 'Where is he?' he asked.

Adisa pointed to Idemudia's bed and began walking back to it. 'He is asleep. He is resting,' Adisa said.

'And you didn't come to tell us?'

'I had no time. I have been here ever since.'

'Well, I can hardly blame you.' Osaro kept his hands

behind his back. 'I ran into Papa Jimoh at Iyaro. He was driving past when he saw me. He told me. I went to the University Hospital. You were not there. I went to your house. Nobody was there so I guessed he must be here. What is wrong with him?'

They arrived at Idemudia's bed. Both stood looking down at him.

'It's fever,' she said. 'Very bad fever.'

'When did it start?'

'I cannot say. I came home to find him already very sick. Did you not go with him to unload the bags of cement?'

'Yes.'

'And this morning the man comes to say ...'

'Which man?' Osaro interrupted.

'I think he is the owner of the hotel, Obofun. He comes in and says one hundred and fifty bags of cement are missing.'

'Don't mind about him. He is lying. Who cares about their cement?'

'Anyway he came back to say he was sorry. That it was a mistake.'

Osaro hissed, 'These people! And how is he? I mean him.' He pointed at Idemudia, lying on his side on the bed.

'I don't know. The nurses have said nothing yet.'

'It's a great pity. I am sure he fell ill because of the rain and the work. He was in both for a long time.'

He pointed at the old man with whom Idemudia shared the bed.

'Who is he?'

'I don't know,' Adisa replied. 'Nobody visits him and all the time he coughs and calls on Anuoha.'

'Anuoha?'

'Yes.'

'That could be the name of a man.'

'I think so.'

'But why does he call on Anuoha?'

'I can't say.'

The old man lay in a heap, on his side. He seemed to be sleeping peacefully but inside him the cough gathered like a storm and soon it erupted like a volcano. He coughed for so long that his eyes watered. Then he seemed to be chewing and grinding his teeth.

'Anuoha! Anuoha! Anuoha!' he called plaintively.

'Listen!' Adisa cried, poking Osaro in the ribs.

'I wonder why nobody visits him.'

'I don't know.'

The old man's coughing woke Idemudia up. But he couldn't speak. He was awake but only semiconscious, like the hours of night before the dawn. His eyes were closed, yet his mind was half awake.

The old man coughed again, and again he chewed and ground at his teeth.

'Anuoha!'

Osaro went to the other side of the bed, where the old man's head was turned.

'Who is Anuoha?' he asked. 'Perhaps he can be sent for?'

The man's eyes flickered. Very slowly, he turned his head.

'He is from Asaba,' Adisa informed him.

'Oh, that is good,' Osaro said. 'I will speak his language to him then.'

'Who is Anuoha?' he repeated in the man's language.

Momentarily the old man's mind cleared of its fog. He noticed the people around him.

'Anuoha,' Osaro said again. 'Perhaps he can be sent for. Who is he?'

'Anuoha?' the old man's voice was like a ruptured roof. 'They killed him. He is dead.'

Silence descended upon Osaro and Adisa and even upon the other visitors nearby.

'They shot him close to the bridge. I found him

111

there. They shot him in the head and in the neck. They killed him! Anuoha!' The old man's eyes watered. 'I told him never to go into the army but he went. He said he needed a job. He was tired of sitting at home, running from place to place – looking for a job. He joined the army to get a job and they killed him. By the bridge. I found him there. I carried him. Alone I buried him. Anuoha! Anuoha!'

Adisa looked expectantly at Osaro. 'What did he say?'

Osaro's voice was heavy as he narrated the story. 'They shot his son,' he explained. 'They shot him in the head and in the neck. He says he found his son by the bridge shot through and through.'

'But many people were killed during the war. Why can he not forget?'

Osaro tried to explain. 'In the war that is gone,' he said, 'the losses were not equal.'

The old man began to cough again. This time it was a long protracted cough. It erupted again and again, increasing all the time in intensity. The old man's hands flew to his chest, then to his throat, while his spine arched and curved from the effort of coughing.

The nurses sat at the desk and heard him coughing. Yet none of them came, at least not for the moment. They were three in number, one of them was the staff nurse and the others were student nurses. They were gossiping about another student nurse. The story gripped their attention, stayed their minds.

At last, unable to concentrate on the story because the coughing of the old man carried still more sharply to her ears, one of the nurses stood up from her chair and walked over. There was no pity in her eyes. 'The dirty old bastard!' she thought furiously. 'The old coughing sack!'

She remembered, however, what the doctor had said.

112

'If he coughs more and more, give him that second injection. At least that's the best we can do for him.'

Adisa and Osaro regarded the nurse as she bent over the coughing man, her eyes hard. The water ran down the man's face and his whole chest heaved and trembled as if it would collapse in a second. The nurse went back to her desk for the syringe.

'I am afraid for Idemudia,' Osaro said. 'He too might catch the cough.'

'I said so, too. Right at the beginning,' Adisa added. 'But they told us it was this bed or nothing. Surely a man comes to the hospital to be cured and not to have other diseases added to his.'

The nurse had come back with her loaded syringe. The old man gasped with pain and Adisa turned her face away as the nurse plunged the long needle into the old man's arm, lower down towards the elbow. Then she squeezed the trigger on the syringe, almost with pleasure. The old man mumbled something. Again his mind was clogged and fogged. And after a few minutes, when the nurse had gone away, his consciousness was gone. He fell asleep.

'Perhaps the man has other people?'

'They would have come,' Osaro answered.

'You are sure they know?'

'Why not, although some of them might not want to come for fear of the expenses. It has happened before.'

Somewhere a bell began to ring.

The staff nurse stood up and like a cock announced that the visiting hour was over.

Idemudia did not come out of his half-consciousness. 'Perhaps they also put some sleep into his blood,' Adisa thought as she walked with Osaro to the door.

'There is nothing we can do for him today,' Osaro said. 'Perhaps by tomorrow he will be better. He must. Idemudia is a strong man. You should have seen him working on that heap of cement. Without him . . .'

'Oh yes, he is a strong man!' Adisa thought bitterly. 'A strong man who can scarcely feed his wife and the only money he brings home has to be used in curing him. God knows who is going to pay the bills for his treatment. Where is the money going to come from?'

'Where are you going now?'

'Home, home,' she answered. 'Where else would I go?' She did not relish coming to this hospital to-morrow, or any other day afterwards. Why did he have to fall ill? Then her conscience slapped her. 'You shouldn't be thinking like that,' her conscience told her. 'You know that everything he has, he has always given to you. Is it his fault that he cannot find a job? Does he not try hard enough? Which man who has seen the inside of a college building for four years would ever have gone to Iyaro? Yet Idemudia had gone there, every day. And you very well know now why he is sick. He was working while you were at your aunt's place, thinking of how to leave him.'

'But I am not going to leave him,' she defended herself. 'And anyway, I went to her because I was hungry. And he threatened to kill me.'

'No, you told him what a woman should never say to her husband,' her mind rebuked her.

'I was angry. I was hungry. He had no right to hit me.'

'That was no excuse to tell him you were going to look for another man. It's never said. Not when a man is still your husband.'

'Oh, come on, shut up,' she said to her other mind viciously. 'I was hungry. A man who cannot provide for his wife . . .'

'How much did they say you would have to pay?' Osaro asked, breaking into her thoughts.

'What?'

'How much will the hospital be charging Idemudia each day?' Osaro asked again, and looked at her sharply.

'Seventy-five kobo a day,' Adisa said. 'Then there will be other charges.'

'That's expensive,' Osaro said, and looked at her again. 'Are you sure you are all right?'

Adisa glanced at him. 'Yes. Why do you ask?'

'It's your face. You look worried. Extremely worried.'

'So I should be,' Adisa said, and looked away.

They came to the traffic lights. Osaro had to go right while she had to go left.

'I will be calling on him again,' Osaro promised. 'If you want anything . . .'

'Oh thank you,' she said. 'If I want anything I'll let you know.'

'You don't know when you will be here again?'

'I should say tomorrow morning.'

'Then, it is goodnight.'

'Goodnight.'

They parted there by the traffic lights.

Osaro went to the right, to his one-bedroom apartment on Upper Sakponba Road. He too had a wife and three children, and his children too were away in the village.

Adisa turned left and went towards the Ring Road.

'You should go home now,' her other mind said to her.

'Yes, I will,' she answered.

'Good. You must not let yourself be tempted.'

'But perhaps he wants to help me?'

'How can you believe that? Didn't you see the look in his eyes when he invited you?'

'No,' she told her other self. 'I didn't see it.'

'Well, I saw it,' her other self said. 'I saw it and it was not good. It was full of lust.'

'Do you really imagine I am going to give myself to him?'

'No, I do not. But you could be tempted. You should go home.'

'Yes. But I need the money.'

Her other self fell silent.

'Well?'

'What do you expect me to say?'

'I need money. Idemudia is sick and we are hungry. Obofun has only promised to help me, nothing more. And you say I shouldn't go?'

'Yes.'

'And what if he really wants to help us?'

Then she came to that part of the Ring Road where Airport Road joined the Ring Road, and instead of walking straight on towards the bank to her house, she turned left and went down Airport Road.

Chapter 10

The Samson and Delilah Hotel stood a little way off Airport Road. It was tucked among very well groomed trees and the chalets formed an arrow head, as though drawn up for battle. First came the main building of the hotel with the bar, the restaurant and the banquet hall. After the main building, the chalets began, running up in numbers.

In the seventh chalet, Obofun waited. He had been waiting since six o'clock. He had come directly from home after Queen had told him the story about their daughter, Lilian.

'The driver comes rushing downstairs and cries that there is trouble,' Queen explained. 'As I am going upstairs, three boys wearing school uniform come running downstairs. I think nothing about them. "If there is trouble," I say to myself, "what concerns a schoolboy?" After all, many of them come in each day to visit Esie.'

Obofun swallowed. He had been sitting on the balcony of the Freedom Motel upstairs. What trouble could have started while he was away?

His wife continued her story.

'Well, I get upstairs to find Lilian screaming . . .'

'Why hadn't she gone to school in the first place?' Obofun queried his wife.

'She complained of a headache. And after all, she is your daughter. You ought to have made sure that she left for school each day before you took to the streets yourself,' was Queen's reply.

He waited patiently for her to continue with the happenings of the day.

'I go upstairs and I find that Lilian has been raped!'

'Raped?'

'Yes, forced and raped!'

'But how? Was there nobody at home? Where was the servant?'

'It was a most brutal assault. Imagine those three scoundrels raping our daughter, one after the other! It is unforgivable.'

'It is punishable!' Obofun himself contributed. 'Punishable and I am going to hand the matter over to the police. At once!'

'But you can't do that!' Queen cried, suddenly.

'I can and I am going to. Those three bastards are going to pay dearly for their crime. By the way, how did they get in?'

'They came in under the pretext of wanting to see Esie.'

'But Esie was at school. In the same school.'

'They came in and clapped for somebody to attend to them. Lilian answered from her bedroom. They went in there and found that she was still in her pyjamas. Then one of them locked the door and they pounced on her!'

'Terrible! Impossible,' Obofun blurted out. 'Impossible! Those scoundrels!' he fumed.

'Well, the driver comes in and calls on Lilian to go into my bedroom to collect some money for me. As soon as they hear the voice calling on Lilian, they jump up, open the door. Meanwhile Lilian is screaming. The driver rushes downstairs to inform me and as I am going up, down go these three criminals, taking the steps two at a time, and one of them even has the guts to stop and greet me!'

'This is a police case,' Obofun repeated angrily.

Queen however had been vehemently opposed to it. 'You can't! Imagine the name of the family. Obofun's daughter raped by three schoolboys. No, never. These schoolboys. They must pay for it in another way.'

He had spent the afternoon going from one doctor's house to another until he found one who came and examined Lilian. But the doctor's report was discouraging. 'Intimacy isn't anything new to your daughter,' the doctor said discreetly. 'But she has some bruises from the prolonged use of force.'

And after going over the whole matter in his mind, he came to the conclusion that it was perhaps best not to hand the matter over to the police. What would his daughter answer if they asked her why she hadn't screamed before the arrival of the driver? After all, the servant had been upstairs and his attention could have been attracted.

'So like her mother!' Obofun cried out. 'So like her. And what does a man do with such a daughter?'

The more he thought about the episode, the angrier he became. Perhaps it was best to forget about it. Yes, he would forget about it. And the rascals? They had to go free. It was a pity. If only ... Oh yes. He was going to contact their parents. They must never come to his house any more. If they did, he would declare them thieves. Nothing more, nothing less. Anyway, 'Let me forget about it' he told himself. 'It is annoying. Terrible. But I think I should erase it from my mind. It is better that way.'

His mind went to Adisa. 'If she comes,' he told himself, 'then I think I am lucky. Oh, what a nice woman. Decent and goodlooking. Rare. How I should love to have her. Just once and then afterwards it will be easy. But the trick had better work.'

The better part of his nature accused him. 'Adisa is married,' it warned him. 'Don't try anything with her. Just help her. You have the means. Help her and forget about her long straight legs. Forget about that.'

Then he jolted himself away from this part of himself, this dissuading conscientious part of a man that always attempts to make him go straight. 'Queen is no wife to me any more. She is no wife, the way she carries on, not caring even if I know she will sleep with any man, any kind of man. Other men take my wife. So why can't I take their wives?' he asked himself. 'I have something that Adisa needs badly. Money, or at least the means to make money. She will benefit from it. She loses nothing by giving herself for it. Absolutely nothing. And I, I will be satisfied. And I didn't give her that lift for nothing. The rain was pouring and I stopped. But I looked at her first. Then I remembered what I had noticed when I stood by her telling her that her husband was a cement thief. She is like a diamond mine in an obscure place. I have discovered her. I have ...'

'Oh shut up!' his better nature told him. 'Shut up and stop thinking about a married woman!'

'But she is not even working-class,' the darker part of him countered.

'And so what?'

'You should be careful.'

He laughed aloud to himself. 'How many of them have I been intimate with?' he asked himself. He couldn't answer his own question because they were many and difficult to remember.

'Anyway, let her come first,' he told himself. 'Perhaps she will slap my face when I circle her but I know that is almost impossible. But if she does ...'

He brought out a pad and was about to write figures on a clean page when the 'phone rang.

Adisa walked up to the main lobby of the Samson and Delilah. A man sat at the receptionist's desk, a 'phone by his side. She walked up to him, then hesitated. The man looked up, askance.

'I have come to see Obofun,' Adisa said.

'You mean the Director?'

Adisa did not know who the Director was. So she repeated her request.

The man picked up the 'phone, dialled and spoke briefly into the 'phone. Then the man said, 'You can go out to see him. He is waiting for you.'

'But I do not know where to go,' Adisa said.

'You go out and count seven houses on this side. Knock on the door of the seventh house.' The man pointed, and Adisa went out of the building.

Obofun stood up when he heard the hesitant steps outside the door, then came the still more hesitant knocking. He drew the bolt of the door backward and called, 'Come in!' and then the door opened slowly and Adisa stood there, her shadow behind her, her face drawn and tight, uncertain and afraid.

'So you have come,' he breathed, and smiled to show that he was relieved and pleased that Adisa should have kept the appointment.

'Oh yes, I have come,' Adisa replied. 'You said I should come and I have done as you asked.' She was a little bit uncomfortable in this room that was so big and so polished.

'Please sit down. Sit down. Then you will have something to drink and eat and after that we shall discuss how I can help you.'

Adisa sank into one of the chairs. The comfort of sitting down there was so great that her back began to ache. She stretched out her long legs, cautiously as a snail senses the outside of its shell, and then looked round the room again.

The chalet had a sitting room, a bedroom, a toilet and a bath. In the centre of the sitting room, there was the low round table which was surrounded by six cushioned chairs. Against the right-hand wall of the sitting room was the writing desk with a white top, a chair with a white seat placed against it. Then there was the almanac on the wall carrying the photographs of the leaders of the country. It was funny, but Obofun had observed that many of his guests who had occupied the room turned the almanac either upside down or face against the wall, so that the photographs would not show. On one occasion, he had been annoyed to find the almanac rolled up and under the bed in the bedroom. Always after one of his guests had stayed in the chalet he found something of this kind.

Then there was the low window with its white curtains, drawn aside to let in some of the fading light of the day. Each window had a mosquito net proofing directly attached to the wooden window frame. Outside the window the grass grew and the hibiscus flowers stood in red and green splendour. And interwoven with the flowers were the pine trees against which the wind blew, producing a whistling in their higher branches. Then higher up and above the pine trees were the birds and the sky.

In the bedroom were a large double bed and a single chair. Against the wall was a giant wardrobe and inside the wardrobe were the cartons where the drinks stood in rows of twelve. Under the cartons were the bales of cloth and below these were more cartons, more drinks, all smuggled across the country's borders and sold at black market prices to people through distributors.

'And so, what will you have to drink?' Obofun asked.

Adisa shook her head. 'I do not want anything to drink.'

'Oh come on,' Obofun insisted. 'Have something, a beer at least.'

'I do not want any beer,' Adisa said, her heart beginning to beat rapidly.

'Then you must have some other drink, something

soft,' Obofun said, and picked up the 'phone.

But before he spoke to the receptionist, he said to her, 'Perhaps you would like something to eat as well?'

Again Adisa shook her head in the negative. 'I am not hungry,' she said. But she was lying. She was hungry. She wanted so much to eat.

'All the same,' Obofun insisted, 'you cannot leave here without eating something.'

Then rapidly, he spoke into the 'phone and gave brisk sharp orders.

'I am sure you will like the food,' he said as he dropped the 'phone, and smiled.

Again Adisa looked round the room. She noticed the polished floor again, then the walls and the high ceiling painted white where the air-conditioner softly blew cold air into the room. Then her eyes came back to the man who was watching her, and finally to her own hands as they rested in her lap, trembling.

She recognised that this place was far, far better than her own. There was comfort and luxury here. At her home, there was nothing but hardness; hardness, pain and disease. They always wanted something, they were always in want. When would it go, this want? She didn't know.

Obofun began to explain. 'I think we can be of use to each other,' he said and eyed her. 'We can ...' and then there was a knock on the door, and he stopped and called instead, 'Yes?'

The door opened inwards and a waiter came in carrying a tray.

'They have brought you a bottle of maltex,' Obofun told Adisa, pushing the glass towards her. Then to the waiter, he said, 'Open it quickly, and fill her glass. Then open the bottle of wine too.'

The waiter opened the bottles in silence, filled up

the glasses and left.

Obofun raised his glass. 'To our mutual understanding,' he toasted and took a sip from the drink in his glass.

Nervously Adisa took up the glass and tasted the dark liquid. It was good on her tongue and even better still against her throat, as it ran down, cold, almost icy.

Obofun sat forward in his chair and spun his glass of wine round on the round table.

'I have some things you will help me to distribute, or to put it another way, sell. For each item you sell, you get a commission. I think you can do it.'

So that was it, Adisa thought. Things to sell. But was that all?

'I will show you what the things are, after we have eaten. Then you can decide whether or not you will like to help.'

Adisa drank some more of the maltex and set the glass on the table. 'I don't know what you want me to sell,' she answered cautiously, 'but if I can, I should ...'

Another knock on the door interrupted her speech. The door opened and three waiters came in, each carrying a tray.

'You will wait here to serve the food,' Obofun instructed them generally. Moments later, he changed his mind and dismissed them.

'It is better that they should go,' he said. 'Otherwise I cannot eat.'

There was the soup, then the main course comprising jollof rice and meat, and then the ice cream and some more bottles of wine.

Adisa found she could not really eat. She was hungry but everything seemed so strange. Was she here or not? 'I am sitting here, on this chair,' she told herself, 'so I must be here.'

Obofun was talking about prices. The price of milk, he complained, had shot up. So also had the prices of meat, oil, eggs. Everything. His workers were demanding higher wages, although they were now eating more than ever before from the hotel's kitchen. No, life was terrible, he concluded and God, if he even knew, could perhaps tell where all these developments were leading the country. There was bound to be disaster.

Adisa heard him but did not take in anything he said. Her mind was in a turmoil.

'You are not eating,' Obofun said at last, pushing his own plate away.

Adisa did not answer him.

'I have told you, you have no reason to be anxious. I want to help you, so why can't you relax?'

'I am sorry,' Adisa said. 'I am not really hungry.'

Obofun shrugged his shoulders and stood up. 'All right then, I'll show you what I want you to sell for me if you will follow me.'

They both went into the bedroom and Obofun flung open the wardrobe doors to show her the stack of whisky.

'For each bottle you sell,' he explained to her, 'you make a profit of at least fifty kobo. You get them from me at four naira a bottle and you sell them at four naira and fifty kobo. And don't worry about whether or not people will buy it. In the big shops, each bottle costs at least six naira. People will come to you once they know you have it. The main problem to be solved is letting people know that you have the drinks to sell.'

Then he drew back from the wardrobe and offered her the chair in the bedroom while he sat on the bed himself. He left the wardrobe doors open so that Adisa could feast her eyes on the cartons.

'For a start,' he told her, 'I can give you at least ten cartons. That makes one hundred and twenty bottles. And if you sell them all, you make at least sixty naira for yourself.'

Adisa thought about the sixty naira and her throat went dry.

'If I give you so many cartons,' Obofun explained, 'that means you are going to pay me some four hundred and eighty naira.'

'But ... but I have no money,' Adisa stammered, her voice trembling.

Obofun lifted one of his legs up to the bed. 'I know you have no money,' he conceded. 'I do not require that you pay me the four hundred naira at once. I merely need an advance. From some people I take one hundred naira as an advance, from others I take more. From you, however, I am going to take less. Much less. Only fifty naira.'

Adisa clasped her two hands together. 'Fifty naira!'

'Fifty naira,' Obofun repeated. 'Or is that too much for you?'

Adisa was silent for a while. 'I have no money,' she said at last. 'Not one single naira. How can I pay you fifty naira? My husband is sick. I am going to need more money. We have no money. Not a kobo.'

Obofun licked his lips with his tongue. He stayed for a moment in deep thought.

'You can look for money somewhere,' he suggested to her.

'From where?' she asked in a small voice.

'From your friends, I suppose.'

Adisa shook her head sadly. 'I wish I could,' she said, 'But I cannot. Nobody will lend me fifty naira at this time. But I can sell the whisky and return the money to you afterwards. I would return all the money I am going to make after selling the bottles of whisky.'

Obofun laughed and shifted his leg back to the floor. 'No, no,' he refused. 'That will not help. You are not the first woman to tell me that. And afterwards, what happens? The drinks are sold but the money never comes back.'

'I would always return the money,' Adisa pleaded. 'Why should I want your money? I would always return what I had sold.'

'I have taken that risk before ...'

'But not with me.'

'I know ...'

'I will always return the money.' She was almost desperate now.

Obofun stood up from the bed slowly and proceeded to pace the room to and fro. Then he came and stood behind Adisa's chair.

'Perhaps you can give me a guarantee in another way,' he suggested.

Adisa's voice was eager. 'How?' She turned round in her chair, as his hands came down slowly but deliberately on her shoulders, gripping them, before slowly going down to her breasts.

'We could do it this way,' he said, breathing harshly and rapidly.

Adisa stiffened for a moment while the voices which she had thought were dormant in her came back to life. 'I'll find out. I'll find you out. I'll find you out and I'll kill you,' Idemudia's voice rang in her head. 'I'll tear out that thing which you think you have got and I'll throw it to the dogs outside.' Then it was her aunt's voice saying, 'Leave him. There are other alternatives to living with a man ... You think you will die.'

And now it was Idemudia laughing, 'So you think you are going to find another man ...' And then it was her aunt who laughed, 'You pack your things and you go out. Men will go after you ...' And then it was her own voice, 'Or perhaps you think you are the only man in the world?' Then her internal voices joined in, 'No. Never. I will never leave him! I will never be like my aunt ...'

'No! No! No!' she cried, and stood up from the chair abruptly.

Her head hit Obofun on his chin, almost knocking him over. Obofun regained his balance and there were both pain and anger in his eyes.

He began to rub his chin and the water almost came out of his eyes. But he laughed and said with the other side of his mouth which was in less pain, 'And yet you complain that you have no money!'

Adisa stood away from him, her eyes wild with her alarm. 'It is true that I have no money,' she said.

'And yet you cannot offer yourself.'

'But how can you suggest that?' she cried. 'I am a married woman.'

'And I am a married man,' Obofun countered. 'We both lose nothing.'

'Two wrongs cannot make a right.'

'What then do you want me to do?' Obofun asked her. 'You have no money and yet I am sure you would like to have the drinks.'

'You said you were going to help me,' Adisa accused him. Her eyes momentarily strayed to the cartons piled up inside the wardrobe.

'In fact, I wouldn't mind selling the drinks to you at three naira and fifty kobo a bottle. That gives you a profit of one naira on each bottle that you can sell.'

Adisa's mind responded to that by thinking of one hundred and twenty naira. One hundred and twenty naira!

'Then perhaps you could have some lace materials to sell afterwards,' Obofun continued relentlessly.

Adisa said nothing still, but the voices were loud in her head.

'Or perhaps you may even need some money to make a start? Some fifty naira? I wouldn't mind giving you all these things. But I need ...' and he moved towards her. Adisa backed away from him towards the open door, leading into the sitting room. 'No, don't come near me!' she cried. 'Don't touch me again! Let me go away from here.'

Obofun followed after her. 'But you lose nothing and yet you gain everything. Tell me, what do you lose? Your virginity?'

'It is adultery!'

Obofun stopped in his tracks and laughed. 'Adultery!' he laughed, pouring all the scorn he could muster on the word.

'This is no adultery. You do it, or let me put it another way. We do it because of something you need. Where is the adultery there? I have told you I'll give you the drinks at the lowest price ever. Then I'll give you another fifty naira so that you can start off in your own trade. Do you call that adultery? Do you still insist that it is indeed adultery?'

'I don't know anything,' Adisa cried. 'I only know that when a married woman sleeps with another person who is not her husband, then it is adultery. I want to go home. Please let me go.'

Obofun put his hands in his pockets. 'No use fighting her,' his senses advised him. 'I will let you go,' he said. 'But you can always come back. Any time you want the drinks. I am not forcing you.'

He came up behind her again and she was afraid that he was going to touch her. But he merely opened the door for her.

She almost ran out of the room, but as soon as she was clear of the chalet, she ran and did not stop until she came to the main road. Her heart pounded within her. She was frightened and weak. The temptation had been so strong!

Chapter 11

'Two men were here looking for your husband,' Mama Jimoh told her as soon as she got home.

Adisa did not look up at Mama Jimoh, but pretended she was opening the door. 'Two men? What for?'

Mama Jimoh was outside pounding the family's food for the evening. She rested her pestle against the wall.

'They said they were from the Freedom Motel,' Mama Jimoh informed her, wiping the sweat off her face with the corners of her wrappa.

Adisa put the key in the keyhole and turned it. She wanted to get away from everybody so as to be alone. 'Did they tell you what they wanted?' she asked.

'Yes, they did,' Mama Jimoh answered, taking up her pestle again. She lifted it clear of the mortar and proceeded to scoop the pounded yam into a plate.

Adisa waited nervously, her back still turned away from Mama Jimoh.

'They said their madam wanted to see Idemudia,' Mama Jimoh said at last.

'Madam?'

'Yes. I guess that must be Queen, Obofun's wife.' Adisa's heart missed a beat. 'Well, thank you,' she said, and wanted to get into her room, but Mama Jimoh's voice arrested her.

'They said they had been here twice before.'

'Yes?'

'One of them said it was urgent.'

Adisa turned round slowly, away from the door so that she faced Mama Jimoh. Could it be the cement issue again? But Obofun had apologised. Hadn't he?

'Well, what should she want Idemudia for?' Mama Jimoh persisted. There was interest in her voice. It was interesting, Obofun's wife sending for a man who had no job.

Reluctantly, Adisa told Mama Jimoh about the events of the morning. She told it up to the point where Obofun had gone down the three stairs of their house. But she was careful not to mention Obofun's name. She said two men had come to ask for her husband and when she appeared, only to talk about some missing bags of cement.

'Don't you think they came again because of that?' Mama Jimoh asked.

'Could be,' Adisa agreed. 'But I don't think so. You see, I met one of the men shortly afterwards and he began to apologise to me on behalf of his wife. He said his wife had realised that she had made a mistake.'

'Then it must be something else,' Mama Jimoh said.

'Perhaps,' Adisa said, and was about to turn away when again Mama Jimoh's voice arrested her.

'They also wanted to know when Idemudia would be back and so I told them I didn't know and then they promised to call again but an hour or more has since gone by and they haven't come yet.'

'Thank you very much,' Adisa said.

'And how is he?' Mama Jimoh asked.

'Oh, who?' Adisa was about to ask and then she stopped herself just in time, and said instead, 'Oh, he is just as he was.'

'You mean there is no improvement?'

'No, nothing.'

'It is the sickness,' Mama Jimoh said. 'But it will pass. It will go away.'

'I hope so.'

'Of course it will go,' the elder woman said. 'But

only with time. Tomorrow he will be better. You will see.'

'I hope so,' Adisa said again, and conscious that the elder woman was watching her now, she went into her room and shut the door. Then she remembered that her clothes were still outside, hanging on the line and as she opened the door to come out, Papa Jimoh himself was standing beside his wife.

'So, how is he?' he asked.

'He is there as he was,' Adisa answered.

'The rascal,' Papa Jimoh joked. 'He doesn't want to get well.'

Adisa forced a smile.

'Perhaps the hospital bed is too comfortable,' Papa Jimoh added. 'They should give them wooden beds with grass mattresses.'

'But some of them sleep on the floor,' Mama Jimoh said.

'Ah yes. You know I have slept there myself once. But those who sleep on the floor want to get well quickly.'

'Idemudia is sharing a bed with a man who coughs,' Adisa said, feeling that she must say something.

'Then he should want to return as soon as he can. I intend going to see him tomorrow. Today was a busy day.'

He went into the house and Adisa was glad to get back into her room. She left the door open after her because it was too dark inside, and then sat on the bed. She held her head in her hands. What was she going to do with herself? Obofun had promised her fifty naira and then the bottles of whisky, one hundred and twenty of them and each one for only three naira and fifty kobo.

Wasn't that money preferable to this hunger, this situation of always wanting? But she had to give her-

133

self to him. Should she give herself to him? She needed the money, not so much for herself but for both of them together. The day would come when Idemudia would leave the hospital and the hospital authorities would demand some money. And where would the money come from? Perhaps it would be possible for Papa Jimoh to lend them some more money. But that would be too much. They already owed Papa and Mama Jimoh some twenty-three naira. That sum had to be repaid. Mama Jimoh had been patient so far but she might not remain patient for too long. She couldn't go to them again for more money. She wouldn't have the moral courage.

But then was it not better to owe Mama Jimoh one hundred naira than to submit herself to Obofun? And if Mama Jimoh was reluctant at last to lend her more money, couldn't she go back to her aunt? Perhaps her aunt would refuse to help her and insist that she took a room in the city, but then she would know that she had tried to get her help. She must reason this thing out coldly, she told herself. She must not act in a way she might later on regret. Idemudia may have failed to provide sufficiently for her but she knew he was a good husband. She knew how hard he tried, and she told herself that she would never deliberately do anything that would hurt him. When she had taunted him with going to another man, she had been angry. She could never commit adultery. Not on her life. There must be another way out, she reasoned with herself. There must be other ways of getting money. Yes, she would go to her aunt once more. Perhaps she would give her some money, at least ten naira. If she could borrow some money from her aunt and from Mama Jimoh, then perhaps she would have enough money to feed herself and to pay the hospital bills when the time came. And when Idemudia became well, he would find a job and pay off their debts. And since she had decided on what to do, why not go to Mama Jimoh straight away?

It is not easy begging for money where money is already owed. Adisa found this out when she went to see Mama Jimoh later.

Mama Jimoh said, 'Please sit down, Adisa. You look terribly tired.'

Adisa refused to look Mama Jimoh in the eyes. 'I am tired,' she confessed. 'But that's not my problem now.'

Papa Jimoh came into the sparsely furnished sitting room where one bed stood against the wall and where Mama Jimoh and Adisa were sitting. He was smoking a cigarette.

'So you are here,' he said to Adisa.

'Yes,' Adisa answered. 'I came to see Mama Jimoh.'

'Then I will leave you to discuss your secrets,' Papa Jimoh said, and tying his wrappa more firmly round the waist, he went out of the room.

The smoke from the cigarette followed him outside.

Both women were silent for a while. Adisa looked at the wall where the photographs of the family stood, nervous, afraid and ashamed to look the other woman in the eye.

At last Mama Jimoh picked up the shreds of conversation from where they had been broken.

'What kind of problem is it?' she asked.

Adisa hesitated. 'I know we already owe you,' she said, 'but we are in difficulties again. We need some money.'

Mama Jimoh was silent for a while. 'I have no money,' she finally declared. 'God knows how many people are owing us some money. They buy things and promise to pay afterwards. But they never do. They always have one reason or the other to give for not bringing me my money. But let me see,' she said, and paused in thought.

'Will five naira be enough?'

Adisa did not think that five naira would be enough but it was more than she had hoped for.

. 'Thank you. It will be more than enough,' she said, lowering her eyes. Mama Jimoh went into the bedroom. The room was dark and crowded. She came out of the room and held a five naira note in her hands.

'That's all I have,' and she handed it over to Adisa.

Adisa placed the money on the chair beside her and thanked her again. 'I really don't know what we would do without you,' she admitted truthfully.

Modesty made Mama Jimoh reply, 'It is nothing. It is absolutely nothing.'

They sat down in silence again. Adisa felt uncomfortable, yet she couldn't bring herself to stand up and go away. Mama Jimoh began to tell her about events in the market.

'There was a big fight today,' Mama Jimoh said in a loud voice.

Papa Jimoh called from the doorway, 'Where?'

'In the market.'

'Who fought?' Papa Jimoh asked from the doorway.

'Two women. Mud flew, they tore each other's dresses. Then the police came.'

'What happened?'

'One of the women is a trader. She said the other woman had bought some crayfish and walked away without paying for it.'

'Is that why they were fighting?'

'Well, the other woman said she had paid. The crayfish was worth only ten kobo.'

'And after that?'

'The trader called the other woman a thief. This other woman was big and fat. She replied by calling the trader a liar. This trader's daughter is sitting by, a schoolgirl. She comes out and spits straight into the big woman's face. "You can't abuse my mother," she cries. People gather round and nobody tries to separate them! They all want to see the fight. And in a second it begins. Mud is flying, clothes are tearing and the little schoolgirl fights by the side of her mother. It is not until they are almost naked that some men come to separate them. Then some policemen come and the fight is over. Everybody runs away at the sight of the policemen. Nobody wants to give evidence.'

'That is bad,' Papa Jimoh said. 'It was wicked of them all. They should have stopped the fight before it started.'

'They wanted to see the fight. The crayfish was gone, scattered all over the place. The trader's wares were overturned. She lost many things. There was a cut on her forehead and the blood came from there and ran down her face.'

'You should have stopped the fight,' Papa Jimoh insisted.

'Nobody wanted to. Everybody wanted to watch the fight and when the policemen came, they all ran away.'

Adisa summoned up her courage and stood up. 'I must be going,' she said. 'I am now going to see my aunt. She does not know that Idemudia is in the hospital.'

'It is goodnight then,' Mama Jimoh said.

'Yes, it is goodnight.'

Papa Jimoh let Adisa get out of earshot before he called out to his wife who was in the other room.

'What did she want?'

'Some money.'

'Some money? What about the twenty-three naira you said she was owing?'

'They haven't paid it back.'

'And did you give her any more?'

'Yes, I did. Only five naira.'

'Only five naira! You should have made sure that they paid back the other debt first.'

'I couldn't refuse. But this will be the last time. I am also sure she will not come back. She is not happy. She was ashamed. I could see that from her eyes.'

Adisa was gone for about an hour before she came back. By that time, the lights in Papa Jimoh's house were out. She opened the door, went inside and then locked it. Then she flung herself on the bed and began to cry, bitterly.

Chapter 12

The morning came upon the city suddenly. The day before, it had been misty, cloudy and soon afterwards rain had poured out of the sky in torrents. But today was different. This morning was different. The sun was up in the sky, not fully out yet. The trees hid it after it rose straight from the earth, where it had buried its flames in the loam that was the earth, filling the whole night with a soft warmth.

Now it rose from the earth like a bird taking off from the grass. It did not climb steeply at once. It spread out its red wings lazily and the leaves of the trees hid the full length of the fiery wings from view. But the way it had taken off was sudden, like a stoned bird where it had been resting. One moment there was intimate warm darkness, another moment there was intimate warm dawn, clear and soft and mellow.

Adisa woke up with a start and yawned almost immediately. She fell back on the bed and stared at the ceiling. Then the memories flooded back, as soon as the sun showered its rays outside, gradually but clearly.

It came back to her. There had been a yesterday and a day before yesterday. Idemudia was ill, Obofun had demanded more than a pound of her flesh, and her aunt had refused to help her. That had been the yesterday, the past, not today. The sun today rose quite clearly. Would the events of the day not take on the same clarity?

She hoped that Idemudia would be better. She hoped that some miracle would happen to change the course of events. Perhaps God would intervene. Was

He not there to protect the poor and the needy? Yes, perhaps He would intervene!

She washed her face in a bucket of water. Papa Jimoh and Mama Jimoh were already out. She too would go to the hospital. She would spend her day there, hear the sight of the sick calling for the pail to urinate into, bear the sound of the man coughing and calling Anuoha. But when would all these things end? When would her troubles be resolved?

She didn't know. Again, she stepped out of their house and joined the stream of haggard faces that were already prowling the street even at that hour.

Adisa was surprised to find that Idemudia was not only awake but sitting quietly on the bed when she got to his ward in the hospital. But she noticed that Idemudia was now alone on the bed, and that the old man was gone, so she asked, 'What happened? Have they moved him to another bed?'

Idemudia shook his head and his eyes were sad. 'They took him to the mortuary. He died in the early hours of this morning.' His voice was a whisper.

There was shock on Adisa's face. 'Died?'

'Yes, he died and they took him away.'

Adisa looked round. There was fear in her eyes. 'They should change your bed,' she said. 'You mustn't sleep on that bed any more!'

'I told them that just before you came in.'

'And then what happened?' Her voice became a thin and anxious whisper.

Idemudia sat at the edge of the bed, on the side he had always occupied, and now that his fever was gone, he was able to reason coherently. He looked at his wife and waved his hands in the air.

'Well, what happened?' Adisa repeated, real dismay in her eyes.

'They said I was lucky to have the bed alone to myself.'

'Do they call that luck?'

'That's what they said. They have disinfected the bed and changed the sheets anyway.'

'That is not enough.'

Idemudia shrugged his shoulders and the bed creaked. 'One of the nurses even explained that if they took his bed away, they would most probably bring another from a ward on which another patient had died. So what is the use, she asked?'

They were both silent for a few seconds. Then Idemudia said, 'I am to be discharged this morning.'

'Yes?'

'That is if I can find the money. In fact, they have already told me to send for my people, my wife, the Staff Nurse suggested.'

Adisa looked at her hands and her eyes were clouded with thought. 'How much did they say?'

'Twenty-three naira, seventy-nine kobo.'

'Twenty-three naira?'

'And what happens if we cannot pay?'

Idemudia shrugged his shoulders. 'I do not know,' he said. 'I did not ask. But I have never ...'

His words were interrupted by the noisy entrance of a man into the ward. He was accompanied by two nurses, one in front of him, the other behind him.

'He is here, Staff,' the nurse in front called to the staff nurse, who sat at the desk towards which they were going. The man murmured something. He wore a check shirt that was open at the neck and his pair of trousers were blue and wide at the bottom. He was tall and lean and he had a small beard that looked extremely laughable.

'So you are Mr Iyokoh,' the staff nurse said, as they walked up.

The man stroked his sparse beard. 'I am Iyokoh,' he admitted.

The staff nurse proceeded to explain. 'The man gave

us your name defore he died. We want you to identify him.'

'But I do not know him,' the man protested.

'Then how did he get your name?'

'Perhaps it's because we are from the same town. Our family is large and well known but we cannot know everybody.'

'Well, well, well,' the staff nurse admitted, 'that is quite understandable. But he happened to have mentioned your first name. Are you not Ernest?'

The man was silent for a while. Then he said, 'Look, I write for the newspapers. It's quite possible . . .'

'This man could neither read nor write.'

'Then how did he get my name?'

'We should be asking you that,' the staff nurse reminded him. 'How did he get your name? He first mentioned it four days ago but we called at your office and you were not there. We left a message. Perhaps you didn't get it.'

'I did not,' the man replied.

Adisa and Idemudia listened as the man and the nurses argued it out.

Presently, the staff nurse turned to the man again. 'So, are you going to identify his body or not?'

The man clasped his hands helplessly and stammered. 'How can . . .' and stopped. 'How can I identify the corpse of a man whom perhaps I did not know in real life? How do you expect me to do it?'

'Nobody will blame you if you cannot recognise him after seeing his body. The most important thing is that you go there to look. In the mortuary.' She pointed outside towards where the mortuary stood, alone and forbidding.

'Look,' the man said, and his voice was firm. 'I am not going to any mortuary to identify any body. If there is any other thing I can do, I will gladly do it. But go

142

in there to look at ...' He shook his head vigorously and left the statement hanging in the air. 'I am not going in there?' he said again and finally.

The staff nurse conferred with the other nurses briefly.

'Then perhaps you can pay his hospital fees?'

The man's voice was cautious as he asked, 'How much?'

'It's not too much,' one of the nurses said and brought out a sheaf of papers. 'These are from the almoner's office. Let me see.' And she looked at the papers. 'It's only sixty-seven naira, eighty kobo.'

The tall lean man whistled. The patients in the room watched him.

'That isn't a small amount,' he protested. 'How many days did he spend here?'

'It's either you pay or his body doesn't leave the mortuary,' the staff nurse declared.

The man considered this for a moment. 'I have a right to know,' he insisted.

This time another nurse answered him. 'Here we talk about what type of treatment he got, not just how many days he spent in the hospital. There is no fixed amount for each day. We are a public hospital. Nobody cheats.'

The man nodded. 'I think I have a right to know,' he said again. 'Here I am called away from my office by a strange message. First of all, you ask me to go and identify a dead body. Next, you ask me to pay over sixty naira and you are angry that I should ask questions. I don't think people should work like that. I am from a newspaper.'

His last statement struck home. The staff nurse immediately apologised. 'We only wanted to explain,' she said. 'Nobody wants to put anything on you. In fact, the man mentioned the name of another person, a tailor, who he said lived on Forestry Road. We have been there several times but no tailor seems to live there. At least not now.'

The tall lean man calmed down. There was, however, a worried expression on his face.

'Where is the almoner's office?' he asked.

'I will show you myself,' the staff nurse said, standing up, and, going round her desk, went in front of him to show him the way.

They passed by Idemudia's bed and the staff nurse glanced at Adisa as she stood by the bed.

'They were talking about the old man,' Idemudia whispered to Adisa.

'I thought as much,' Adisa said. 'But how did he die? You were awake?'

'No, I was asleep,' he said. 'I woke up to find the nurses and his body being hauled onto a stretcher. All the time our bed is sealed off.'

Idemudia closed his eyes for a second and covered his face with his left hand. 'If only I had known he was going to die!'

'Did he do anything to show that he felt it?'

'Oh yes he did. He woke up, hours earlier. I was surprised to find him digging at my side with his hands, almost frantically.'

'Was that during his last moments of life?'

'No, much earlier. He wakes me up and his voice is clear and strong. I think he has fully recovered. His cough is gone. He is quiet but his voice is clear and steady. He says, "We have spent a few days here together and we scarcely know anything about each other. But that is not necessary now. I am sick. I feel that my end is near!" I am afraid but I tell him he has never been better. Surely he is going to recover!

'He simply stares at me. "I do not want to recover!" he says, "What for?"

' "Why, to live," I answer.

'He shakes his head. "I have seen a lot of life," he says. "My father was a farmer. I took after him. I was married to two wives. Then the priests came and said that that was heathen. A man had to marry only one wife. So I asked my senior wife to go. Although she had come first, she had not had any issue for me." The old man seemed in a hurry to unburden himself. He spoke quickly and in pidgin.'

'And what happened after that?' Adisa asked, sitting down on the edge of the bed close to her husband's feet.

'What happened?' Idemudia repeated. 'A lot. He told me about his home town, about his wife and daughter and finally about Anuoha.'

'What about his wife and daughter?'

'Well, one midnight just before the coup he was in his house when a noise in his sitting room woke him up. "I went out there with a matchet," the old man said, "but I found about nine men in the parlour. They came in through the front door. At that time there were the political troubles. These men, nine of them, my matchet was useless against them. I asked them what they wanted."

' "What party do you belong to?" they asked.

' "I was sick during the last election. So I did not vote," I told them. They said they knew that but now I had to belong to a party. If I did not, then I had to join their own party by paying five pounds. Of course I told them I had no money. I told them about the leaking roof of my thatched house. If I had money I said, I would put a new roof over my head.

' "At this time Ifeanya had heard the noise. She came in." '

Idemudia paused in his narrative and supported his head on his two hands. 'The old man nearly wept here,' he said thickly.

'Did they kill his wife?'

'No, they asked his wife to pay up the five pounds. When she couldn't five of the men jumped on the old man. At that time, he wasn't so old and I doubt if he was even old now. I saw the nurses writing down forty-five years against his age. Well, they held him and then the other four went to his wife. Then one by one, they raped her. The whole nine of them, and they made the old man look. By the time the last of them was finished with his wife, he was nearly mad. His wife was unconscious on the floor. And in the morning, she was dead. She never recovered.'

Adisa was breathing harshly. 'That was brutal!' she cried.

'And that is not the end of it. These men went parading about that they had slept with the man's wife. Yet when she died and the police stepped in, nothing ever came of the case. They were discharged and acquitted for want of evidence. "I was happy when the coup came," the old man said. "I thought that things were going to change. I never forgave the politicians for raping my wife, for killing Ifeanya. These soldiers will be better, much better. So I thought until one day when my daughter went out to fetch some water from the pump. Itetah had been gone for nearly thirty minutes and I was angry. I went out of the house. Two little girls came running towards me. That time the war had already long started and spread to Asaba.

' "The two girls came running up, crying 'They have carried Itetah off! They have carried Itetah off!'

' " 'Who has carried Itetah off?' I asked.

' "And the little girls tell me the story. 'We are out drawing water from the pump. Then this jeep draws up and beckons to Itetah to come to them. Itetah hesitates, then goes towards them. They ask her the way to the Obi's house. They are all soldiers inside the jeep. Itetah points. "It's at the other side of the town," she tell them. "You come with us to show us the place," the soldiers answer back. Itetah does not want to go. She says she is coming to tell you first. But the soldiers will not allow her. Two of them point guns at her and tell her to get into the jeep. Itetah is crying. We stand off. We are afraid. The men seize her hand and pull her into the jeep. Then they drive off. We can still hear Itetah wailing. She is crying and screaming. We also saw one of the soldiers in front of the jeep. He has two stars on his shoulder!'

' "The little girls tell me this story and I hurry as I am to the Obi's house. I get there but find out that no jeep carrying Itetah has called there. I go round the whole town. Itetah is nowhere to be found. Up till to-day. The war has ended but Itetah has not returned home. The war has ended and daughters have returned to their parents but my Itetah! Where is she? Where is Itetah? The war has ended for everybody else but me!" '

'The next moment, the old man is crying out, "Anuoha! Anuoha!" I am deeply worried because I have heard the name before.

'And the old man tells me the story. "Anuoha couldn't get a job. For two years after he left secondary school. Then he went into the army. He promised he would find Itetah. I let him go because of that. He was away for a year, then he came back. He had searched everywhere for Itetah. He didn't find her. Then, he shouldn't go back to the army, I advised him. But he wouldn't listen. Already he too had stars on his shoulders. He couldn't run away, he said, at least not then. Then that morning, he was going back. We heard a shooting at the bridge. And there I found him, shot through the head and the neck. First it was my wife, then Itetah, then Anuoha. They were all gone. My farm suffered. I couldn't be myself again. I never have been myself ever since. This cough came, other diseases followed it. There was no money, not one single penny, to eat with. And I lived there alone, with the memory of my dead!"

'The man continued to talk. But they always gave me drugs to sleep,' Idemudia said. 'So I did not hear him finish his story. I fell asleep and later on, something made me wake up. Then I saw the nurses and they were hauling his body onto the stretcher.'

He fell silent. Adisa looked at her hands and then at the floor. Idemudia found himself putting himself into the place of the old man. 'But the man was a farmer,' he told himself.

'And he had no money like you,' his other mind reminded him. He now saw clearly that the man had not been old. His grey hair and wrinkled face, together with his crumpled body structure, were all the results of his sufferings, not of his age. The wrinkles in particular. Or the grey hair. He saw the old man being hauled by the nurses onto the stretcher. He saw them covering him with a white sheet. He shivered on the bed.

'I borrowed five naira from Mama Jimoh yesterday,' Adisa said and brought him back to the present.

He did not answer at once. Then he said, 'How much do we owe her now?'

'Twenty-eight naira.'

'Twenty-eight naira?'

'Yes. Did you think it would be less?'

Idemudia looked at her and did not make any reply.

The tall man from the newspapers came back into the ward with the staff nurse, but instead of continuing with him to the nurses' desk at the other end of the room, the staff nurse came straight to Idemudia's bed. 'So this is your wife,' she said to Idemudia.

'She was about to say something, but hearing the

man whom she had taken to the almoner's office talking, she turned to listen to him.

'I was told to pay sixty-seven naira,' the man was saying. 'I mean by you here. I got there and the girl in the almoner's office insisted that it is seventy-three naira.' His voice became bitter. 'I don't know why a man has to pay for the treatment of a person who dies while on treatment. One already has a tragedy on his hands, then another one is heaped on top. While he is weeping for his dead, he has to go on looking for places to borrow money to pay off your charges.'

'That is the regulation of the hospital,' the staff nurse said from where she was standing beside Idemudia's bed.

'It is unfair,' the tall lean journalist protested.

'If you say so, why don't you put it in the papers? After all, you work there.'

The tall man walked over and as he faced the staff nurse, his eyes were hard. 'I promise to do just that. I will certainly write about it and with your assistance. I merely came back here to make sure that every one of you knows what I am going to do.'

'Then go ahead and do it,' the staff nurse replied. 'But not with our assistance.'

The journalist left the ward, angry and promising to expose everything to the public.

The staff nurse snorted at the journalist's retreating back. 'Irresponsible people!' she hissed and then turned back to Idemudia and Adisa. 'So have you told your wife about the money?' she asked.

Idemudia looked at her and then away, 'Yes,' he said. 'But we have no money.'

The staff nurse laughed. 'So you have no money! And you came to the hospital?'

'So should I have stayed at home and died?' Idemudia asked.

'Look Mr Man,' the staff nurse told him angrily. 'I have my own husband at home and what happens to you is none of my business. But if you come here, you must be prepared to pay the charges. Otherwise, you will not get discharged! I will see to that!'

'You can see to everything you like,' Idemudia answered back angrily.

That really infuriated the staff nurse. 'You will rot here,' she cried. 'I will see to that. You dirty ...'

'Madam!' Adisa cried.

'And you better clear off from the ward!' the staff nurse turned on Adisa angrily. 'Get out of the ward before I send for the Security Officers to come and throw you out!'

Both women looked at each other angrily and then Adisa stepped away from her.

'Go round the window and we will talk from there,' Idemuia said to Adisa, 'and ignore her. That is how they are, callous and unfeeling.'

Adisa went out of the ward and walking along the corridor came to Idemudia's window and stood there.

'So they will not let you go?' she said in a subdued voice.

Idemudia moved the pillow away and sat at the head of the bed. 'No,' he said. 'They will not let me if that nurse has her way.'

'But how can they hold somebody against his will!'

'I do not know,' Idemudia said, 'but perhaps they can do it. Didn't you hear what she said about the body of that man? They will not even let it out of the mortuary. And that is a dead man.'

'My God!' Adisa cried. 'Oh my God!'

'I think you had better go and see Osaro. If he has any money, he will help.'

'And if he has none?'

'Then you come back here in the evening and bring some clothes.'

Adisa nodded quickly with understanding. 'Yes, I will bring you some clothes. But where will you be?'

'There is a concert here in the evening,' Idemudia said. 'They say this is Florence Nightingale week and again the hospital is twenty-five years old. So they are celebrating it and there will this concert in the big hall. All the patients that are well enough have been told that they can go to the concert. I will be there but I will sit near to the entrance. You bring the clothes in a bag there.'

'Are you sure that will be the best way?'

'Yes, I am sure. Now, please hurry and go to Osaro's house. See him and if he can help, perhaps I will not have to run away.'

Chapter 13

Idemudia sat on the corner of the bed and looked out of the window into the evening. The young man of twenty-four whom they had brought in in the afternoon and who now shared the bed with him was asleep. He had been heavily sedated because he had been quite excited when they brought him in. He had wept and cried and called on Jesus, instead of remaining quietly to be given his drugs. So the doctors sedated him and now he slept heavily. From his nostrils a whirlwind was blowing and the window curtains fluttered easily. He had been involved in an accident.

Directly outside his window was another ward and beyond it was the tarred road where the traffic moved and the truck pushers pushed their trucks. On the other side of the road was the church and beside the church was the big supermarket that was always crowded. In front of the supermarket was the road along which Queen had established her own hotel and beside that hotel was another church that was by far larger than the one that stood beside the hospital itself.

Idemudia could hear the noise of the traffic outside, the car horns and the voices of people but he could not immediately see the cars or the people because of this other ward that blocked his view. But he could see the tall buildings, the clouds and the sky that were again darkening, and he knew that very soon it would rain. He sat and watched the clouds gather like an army of locusts and he became nervous because he knew that if it rained, then perhaps Adisa would be delayed. He did not want to think about what he had planned to do. Thinking about it made him feel ashamed and bitter.

Momentarily his mind went to Iyaro, to the petrol station, to the tyres on which they sat, to the loose stones by the water tower on which they sat, to the gutters, filled with refuse by which they stood, to the rain and to the sun under which they all gathered and waited. He saw himself sitting there and it was early on a Monday morning and there were hundreds of others like him waiting, on the lookout for any car that would stop. Then he saw a car now and it was a blue Lada and he scrambled to his feet and fought his way through the other hundreds of labourers to the front window of the car. He saw the owner of the car, a young man in his mid-twenties, hurriedly rolling up his window half-way, embarrassed and for a reason he could not understand, angry.

He saw himself straining his neck forward and looking directly into the embarrassed eyes of the man and asking, 'You want labourers, sir?'

He saw the young man more embarrassed than ever now, shaking his head and saying, 'No, I am sorry, I do not want any labourers. I have come to check the pressure in my tyres.'

And then as he fell back from the car, he saw the man shaking his head and then all of a sudden, he understood why the anger had been in the man's eyes but he had not given himself time to reason out why the man should have felt concerned because a tipper had drawn up and he had become involved in a great struggle with the other labourers to get as near to the tipper as he could. He saw himself struggling, fighting, cursing and sweating and anxious, and his mind grew more bitter. How could he go back to all these things, to the overpowering heat of the sun, to the numbness of hunger, to the despair of returning home each evening after a day's long wait? How? What alternatives had he? And what hadn't he done to earn money? He had even sold his blood to make money. Yes, given out pints of his blood for as little as fifteen naira a pint. Sold his blood so that he and Adisa would not starve, so that they could survive. And this he had done not once nor twice but many times. Always, the men who wanted the blood came to them at Iyaro in their big long cars. Always, they were hesitant to say they wanted to buy the blood.

'We want some . . .' and the men would hesitate, looking at the hard set faces of the labourers. But the labourers understood, always.

Always, after they had decided to sell their blood, they would stand in the shadow of the water tower, away from the main body of the other labourers and as they waited, their faces hard and set, they would be hungry, frustrated and silent. Always.

The last time he and Osaro had gone to sell their blood, it had been to a man in a big Mercedes Benz car. The car had drawn up close to where they were standing and in the car were the driver, the man and a boy. The man and the boy sat at the back of the car and then the man had rolled down the window glass and beckoned to them.

He saw it again clearly now, very very clearly, the man, the boy and himself and then the hospital.

'I want . . .' and as always, the man hesitated.

Idemudia saw himself nodding and saying, 'Blood, sir?'

'Yes.'

'How much will you pay?' Osaro asked.

'How much do you want?' the man replied. 'I want as many as four pints.'

'It is twenty-five naira a pint,' Osaro said.

154

The man laughed. 'Twenty-five naira! That is too expensive.'

'Then how much can you pay?'

'Ten naira a pint, nothing more, nothing less.'

Idemudia shook his head then. 'No, sir. Ten naira is too small. You are buying blood, you know. Our blood.'

'All right then,' the man said while the child leaned forward. 'I am prepared to pay twelve naira for a pint.'

Idemudia and Osaro shook ther heads.

'Thirteen naira then.'

'No, sir,' Osaro said now and shook his head again. 'That is still not enough. We are prepared to accept fifteen naira and nothing less.'

The man in the Mercedes car considered this for some time, then nodded. 'Okay, fifteen naira, but I want you at the hospital straight away. I am going to give you twenty kobo so that you can take a taxi. I will be at the gate of the hospital waiting for you.'

And then as he made to hand over the twenty kobo to Idemudia, the boy said, 'Are you sure Grandma will be all right, Daddy?'

The attendants who ran the blood banks always wore white overalls and this last time that he and Osaro were there, it was the tall woman who had approached him.

'Make your hand into a fist and then open . . .' and he had rolled up his sleeve, his face averted, so that the woman would not recognise him. Then he had watched from the corner of his eyes as the woman tied the short brown rubber tube round his arm and with the cotton that was soaked in the methylated spirit wiped clean the surface of his skin where the veins stood out, clear and pulsating like the current of a stream.

'You are sure you have never been here?' the woman asked as she selected a needle from the tray.

'Yes, madam.'

'You are quite sure?'

'Yes.'

The woman picked up the needle and looked at him. 'I say this for your own good,' she said. 'Some men come here two or more times in a single month. It is not good for their health. Last week a man collapsed here and nearly died. It turned out he had been here the week before.'

Idemudia did not answer her.

Momentarily, he had shut his eyes and shivered from the sudden pain when the woman broke the surface of his skin with the sharp end of the big needle before plunging it further into his vein and then as she removed the small brown rubber tube from his arm and attached the narrow but long transparent tube to the needle, he had watched his blood gradually flowing through the tube into the bottle below and his eyes had become dilated, his breathing quick and sharp, his mouth open, his throat dry.

He had watched his life flowing into the bottle and he had tried hard not to think about what the small boy had said to the man in the car. 'Are you sure Grandma will be all right, Daddy? Are you sure Grandma ... ? Are you sure ... ?'

The bottle always seemed to take a long time to fill up, a long time when his heart seemed to clash like cymbals as it beat violently in his chest and everything always seemed to stop, including his life. And always, particularly when they fixed up the second bottle to the long tube, he always felt like going to the toilet to urinate but he never always could because of this needle that was sitting under his skin, gradually draining his life away.

And funnily enough, he never ever went to the toilet afterwards but always felt very weak and exhausted, completely. And each time after he had sold his blood, he had returned home, subdued and for a reason he could not understand, ashamed. And he never told Adisa that the money he brought home had come from selling his blood at fifteen naira a pint. But he guessed that Adisa knew. The defeated, furtive look in his eyes told her. The bottle of Guinness Stout which he always bought and brought home to drink afterwards also told her. The punctures that the needles made on his skin told her. Yes, everything told her, including the gradual thinness of his body. But Adisa never ever said anything about it to him. Not once.

'The things an empty stomach can drive a man to,' he said to himself now, and shook his head. 'The things hunger can make a man do!'

And now? What was he going to do? He couldn't continue to sell his blood. There was bound to be a limit somewhere. What was he going to do?

'Oh yes, I know what I am going to do,' he said to himself. 'I am going to escape somehow from this so-called hospital in which I am being held as a prisoner is held because I cannot pay their charges. I am going to escape and then I am going to see what happens.

'But I am not going to give up,' he swore to himself. 'I am going to continue to struggle, to fight. And where I cannot fight because I am held as I am held now, I am going to escape. Escape and then what? What happens after? What . . . ?'

The chain of his thought was broken by the entrance of the staff nurse into the ward. She was smartly dressed and she went to the centre of the ward and announced: 'It's time now to go out to the hall. Those of you who were told this morning that they could go should now get ready and accompany me.'

The Hospital Hall had formerly been the ward for psychiatric patients. But the ward patients and all its staff had been moved to Okeso and the ward had been converted to a hall for receiving and entertaining very important personalities.

It had been repainted, a deep, deep blue, different from the buildings in the hospital grounds. Flowers were planted at its entrance, hibiscus and Pride of Barbados flowers. The hall itself was surrounded by a thin strip of grass on each side. The grass was fenced round and many little black and white posts were mounted warning, 'Do not trespass on the grass.'

The small wooden windows had been broken down, the window wire fencing removed. New glass windows, wide and low, were built in and blue Venetian blinds installed. Directly above each window was an airconditioner and overhead on the white ceiling were the fans, also of blue and whining even when the airconditioners were on.

The hall was not large. At the lower side were the long wooden benches, all of them high, on which the ordinary people sat each time an important visitor was being entertained or received. They were arranged in two rows, one on either side so that a passage was created. And then there were the rows of low, soft, rich, deep-blue seats, two on either side on which the very important people sat and crossed their legs each time an address or a speech was being made from the raised wooden platform which was the stage. Cutting off the stage from the rest of the hall was the long blue curtain, manually operated by two people each time. And just where the stage ended were the two doors, high, which led outside to some five steps on which a person must climb from outside before getting on to the stage.

Always the ordinary people did the entertaining while the very important people did the receiving. Always the gratitude and acknowledgement went to the reception. Always.

And now Idemudia was sitting in the hall close to the entrance and at the outer end of the long wooden bench, by the passage. 'She should come about thirty minutes from now,' he said to himself and already in his mind's eye, he could see himself going out into the darkness and taking the pack of his clothes into the toilet . . .

The hall was quiet and subdued as the people waited for the guest of honour to arrive. And soon he came with his entourage, this commissioner, a small plump man in a lace agbada. He arrived in a large Mercedes Benz car and as soon as it was parked, small, lean, hungry-looking children surrounded it and regarded it.

The audience rose as soon as the commissioner entered the hall and Idemudia watched the small fat man in his agbada walking up to the soft blue seat reserved for him. Photographers hurried to and fro. There were small flashes of light all over the hall, as his photograph was taken. Idemudia watched the entourage also file past, most of them finely dressed in lace and brocade material. They were mostly women, heavy, fat women with oily, polished skins, their eyes scarcely looking at the floor on which they walked. They passed by smelling every inch a thousand naira, the heavy black handbags hanging loosely from their shoulders. 'Here is money,' Idemudia thought. Money! If only he had some, he told himself, he would pay off the hospital bills. He wouldn't be here anyway. Ah, how could he? He would be somewhere else. There wouldn't be this hunger, this emptiness, this helplessness of watching even his control over his wife slip away. Oh yes, his control over Adisa was thinning out. And there was nothing much he could do about it. But if he had some money! He would open up a small shop and there Adisa would sit on the counter. He would come in to her at the end of each day and ask her: 'How much did you sell today?' Then she would show him the books. He would look at the figures and he would see that everything was all right.

Of course that one room into which their lives were crowded would go. At worst they would live like Papa Jimoh. They would have a bedroom and a parlour. And their son would live there. Then at the end of each month, he would send money to his mother. His father would not receive anything from him. Nothing at all.

'That cruel, useless man,' he thought bitterly. 'A cruel and useless man. I will see him dying one day. Then I will remind him of all his wickedness, of all his heartlessness. He will plead for forgiveness on his death-bed but I will shake my head. I will remind him of my mother crying, screaming. I will show him all the gashes, now healed perhaps, that he inflicted on her. The dirty bastard! The heartless, cruel and wicked bastard!'

Then his memory and conscience jarred him. 'You mustn't think like that about your own father! Remember he was good to you. At least he sent you to school in the first place.'

But this other bitter part of him fought back. 'And so what? What did his goodness amount to? Expelling my mother and my brothers and sisters away from our home? Was that goodness? Letting me sit in the cell, I, a child only?'

'I must not be bitter anyway,' he reminded himself. 'It does no good to be bitter. I should have quiet and peace in my mind. Then I will be able to think about my problems and see clearly how they can be solved. If anybody is to blame, it is the police who arrested my father in the first place. Those unfeeling people. The police who locked me up for being my father's son. Those policemen. If only thunder could get at them and wipe them out. Raiding a whole village and knocking on the doors and waking everybody up. Driving the people into the bush. Only for taxes. After all, who would refuse to pay a tax if he had the money. The police were to blame. Those unfeeling and hardhearted people. But for them, I would have completed my schooling, at least got the school certificate and with that I could have been anything today. But the police have their instructions from the government,' he remembered. 'Our government,' he thought cynically. 'Our government!'

He halted again. 'I am being bitter again,' he told himself. 'I shouldn't be. I should be thinking of how to solve my problems. I should swallow this bitterness. It only makes things worse. I know I am not responsible for it. Circumstances have brought it upon me, but I cannot afford the luxury of being bitter. I simply cannot. And so,' he paused, 'I go back to Iyaro. But for how long? For how many years can I continue to go there to queue up and wait for a day's job? For how many more years can I continue to sell pints of my blood?'

Again he saw himself sitting on one of those unused tyres, his head bent low, the sun fiercely striking at the nape of his neck, like one whose head is held down, waiting for the blades of the guillotine. Then after the sun, the rains came. He saw the wetness, his hair dripping with the water, his face black and empty and he had to go back home to Adisa to tell her, 'No luck today. Nothing.' Then he had to keep quiet about his hunger. The hunger would gnaw at him, chew at the

161

walls of his stomach until he would be forced to gasp, 'I am hungry!' Like a child. Almost like a helpless child.

A shrill voice sliced through the circle of his inner thinking. He started up from his seat and then he fell back. It was the nurse reading the address of welcome, thanking the government for all it had done to provide health facilities for the people, praising the government for building new hospitals. The address did not mention that in the same government hospital, some people slept on the hard floor or shared beds while others had single rooms to themselves which were almost invariably never occupied. The address said nothing about the fees, about the congestion in the mortuary. No, it thanked and praised the government again and again. 'Generous government leaders' it talked about. 'Our courageous and learned Commissioner' it eulogised.

Then it went on to give the life history of Florence Nightingale, to whom it referred as the 'Mother of Nursing'. To commemorate the life and activities of this great warm-hearted lady, one of the three plays lined up for the evening would be devoted to her. The first play would feature two patients. The play had been written by one of the nurses and it was entitled, 'Had I Known'. The second play would, as already announced, be about Florence Nightingale. The third was a comedy and it had, funnily enough, been written by a patient who had left the hospital three months ago. It was entitled 'Violence'.

At that there was a murmur from the audience. The nurse paused for the murmuring to die down. Then she smiled and invited everybody to sit back and relax and watch.

There followed the clapping of hands, voices of people laughing. Unconsciously Idemudia found himself clapping. But after a few minutes, his mind slipped away again from the hall to the streets, to Adisa. When was she going to come?

Chapter 14

It was nearly seven o'clock when Adisa left home. She hurried along Owode Street and joined the main stream of traffic going up Ekenwan Road towards Oba Market. She noticed that the clouds were growing dark and she knew it would rain, so she hurried. She hadn't gone far when the white Cortina drew up in front of her. She immediately recognised Obofun.

She hesitated, then walked up to the car. Throughout the whole afternoon as she ran from pillar to post looking for somewhere to borrow some money, she had kept Obofun at the back of her mind as a last resort and now that he had stopped directly in front of her, her mind was in a turmoil. Was this destiny?

'I saw you as you left your house,' Obofun said as she drew level with the car, her head bent downwards, as the tall stalks of maize are bent downwards in a windstorm. 'But you walk very fast, even faster than a car.'

Adisa forced herself to smile and still she stood beside the car, her eyes confused as she bent her neck forwards, the dark of her lips darker still, her heart beating confusedly, like chaos. She moved sideways, away from the car as Obofun pulled the door knob towards himself and then pushed the door outwards, to open it for her.

'I'll drop you wherever you are going,' he offered and continued to hold the door ajar. Adisa opened the door wider and slipped into the car.

They were both silent for many long minutes as the car bounced and joggled on the rough road. Adisa could think of nothing. Her mind was in utter, indescribable chaos.

Obofun's brain was heated up like a blacksmith's forge. His passions fanned the forge, his reason, that part of a man's mind which always stands for the truth, hammered at the scrap metal that was in his heart, in his passions and attempted to beat them clean.

'What do you want with her? A poor woman, she is nothing to you. She is married. Leave her alone. If you won't then don't help her. But let her go. Let her be. She is married to another!'

To which his passions retorted, 'She is beautiful! Look at her black lips, her long jet black hair and her black sensuous eyes. She is a black wild cat. Look again at those breasts. Oh God, look at them and then remember the roundness, the fullness of her hips. You must have her. A woman is not married when her husband cannot take care of her. She is not married!' Then his better self cried out, 'You know you are lying. Poverty does not dissolve a marriage, but people like you do, your actions and the temptations you offer do. If you touch her, you are offending God!' His passions would have none of this reasoning. 'You do not offend God,' they shrieked. 'You are helping her. She will sell your whisky. You will give her another fifty naira, you can even make it a hundred naira. What is money to you? But Adisa is something. Don't miss her!'

And his better half insisted. 'Drop her where she wants to go. Drop her at the hospital and forget about her!'

His passions laughed. 'How can you drop her now? Look at her. She is confused. She is already half won. You can easily tilt her now. Take her home, to the Samson and Delilah!'

And now his whole body, mind, passions and reason were involved in the argument. He had to reach a decision quickly. Very soon they would be at the roundabout. He had to decide quickly, now. He reached the roundabout and slowed down, then all of a sudden he accelerated. Adisa turned to him.

'We'll go to my place,' he said in a voice that shook at the bottom.

'But why? I want to go to the hospital,' she said, clutching the paper bag she held to her.

'Oh yes, I know.'

'Then why are you not taking me there?'

'We won't be gone long. We'll have a drink and then I will bring you back.'

'I don't want a drink.'

'I know, but does it matter?'

'I do not want to drink anything,' she said again, but it was from the corner of her mind. And the broad knowing side of her mind replied, 'I know, I know. But why are you worried? We will not go for long. Only a little patience. Yes, just be a little patient.'

Her hands hung limply in her lap. She was determined not to give in without a struggle.

'You must take me back!' she cried. 'My ... Idemudia expects me.'

And again the monotony of his reply dulled her mind. 'I know. Just be patient.'

He drove quickly down Airport Road and plunged the car, tyres screeching, into the lane along which was the Samson and Delihah. Then he drew up beside the chalet, and wiped his face with the broad of his palm. He was sweating. 'Why don't you come down?' he asked her.

Adisa sat in the car, her mind busy and anxious. 'I will wait here,' she said. 'I will wait for you in the car. You say you won't be long. I will wait here. You can go and come back.'

'I do nothing to you which is against your will,' Obofun said.

'Then why don't you leave me alone?'

Obofun considered this for a moment. 'It is because I wish to help you,' he replied slowly. 'I want to help you and you do not let me. You have made up your mind about something. You are determined not to relax. But I ask why? Surely you can come down. We shouldn't argue here. I have told you that I will not do anything to you that is against your will.'

A man was walking down the gravel path towards them. The noise his shoes made on the stones increased the tension inside Obofun. 'Oh Adisa!' he cried. 'Please come down. Do not treat me like this.'

He took a few steps to the door of the chalet and quickly inserted the key in the lock. He turned the door's handle and pushed the door backwards so that it yawned open.

Adisa came down from the car.

'You must be quick,' she said. 'My husband is expecting me.'

'I know, I know!' Obofun cried. 'We won't be a minute longer than necessary. Please come inside. Quickly, for we must be fast.'

He shut the door behind him just as the man who had been walking down the gravel path drew level. Normally, Obofun was not nervous with women. He knew what he wanted and how to get it. But Adisa shattered his self-confidence. She made him nervous.

'I am sure you won't object,' he began, and then stopped.

'What is it?' Adisa asked, looking at him.

'I am hungry,' he said, looking at her where she stood. 'I hope you will not object to my having a quick sandwich. I will eat quickly. Then we will go.'

Adisa did not answer, and he took her silence for acquiescence. He picked up the phone and began to dial hurriedly.

Adisa looked round the room and again she was

overwhelmed by the flagrant display of wealth exhibited here. And so one man could live so well while others like her starved to death. 'What makes the difference?' she asked herself. She didn't bother herself trying to find the answer. She didn't know.

Nor could she understand why this man was so obsessed with her. 'Fifty naira! Heavens. Only to sleep with me!' She looked at him as he spoke rapidly into the telephone.

'And what have I got to lose?' she asked herself. 'Nobody will ever find out. Nobody will ever imagine that I can be involved with such a man. We need the money and I must have something I can always do. A small shop of my own. Nobody will find it out. Nobody ... Not even Idemudia.'

'The sandwich will soon be here,' Obofun announced, breaking into her thoughts.

She stared at the floor, at the rug, she couldn't look at his eyes, she couldn't bear to. Within her, she knew she was defeated. Only Obofun did not know this. He thought she was uninterested and hostile, even now.

'I will give you the cartons of whisky,' Obofun said in a small voice.

She looked up at him quickly.

Then he added, 'And one hundred naira ... for you to start off.'

She couldn't speak. She didn't know what to say. There was a knock on the door and then Obofun also stood up and when he opened the door, a waiter came in, and on the tray he carried two club sandwiches, a bottle of beer and a bottle of maltex. He set them down on the centre table and without a word, he left the room. Obofun shut the door after him.

'They brought a sandwich for you,' Obofun said. 'And a bottle of maltex.'

'I do not want to eat,' Adisa said. 'And really I must

go now.' She stood up and very quickly circled the table.

Obofun stood up quickly, and went and stood by the door.

'Really, I must go,' she said, but her voice was weak and she knew she could never fight Obofun now.

'So, one hundred naira means nothing to you? And the whisky . . . ?'

'Please let me go! Please!' she cried.

Obofun stood where she must pass and Adisa knew that if he grabbed her and embraced her, she would be unable to fend him off. Not with her mind the way it was.

Obofun looked at her intently and then shrugging his shoulders, made way for her to pass. Surprised, Adisa sighed with relief and very quickly grabbed the door knob and turned it. But the door would not open.

'Adisa!'

She looked back at him. 'Please open the door!'

'Adisa!' He moved towards her.

Her hand grabbed the door knob more tightly. But already his hands were round her and gripping her shoulders, forcing her towards him. She felt her hand falling away from the door knob, and she knew that she was beaten. She let him drag her into the bedroom. But when he made for her clothes, she fought him. It was an unconscious fight, her consciousness had already given in and so the fight was weak. Then, suddenly, the telephone bell began to ring. It rang shrilly, then stopped. It rang again. Obofun cursed the telephone mentally and ignored it. 'You can ring a million times,' he cursed. The phone continued to ring.

And now, the panic built up inside Adisa. She struggled once more and attempted to break free but it was no use. Obofun weighed down heavily on her and her fight was nothing but the last spasmodic movements of a dying animal. She gritted her teeth and her body was tense but cold and her eyes were vacant, as if she was not here but far, far away.

And then after some time, there was a knock on the door outside and although Obofun was lying now by her side, he did not get up to answer it. The knocking grew louder, more insistent, and then he heard voices but still he would not get up. He felt curiously empty and dissatisfied with himself.

Adisa did not hear any knocking. Her face was buried against the pillow and she was weeping.

'You must not cry,' Obofun said, and turned to her.

He had conquered her. Yet he felt deflated. To him, there was nothing exalting in what he had achieved. The woman had been impassive, he had felt at one stage as if he was making love to a dead woman. And so he had moved to hurt her. He became rough and harsh. But still Adisa had closed her eyes and had not responded.

'You must not cry,' he said now and his voice was rough and harsh. 'You have lost nothing.' Then he turned her over with one hand. Adisa held the dress tightly to her body and with the other hand, she covered her face while the tears came out of her eyes and down her cheeks, slowly.

Obofun scratched his head. He had never felt like this before. This woman was a direct challenge to him. He was going to pay her one hundred naira and yet she was weeping! Worse still, she had not really given in to him. He had given in to her. He had been passionate and very emotional, she had been dispassionate and cold.

He stood up from the bed and went into the toilet. He entered the bath as he was, stark naked and turned on the shower. He watched the water going all over his body. His head was bowed. Christ! He had never felt so depressed in his life! Slowly he began to rub the soap on his body.

He found her sitting on the edge of the bed when he came out of the bathroom. She was already wearing her dress, her eyes were dry but her face was taut and sad, like one who had lost a child. He tried to joke as he hurried into his own clothes. He did not wish to stand before her naked.

'The water is colder than ice,' he said. 'Although of course the heater is on.'

She did not answer.

'Did you not hear some people knocking?'

Slowly Adisa shook her head.

'Ah, I thought they were going to tear the place down!' he laughed, but there was no warmth on his face.

Then he remembered. He went to a side drawer and drew out an envelope. He threw it on the bed beside her. 'There is a magic paper inside there,' he joked. 'Do not open it until you get home. You will be surprised with what you will find there, that is if you obey the magician's instructions.'

Adisa did not touch the envelope.

'I will get one of my pick-ups to send you the cartons of whisky tomorrow morning. Around ten o'clock. You should be outside to receive them.'

He finished putting on his trousers. Next he began to button his shirt. 'You do not have to be sad nor ashamed of what we have done,' he said to her, his voice serious now. 'You can regard it as something that was necessary. And once you come to think of it in those terms, the next time will always be better than this time.'

Adisa did not answer him but she picked up the envelope, and stood up.

'I will drop you at the hospital,' he offered her.

But she shook her head. Suddenly she didn't want to be seen with him. 'I will walk,' she said. 'I don't want you to take me there.'

Obofun shrugged his shoulders. 'Then, let one of my drivers take you there.'

Adisa still refused. 'No, no,' she replied, going towards the door. 'I will go there by myself. Thank you.'

She crossed the bedroom door and went into the sitting room.

'I have the key here,' Obofun called from behind her. He drew the key out of his pocket. 'You know where you can always get me. Here. As soon as you tell the receptionist your name, he will get through to me quickly, wherever I may be.'

He walked up to her and she drew away from the door. Silently, she watched him put the key in the lock. He turned it and turned the handle, then pulled the door towards him inside.

'My paper bag is in the car,' she said.

'Your paper bag?'

'Yes. I want it.'

He went outside with her and then opened the car door and brought her paper bag out and held it to her.

'You must let me know how you are selling the drinks,' he said. 'As soon as you have sold enough, you must come here to see me.'

Adisa did not say anything as she took the paper bag from him, but looked round very quickly to see if anybody was out and watching them. She did not see anybody and very quickly, she walked away from him. But when she drew level with the main entrance of the Samson and Delilah, she did not see Queen who was standing in the darkness thrown by the white pillar against which she was leaning, her black handbag hanging down from her hand, like a tree's branch that is weighed down by the leaves and the fruits. She did not see her but hurried down the gravel path towards the main road, her feet scattering the stones and the stones clashing in small echoes.

Arriving at the main road, she noticed for the first time how much time had passed. Darkness had fallen and she told herself that with what had passed, she couldn't go up to the hospital to face her husband. She would go home instead. Tomorrow morning, she would go and see Idemudia and explain. Yes, explain ... but what?

Chapter 15

Now, it was the third play and as Idemudia watched, he grew restless. 'What is she doing?' he asked himself. 'Has something happened? And if something has indeed happened, what could it be? Has there been an accident? Has Adisa been involved in an accident?' He shifted uneasily in his seat because he didn't know.

He should have stood up and gone out to find out but what if she came while he was away? There were three entrances to the hospital and he couldn't know through which one she would come. His hand moved restlessly from his chin to his lips and from his lips to his nose. What was Adisa doing?

'Will the accused speak for himself or will he prefer that his lawyer should speak for him?' Idemudia heard the loud voice of the Judge booming across the hall and he couldn't concentrate any more on his personal thoughts.

He looked up and he could see many policemen and lawyers, and a small audience on the stage on which the tables and the chairs were arranged as in a court room. The Judge sat away from the rest of the court, on a raised dais and on either side of him, but lower down were the court clerk and other court officials. Idemudia could see a man dressed in torn clothes standing in the dock.

'It's just like a court room,' a man said to the right of Idemudia. 'Just see how the lawyers are dressed.'

'Sh ... shh,' came another voice in a whisper and Idemudia turned sharply half expecting to see Adisa. But there was nobody there and the voice had come from the audience.

Idemudia turned back to the stage and he could see the lawyer consulting with the man in the dock.

'The accused will speak for himself where necessary,' the lawyer announced loudly. 'I will speak where the accused wishes me so to do. This shall apply in the other cases as well.'

'Very well,' the voice of the Judge boomed back. 'I want this point made clear because the trial of people accused of robbery with violence often follows different procedures from those adopted in normal civil court procedures. In this kind of case, for example, the Judge is free to cross-examine the accused if he so wishes. You will see that this is necessary since he acts as both Judge and jury. If this is understood, then Counsel for the Prosecution may proceed with the cross-examination.'

The prosecuting lawyer stepped forward. He wore glasses and held a sheaf of papers. Beside him was a desk and on it, piled high, were fat large books.

'The accused is aware of the offence he is charged with,' he announced. 'He is alleged to have robbed with violence. Does he plead guilty?'

The hand of the Counsel for the Defence shot up.

'Yes?' enquired the Judge.

Counsel for the Defence cleared his throat. He took quite some time doing it and the audience laughed. 'I find the last question from my learned colleague preposterous. The accused, I mean my client, has stated times without number that he is not guilty.'

The Judge brought his hammer down with a loud bang on the table. 'The submission of Counsel for the Defence is upheld. You may proceed.'

The audience laughed.

Counsel for the Prosecution thereupon advanced towards the accused, pointing his five fingers at him. 'What is your age?'

'Thirty-eight years old,' the accused answered.

'Your trade or profession?' His face was very serious.

The accused wiped his face with his hands, pretending to be sweating; 'Labourer.'

'And how much are you paid monthly?' the prosecuting lawyer bellowed.

'Fourteen naira.'

Counsel for the Prosecution looked satisfied. 'Oh yes, I see,' he said. 'Fourteen naira for thirty days' work, ha? Does that not mean that you are lazy, always late to your place of work, and rude to your supervisors?'

'Such a statement is wrong,' Counsel for the Defence spoke for his client now. 'My client is a good and conscientious worker. He works from the earliest hours of the morning to the latest hours of the day. There are hundreds of workers who like my client receive so little pay for so much work done.'

Counsel for the Prosecution nodded understandingly. 'Why is he paid so little if he works so hard?'

'He is paid so little because he accepts it. And he accepts it because he would starve if he refused it. Even if he refused it there would be many more people who would accept it,' Counsel for the Defence concluded.

'I wish to end my cross-examination here,' Counsel for the Prosecution said. 'However, the accused is to stand by since he may be called upon to appear as a witness.' The audience again murmured.

'Does the Counsel for the Defence wish to interview the accused?' the Judge asked.

'Yes, my lord,' the defence lawyer said.

'You may proceed,' the Judge said.

Counsel for the Defence smiled benevolently at the accused. 'I want you to tell us if you are married,' he said.

The accused shifted in the box. 'Yes, I am married.'

'And how many children have you got?'

The accused scratched his head. 'Three. I have three children.'

'And how are they fed, clothed and educated?'

The accused smiled sadly. 'My children do not go to school: They are always scantily dressed and as for feeding, they are always hungry. We have no money.'

'Was that why he decided to go on this dangerous road of robbery with violence?' the Judge cut in.

Counsel for the Defence stared with surprise at the Judge. 'My lord ...'

'The accused will answer my question,' the Judge said.

The accused's face was set, his eyes brimmed with anger. 'Has your child ever fallen ill or wept and cried from hunger? Has your child ever died in your presence simply because he could gain no access to a doctor? Has ...'

The Judge was very angry. 'What!'

The lawyer for the accused put up his hands. 'The accused, my client, would like to know if the children of your lordship have ever suffered or died from the effects of hunger and malnutrition in your presence?'

The Judge rose from his seat. 'That is a stupid and foolish question which has no bearing on the case. Take him out of the witness box and chain him.'

A murmur went up from the audience. Then as he was bullied out of the court room, there was laughter.

The Judge brought down his hammer with a harsh bang. 'Order!'

A great clapping of hands went up in the hall. On the front and foremost seats, however, the commissioner sat, unsmiling.

'Who did they say wrote this play?' he enquired of the man sitting next to him.

'A patient,' the man replied.

'A patient?'

'Yes, a patient. He was here three months ago. Now he has recovered and he has gone.'

'What is his name?'

'It wasn't mentioned.'

'But we can find out?'

'Oh yes. Very easily. But look, they are now on to the second accused.'

They both fell silent as the voice of the Counsel for the Prosecution vibrated across the length and breadth of the hall.

'Profession?'

'He is a school teacher.'

'That's interesting. Very interesting,' Counsel for the Prosecution repeated, licking his lips. The court room was already moderately charged. 'A school teacher and a thief! Now may I ask what impelled the learned professor to the dark roads of crime?'

The voice of the defence lawyer snapped back, 'You do not need to insult my client to cross-examine him. And by the way, your questions already presuppose that the accused is guilty. And may I add that my client has taught betters than you?'

'That is contempt of court,' the Judge chimed in.

'If you'll let us explain, your lordship ...'

'Well ...' the Judge said, and adjusted his wig.

Counsel for the Defence adjusted his wig too, 'My client taught Igreki.'

The Judge sharply caught his breath, 'Igreki, the army general?'

'Oh yes. And you know he was retired last year,' Counsel for the Defence informed his Lordship.

The Judge feigned ignorance. 'I cannot recall for what reason.'

'He was retired with full benefits after embezzling substantial government funds – amounting as many sources have it to nearly two hundred and forty million naira.'

'I hope you are aware of the danger to your career by mentioning the name of a man who could well sue you for slander.'

Counsel for the Defence nodded. 'I am aware, fully aware, and I intend to go further.'

The Judge bowed stiffly. 'You have my permission.'

'Azonze was also a pupil of this teacher,' Counsel for the Defence revealed.

'Azonze who was dismissed last week?'

'Oh yes. He owned over two hundred houses which he used public funds to build. He also owned several farms which were worked with government equipment and labour, and yet whose expenses and maintenance were charged to the government treasury.'

'Where is Azonze now?' the Judge asked, laying emphasis on the word 'now'.

'On his farms. Also dismissed with full benefits.'

The Judge cleared his throat. 'What then are you trying to imply?' he asked. 'That the accused went on this course of crime because his former pupils could not only steal with impunity but profited by it?'

'Your lordship ...'

'Does it not appear to you that the accused being a rogue brought up rogues? It is natural. It is no surprise then that he should have ...'

'Your lordship! It would be unfair to conclude thus. Greater crimes, we will agree, lie unpunished. But what I want to stress here is that the whole society is sick. Charging one man or four of them with an offence such as this does no justice to the system. In fact ...'

The Judge cut Counsel for the Defence short, 'I find your arguments preposterous,' he began, and the whole audience laughed.

'That other rogues do not get punished is no reason why this particular one shouldn't be found guilty. And so if you please ...'

'My lord,' pleaded Counsel for the Defence, 'if you

179

will now permit us to go into the circumstances of the life of the accused ...'

The Judge put up his two hands. 'I cannot grant the time.'

The voice of the Counsel for the Defence was grave. 'This is a matter of life and death,' he declared. 'To do less justice to my client would, I am afraid, leave some moss on all our consciences.'

The Judge seemed to relent. 'Well?'

Counsel for the Defence continued. 'I wish to state that the accused was faced with a lot of hardship for over thirty-five years. And I would like to mention concretely what some of the problems were.'

'Surely you know that he is not the only one standing trial?' the Judge asked, looking down at the next of the accused.

Counsel for the Defence smiled. 'Oh yes,' he answered. 'I know that the whole society here stands on trial. I know that there are other people who you could say have greater justification to commit robbery with violence, people who you could say have enough reason to burn down the present edifice ...'

There was great agitation among the audience. Many of them sat forward on their seats. They wanted to hear more. They no longer thought that the play was funny. They began to identify themselves with it. And so did the commissioner who sat, very uncomfortable, in his comfortable seat.

'I find your language going against the law,' the Judge warned and Counsel for the Defence pretended to be sorry.

He crossed his two hands as if in prayer. 'My sincere apologies,' he cried in a heavy voice. 'But no lesser language can describe the plight of the majority of our citizens, millions of them who you know ...'

The Judge lost some of his patience. 'You are now

going outside the premises of this particular case,' he warned. 'You must come back or else whatever you say now will not stand the accused in good stead.' He brought his hammer down.

'Order!' the Court Orderly shouted.

The audience laughed derisively. But the face of the commissioner was hard and cold.

'Your lordship!' Counsel for the Defence began. 'I did intend to come back. I just wanted to make it clear that the majority of our people have more than enough reason to go on armed robbery, to rob with violence ...'

Again the Judge called him back. 'I wish to remind you that you are defending the school teacher only, not the majority of the people.'

'But the plight of the school teacher, the worker, the farmer and the last of the accused whom I shall soon be calling in evidence personifies to a greater or lesser degree the fate of at least fifty million of our citizens,' Counsel for the Defence argued.

'Will you then call the last of the accused?' the Judge asked.

'When?'

'I mean now.'

'But I have not finished with the school teacher yet.'

The voice of the Judge was grim. 'I do not wish to listen to any more evidence on behalf of the accused. Call the last of the accused!'

'But...' the voice of Counsel for the Defence went up in a plaintive cry.

The Judge waved his hands to indicate that he did not wish to hear any more.

The audience murmured disapproval. The commissioner was, however, smiling. The school teacher was roughly taken out of the witness box, and a third man, dressed in rags with his hair uncombed, was led into his place. He was tall and lean, his hair already greying a little. His eyes were sad and his hands were folded across his chest. He waited like one condemned, ready for the scaffold.

The Judge briefly consulted with the Counsel for the Prosecution. 'I will conduct the cross-examination,' the Judge asserted to the hearing of everybody.

Counsel for the Prosecution nodded his head vigorously, and withdrew to his table where he sat down by his fat books.

'Educated?' the Judge asked, looking from the accused to Counsel for the Defence.

Counsel for the Defence briefly riffled through his file. 'Yes,' he spoke up. 'Educated. West African School Certificate.'

'When then did he complete his schooling?'

'Sixteen years ago.'

'That's many years ago,' the Judge commented dryly.

'Oh yes, many years,' Counsel for the Defence agreed.

'What has he been doing since then?'

'Unemployed.'

'Unemployed? What do you mean?' asked the Judge surprised.

Counsel for the Defence smiled, but his eyes were hard and angry. 'Unemployed means unemployed,' he said. 'He has been jobless.'

'But did he try to get a job?'

Idemudia who was sitting far behind in the big hall shifted uncomfortably on his bench. His mind was on the play now. All of his mind.

'Of course,' he heard Counsel for the Defence reply.

'And he didn't get any?' the Judge persisted.

'No, he didn't get any.'

'Why?'

'Well, there were no jobs!'

'Did he try a few of the places I know, Iyaro, for instance?'

'You mean where they hire casual labourers?'

'Yes.'

'Well, he did.'

'And he found nothing?'

'Well, sometimes he did. In a month, for instance, three times if he was lucky.'

'And how much did he make from that?'

'Sometimes, three naira a day. Depending on the employer.'

'So that means nine naira in a whole month? Incredible!' the Judge laughed in disbelief. 'I pay my own driver twenty naira a month,' he announced. 'Plus feeding,' he added with pride and dignity.

'Does your driver work every day of the month?' Counsel for the Defence asked.

'Of course he has to. He earns twenty naira! So you can see that if the accused really wanted to work ...'

'I am sorry to have to interrupt you,' Counsel for the Defence broke in, 'but since this has degenerated to a more or less personal conversation, may I ask how many drivers your lordship can employ at once?'

The Judge removed his spectacles and cleaned them speculatively. 'That question does not arise,' he said slowly.

Instantly the audience hummed.

Counsel for the Defence put up a forefinger. 'It does,' he insisted. 'It arises because I am sure there are at least ten drivers in this court who are at the moment unemployed and would be only too glad to benefit from your generosity.'

The voice of the Judge suddenly became stern. 'I warn you to carry on with your defence.'

'But, your lordship,' Counsel for the Defence protested, 'you were asking all the questions.'

'Oh yes, let me see. Let me see,' the Judge repeated as if something blocked his view. 'So he has been out of a job for some time.'

'That, your lordship, is putting the situation mildly. My client has never had a job in the true sense of that word.'

'And did he think he would get a job by committing acts of violence against society?' the Judge asked sharply.

The forefinger of Counsel for the Defence shot up again. 'I beg to disagree with your definition and understanding of violence, what constitutes it.'

The Judge sat back in his chair contentedly. 'I have yet to hear of a much better and more correct understanding of what constitutes violence or a violent act,' he pontificated. 'Here is a society that offers limitless opportunities to its citizens and the accused here make use of such opportunities by committing acts of hooliganism, terrorism, totally irresponsible and barbaric acts.' He paused for a second, then continued, 'They carry firearms about and threaten the lives and property of people. With such men about and free, no man who has property can ever be safe. I repeat, no man who has property ...'

'My lord, but not everybody has property and ...'

'Yes?' the Judge sat up.

'What are these limitless opportunities that your lordship so glowingly talks about?'

The Judge evaded the question. 'They are everywhere,' he said. 'A man only needs industry, not violence.'

Counsel for the Defence moved to the centre of the stage. 'As I said before,' he declared, 'I disagree very strongly with your understanding of violence. Even your cross-examination of the accused has shown and proved conclusively that it is definitely the lack of

184

opportunities that drives people to crime, madness, prostitution and adultery.'

The Judge smiled sarcastically. 'Is that then your own understanding of violence?'

Counsel for the Defence nodded his head. 'Yes,' he said. 'In my understanding acts of violence are committed when a man is denied the opportunity of being educated, of getting a job, of feeding himself and his family properly, of getting medical attention cheaply, quickly and promptly. We often do not realise that it is the society, the type of economic and hence the political system which we are operating in our country today that brutalises the individual, rapes his manhood. We often do not realise that when such men of poor and limited opportunities react, they are only in a certain measure, answering violence with violence. What I would like to see, however, is not just for a handful of men to take up arms to rob one individual. I feel and think it is necessary that all the oppressed sections of our community ought to take up arms to overthrow the present oppressive system. The system has already proved that it operates through violence ...'

The voice of the lawyer was passionate and it carried far.

The commissioner half rose from his seat. 'The play must be stopped!' he cried, but in a suppressed voice. 'Stopped! It must cease immediately! This is not a comedy! It is a tragedy, a calculated attempt to ridicule the government!'

The man who sat beside him rose with him, and whispered fiercely in his ear, 'But Your Excellency, we are guests. We shouldn't stop the play! Let us see the end of it.'

The commissioner's voice was weak and it shook with emotion, 'The bastards!' he cried. 'The bastards are using this forum to preach ...'

'Your Excellency!'

A commotion had started among the small audience on the stage. There was booing. Chairs were being lifted, ready to be thrown. But gradually, the commotion died down. The anxious voice of the Judge carried forward. During the short period of confusion, he had already gathered his papers, pretending he was going to leave the stage.

'Enough! Enough!' he cried out now, as if to everybody in the hall. 'What are you calling for? Anarchy? Is that how you defend the irresponsible acts of these men? By calling for anarchy ...?'

The voice of Counsel for the Defence went on unabated: 'When in one public hospital, in the same society, one patient can sleep in a large air-conditioned room whereas other ordinary patients – men, women and children – have to sleep in corridors, on mats, on the hard, cold and roughly cemented floors or share beds, this is violence ...'

The Judge cried out, 'I warn you ...'

But Counsel for the Defence continued: 'When in the same society, whereas one man has more than enough to feed himself, his dogs, cats, children and monkeys and many other men are weak and thin from hunger and their children are suffering from kwashiorkor, this is violence ...!'

The Judge now sat up straight on his chair, hammer in hand. 'I warn you to desist from ...!'

But Counsel for the Defence was not yet done. 'It is,' he continued in a passionate voice, 'a violence consciously maintained, whetted and intensified by those who operate the system. And to cease to recognise this or to pretend that it is not so only shows the extent to which we are ourselves part and parcel of the system that thrives and survives on violence. It is ...'

186

The combined effect of the hammering on the table and the screaming of the Judge as well as the angry voices of the court clerks managed at last to drown the voice of Counsel for the Defence.

'This is unpardonable contempt of court!' the Judge cried. 'And it is punishable ...'

'Your lordship!' Counsel for the Defence cried back. 'I agree that our present system penalises the boldness to speak the truth. It has ...'

'Orderlies!' the Judge and the Prosecuting Counsel shouted in unison. 'Make him shut up! Silence his mouth! Use force if necessary ...'

'The accused are sentenced to death!'

'No! no! no!' came from the audiences both on the stage and on the floor.

'Take them out! Take them out!' the Judge cried louder.

The orderlies hesitated.

'But your lordship! Your lordship!'

'Order!'

'Your lordship!'

'Order! Silence in court!'

The hall gradually grew silent. But the audience was standing to see what would happen next. The commissioner stood, undecided, but the anger was bright in his eyes and he felt insulted. He was sweating and openly mopped his forehead.

A man strolled on to the stage, carrying a radio. He went over directly to Counsel for the Defence and whispered quickly in his ear.

'When?' Counsel for the Defence asked aloud.

'At nine o'clock,' the other man replied in the same tone of voice.

'That means thirty minutes ago! Just before the final verdict!' Counsel for the Defence cried out.

The Judge frowned. He too was standing now.

'What is it?' he asked in a nervous voice. 'I ordered that the accused be taken out ... They are condemned to death by firing squad.'

'Your lordship!' Counsel for the Defence called in a patient voice.

'Yes?' the Judge barked.

'I wish to inform you that just before you started to give the verdict ...'

'Yes, the verdict. What then ...?'

'An announcement came over the radio.'

'What announcement? What did it say?' the Judge demanded.

'It said ...' and Counsel for the Defence deliberately stalled.

'What did it say?' asked the Judge in a harsh voice.

'It said that for not sharing your bribes with your superiors in the Department of Justice you have been dismissed from the service with immediate effect!'

A great roar went up in the hall. The audience screamed with laughter as the Judge, wig in hand, collapsed on his table.

The play was over. The curtain fell. The commissioner's face was flushed with sweat and anger on the front seat. His hand gripped the luxurious arms of the chair.

Idemudia did not wait for the vote of thanks to be moved. Very quickly, he went out of the hall through the back door. Though he was excited by the last play, he had not really enjoyed it because Adisa had been at the back of his mind all the time. Why had she not come? Or had she misunderstood him and waited for him in the ward instead? He hurried towards the ward but when he came into it, he saw no one but the student nurse sitting at the nurses' desk reading a novel.

She lifted her face to look at him, and then she shook

her head. 'No,' she said. 'Nobody came to visit you. Your wife? No. Nobody came.'

Idemudia went back to his bed and the other patient with whom he shared the bed was asleep. He sat on the bed and then after some time, he lay back. It wasn't too late. Perhaps Adisa would still come.

Chapter 16

At the Freedom Motel, Queen recounted her experiences during the day to her husband.

She held a letter in her hand. 'I came straight to the hotel to show you this,' she said, 'but you were nowhere to be found.'

Her husband made no reply.

'Your car was parked outside the reserved chalet,' she continued. 'We knocked but there was no answer.'

'How long ago was that?' Obofun asked.

Queen crossed her legs. 'About an hour ago. Where were you?'

'I was in another chalet with a friend,' Obofun said.

'Somebody saw you enter the reserved chalet with a woman,' Queen said, looking her husband directly in the eyes. Still she avoided mentioning that she had actually seen Adisa come out of the chalet.

Obofun avoided her eyes and laughed.

'So you were in there,' Queen accused him. 'You were in there with a woman!'

Obofun's face grew serious. 'Stop it,' he cried. 'I never ask you what happens to you. Do I?'

Queen stood up. 'You do not ask because you do not care.'

'And why should I care?' Obofun asked. 'Anyway, let's stop it. There's nothing we can do about it. Besides we have already agreed ...' He stopped. 'What do you want to do about that?' He pointed to the letter which Queen had placed on the table.

Queen looked at him and her face was drawn and tight.

'Don't you want to discuss the letter any more?' he asked, and his voice was cold and impersonal.

Queen's eyes were angry and bitter, and she crossed her legs and looked fixedly at the letter.

Obofun took up the letter and very quickly went through it. 'So this is it,' he said to himself. 'Another ultimatum.'

'Why don't you take on more people? You could get those men who helped you to off-load the cement,' he said to her, and placed the letter back on the table.

'You mean the husband of that woman and ...' Queen came out with it now, openly, angrily.

Obofun stopped her short. 'Whose husband?'

Queen looked at him scornfully. 'The husband of the woman who was with you. Poor people! If they knew what you are!'

Obofun was angry but he kept his voice level. 'I don't know how you still find time to sympathise with people,' he said bitterly.

'And you? Do you ever find time for anybody but for yourself? What do you do but run around with other people's wives?'

He stood up threatingly. 'Stop it!' he cried. 'There is none of my friends who hasn't ...' He checked himself. Lilian had come into the sitting room. He sat down.

'Lilian!' Queen called. 'Go to your room and stay there!'

Lilian stood up and went out of the room.

'Well, go ahead and say it,' she demanded, little flames dancing in her eyes. 'I have slept with your friends! I have enjoyed myself as much as you have. And whose fault is it? I should have sat here, shouldn't I, washing your pants after you had soiled ...'

Obofun quivered with laughter. 'I hope you know he is sick,' he said, still laughing. 'I know you will take any man. But thank God, Idemudia is sick. So you will have to wait for some time before you can have him.' His laughter was full of bitterness.

She also laughed and stood up. 'You have nobody to blame but yourself.' Her voice brimmed with hatred. 'I will take him when he comes out. I'd rather sleep with him than wash your pants which you have soiled by sleeping with other men's wives.'

She walked across the sitting room and went to the balcony.

Obofun sat where he was and watched her go, his mind full of hatred. Oh, he could murder her! 'The bitch is still beautiful!' he told himself, and knotted his hands into fists. 'And if I could tear it away from her. Tear it! But am I to blame? Ah, the bastard knows how to shift responsibility. She won't accept anything. No, not only your life. I must be blamed. Not her. The bastard of a bitch! Why did I ever marry her!'

He twisted his mouth. He had gone all over this before. They had fought like this before. What was the use? He had come to learn to put up with the situation. It had been a shock when he had first found out but then he had found out too late. Too late, because by then he had established all his businesses in her name. Divorcing her would have meant losing all his businesses. And he knew it would have been useless, just as it was useless now fighting each other. And he knew that she knew it. It was too late. Other people took his wife and he took the wives of others. It was an eye for an eye. 'The iron law of Moses,' he thought to himself.

Yes, it was wrong to be bitter at this stage of their lives. They had decided to live together irrespective of everything. They had to keep to the decision. But he couldn't understand her jealousy now. What did it matter to her what woman he slept with? He rose from his seat and went out to her on the balcony. They had to talk things over. He wasn't interfering in her life. She mustn't interfere in his. They stood silently beside each other on the balcony, and gazed out into the rapidly falling darkness, while he decided how best to tackle the problem.

But was he actually to blame? 'Am I to blame?' he asked himself. Was he wrong to have invested his money in businesses under his wife's name?

Obofun had introduced his wife into the business world several years earlier. It had been on an evening like this and they had been sitting, only not standing, on the balcony, just like this. At that time there had been nothing like the Freedom Motel. It had just been a house, a house to live in and nothing more.

He remembered now, clearly. The table stood against the railings where both of them were now standing. They had just finished supper and Queen looked at her husband over the empty plates.

'There will be many stars tonight,' she observed, pushing her chair backwards so as to give her legs more room.

'The darker the night, the more brightly the stars shine,' Obofun contributed, also pushing his chair backwards.

'Richard!' Queen called. There was no answer. 'Richard! Richard!'

Obofun looked at his wife and she said, 'He never seems to hear. I think he pretends because sometimes he is standing right behind you and when you call him, he does not answer.'

'Then why do you continue to keep him?' Obofun asked.

There was a matchbox on the table. He picked up a matchstick from it, broke off the dark end of it and began to pick his teeth. 'You should fire him,' he advised his wife.

'And how do I get another one?' she asked. 'It is not easy.'

'I will get you another one,' Obofun promised.

But Queen refused. 'No,' she replied. 'That will not do. It is better to have a bad servant who you know well than get a new one each time the one you have misbehaves. Every servant leaving a house takes something that belongs to the master along with him.'

Obofun shrugged. 'Well, if you want to keep him, you can.'

Richard appeared and so the conversation was broken off.

A woman was passing below. She called out generally, 'Milk! Milk for sale here. And eggs too!'

Obofun stood up and gazed down at the woman. She carried a kerosene lamp in the centre of her wares. Queen also got up and went to stand beside him.

'Have we got any milk left?' Queen asked, turning to Richard.

Richard straightened up and wiped his face with his hands. 'We have six tins of milk left, madam,' he replied.

'And eggs?'

Richard thought for a while. 'I think there are two or three left. For tomorrow's breakfast only.'

Obofun turned to his wife. 'Why can't we just open a supermarket here? We could use the lower part of the house. You could manage the supermarket and really have something something to do. At the same time we wouldn't have to get our provisions in small quantities. They would also become cheaper for our use.' He saw that Richard was still standing, so he said to him. 'Clean that table quickly and go after that woman for some eggs. Take two dozen eggs from her.'

Queen called out to the woman from the balcony. 'Woman! Please wait. We want some eggs!'

Two weeks later, Obofun withdrew twenty thousand pounds from his account. Most of this money had come from companies to whom he had given government contracts. However, in another month, the supermarket was opened but he had registered everything in the name of his wife.

During this time Queen had to go out to make the big purchases. She found out that getting the things she wanted was not as easy as she had thought. Commodities like milk and beer were scarce and she had to go through the back door if she was to get them at fair prices. Then the government established agencies for marketing some of the commodities. To her consternation, things were much worse at the government wholesale centres. The men there openly disregarded the notes her husband wrote to them. They wanted her and promised her many things. Did she not want contracts? Only twenty thousand naira. Easy to get, the men said, if only ... She didn't want to at first. But the men persisted and the money they offered rose higher and higher. And gradually she changed. After all, she was going to do everything in the name of her family.

She began to yield to people who helped her and she got the things she wanted. Then like an explosion, she realised that she had an important weapon in her hands. Men were so weak! She could get whatever she wanted. She only had to look and say, 'This is what I want. If you give it to me, you will ...' The men also understood and gave in to her, did the things she wanted for her.

In the beginning her conscience nagged her each time after she had gone out and had an affair with a man. But gradually, she lost her conscience in the thousands of naira that poured in to her, in the confidence that she could use what she had to get a man, any man, to do what she wanted. She didn't have any scruples any more, none whatsoever.

During the whole period, Obofun suspected nothing. He was both surprised and pleased at his wife's successes. He thought his notes were working wonders, that people respected him. And each time his wife came home and narrated how pleasant and helpful one of his friends was, he immediately picked up the phone and rang to thank the man 'for being so helpful'.

Obofun also found out that using the name of his wife in his business dealings was extremely important. He knew about the frightful problems which usually came with each change of government. So he had to be careful with the way he spent the vast sums of money he received as percentages from those contractors to whom he awarded government contracts by virtue of his position in the government. His wife had provided the invaluable safety net through which he had been able to dispose of these large sums of money. He had paid all his money into his wife's account in the bank.

Five years after opening the supermarket, they had had to move the supermarket to the city centre because it had become too noisy. But again, he had converted the lower part of his house into a motel. 'Freedom Motel' was known all over the city. Next came the Samson and Delilah Hotel. For the building of this hotel, he had to come together with two other government officials and his major claim to the hotel lay in the fact that everything about the Samson and Delilah was in his wife's name. Of course, he also had some money tied up in businesses elsewhere, but these were mostly small businesses and amounted to little when compared with the property he held in his wife's name.

He didn't really realise how cornered he was until he had consulted lawyers about what would happen if he divorced his wife. He was cornered. He knew it, and he had to live with it. There was nothing he could do.

They could never leave each other now. At least, he couldn't afford to. They were no longer husband and wife in the true sense of the word. They were strangers to each other in many respects. The sun had gone out of their relationship and there was nothing left now but the darkness and the coldness. The stars were the memories of earlier years and they crystallised now because they had been so full of promise.

Now there was nothing but the bitterness, the hatred, the anger, the frustrating knowledge that he couldn't divorce her. Even apart from his property which was held in the name of his wife, there were the children growing up. No, he told himself, there could be no question of separation. They would continue to live together as husband and wife. The business that had forged the gap between them also tied them together. There was nothing they could do about it. Business had to grow on them. And the more it grew, the colder and more impersonal they became to each other and yet the more tied together they also became.

He looked past her at the surrounding houses that were now merging with the darkness, and he sighed. She placed her hands on the railings and turning her head, looked at him.

'What is it?' she asked.

Obofun looked back at her. 'Nothing,' he answered. 'Nothing.' Suddenly he didn't want to discuss the problem any more.

Queen continued to look out at the surrounding houses and the darkness that was swallowing them up. 'The bitch is still beautiful!' he said to himself bitterly again. 'She hasn't changed, not one bit.' He wanted to reach out and push her over the railing. 'That would kill her,' he said to himself, but swiftly he turned away from her and walked into the house.

He was now thinking of Adisa. The more he thought about her the more empty and depressed he became. No woman had so thoroughly conquered him as Adisa had. In her passivity, she had made him appear a rapist, inhuman, cold and exacting, a Shylock. She hadn't done this consciously and that to him was the most defeating aspect of it. She hadn't said a word more after he had finally overpowered her. She had merely stared at him, unmoving as if saying to the vulture that was his spirit, 'You can pick my flesh. I am dead. I am not alive.'

But was it possible for a woman to be so detached at a moment when she gave away her most invaluable jewel?

Was it possible that a woman could be so devoid of feeling, physical, sensuous feeling, not exaltation or the peaked chaos that comes from real love and deep emotion, just the ordinary physical animalistic feeling of a human being that comes from well ... Oh, he didn't know. He told himself that Adisa had conquered him and that he would remain conquered and depressed and dissatisfied until he had struck with his burning match the flint that was in her, until he had exerted and extracted from her one single cry of pain or pleasure.

'I was like a vulture picking at the flesh of a dead prey,' he said to himself as he went towards the cupboard in his room.

He cursed aloud. The electricity was still cut off, as turning on the switch that stood beside the cupboard told him.

He called out to Richard to light a candle and to

bring it to his room. When the candle had been brought and set upon the table in an empty tomato tin, he opened the cupboard and drew out a bottle of whisky. He nearly filled the tall glass that stood on the table beside the burning candle. The candlelight turned the colour of the whisky to a brighter yellow. It seemed to burn, the drink as it stood in the tall glass. 'Here is to me and to Adisa!' he said and tossed half the glass of whisky down his throat. The whisky burned his tongue and he could feel it flaming down his throat. He coughed and his eyes watered. But he instantly felt better. In two straight gulps he emptied the rest of his drink and set the empty glass against the bottle and the burning candle. Then he went and sat on the bed.

He thought it was still too early to go to bed. Only half past eight, but Christ, the clock had stopped. He went over to the table again and wound the clock, then he set it and put it back gently on the table.

'I was like a vulture,' he repeated to himself and smiled. 'But is her flesh beautiful! God! Is her body beautiful! Soft and hazy like dawn. Oh yes, softer than anything I have ever touched! And I must touch her again. I must have her again!'

After some time, he shook his head slowly from side to side. 'No,' he told himself. 'I am not thinking properly. I must apologise to her. I have offended God and the earth. I was like a vulture picking at the flesh of a helpless prey. I must see her in the morning and tell her how sorry I am that I forced her against her wish. I will kneel down before her and say, "Adisa, please forgive and forget. Only God knows what entered my head. You are beautiful but helpless. I shouldn't have taken advantage of your piteous situation. Honestly I am sorry. Please forgive me." And she will look at me and smile and then it will be over. My conscience will be cleared. I will then be able to help her properly and openly. I must do that tomorrow morning. I will drive there straight on my way out.'

He lay back on the bed, his head on the second inner pillow, his legs hanging over on the floor, his eyes staring at the white ceiling. His mind was clear. He reasoned clearly and simply. He wanted the day to break quickly so that he could go to Adisa and explain to her. He was impatient with the night. He kicked off his shoes and lifted his legs to the bed.

'And I must discuss things with my wife,' he told himself. 'Tomorrow will see the beginning of a new day. I will call Queen and discuss matters with her. We will take stock of our feelings for each other. We are husband and wife still. She is still jealous. Hear her asking where I was! I am sure that something is still there. The river is dry but the banks still remain, the river bed cannot be taken away. Come another rainfall and the current will start to flow where it first left off. Yes, I will patch things up with her ...'

He drifted into sleep but a few minutes later, he was awake. The lights were on now. He remembered that he still hadn't closed the hotel for the night. 'To hell with the hotel!' he told himself. 'Queen will close it up. Oh yes, Queen. Beautiful bitch, sleeping with all my friends! How can I be sure the children are mine? Look at Lilian. Remember that scandal with the schoolboys? Three schoolboys raped her. At least, so she alleges. And so like her mother. Oh God, I am so unhappy, so unfortunate! But why couldn't I have been more fortunate? Why am I so unhappy? Oh God why ... ?' He stood up again, filled the tall glass with the whisky and emptied it.

Queen stayed on the balcony long after her husband had gone. She sat on the bamboo chair and drank in the incense of the darkness. She watched the customers come and go. She was sick of them all, their stares, their unspoken desires. She could always see it in their eyes, this desire to lay her at any price, just for the experience of it and because what she had was peculiar to her. But why was Obofun angry with her? Hadn't he known what would happen? Why had he opened the Crown Supermarket and put her in charge of it? Why had he introduced her to all his powerful friends? He was to blame, not her.

She looked at her wristwatch. 'Christ!' she hissed, 'Time to be closing up for the day.'

She was tired anyway and she didn't want to go downstairs. She would wait there until Richard came back, then she would go and sleep. The boys could lock up on their own.

Except for an occasional glimmer of light, the surrounding area was black with the darkness. She told herself that the electricity people were a problem. They took away the light any time they wanted and brought it back too any time they wanted. It was nothing but pure chaos. Chaos and confusion. They should have used a generator of their own. It wasn't too expensive. The only problem would be their neighbours' attitude. They would complain about the noise and the generators usually were very noisy.

She didn't hear Richard come in until he said, 'Madam, I have come back.'

She half turned, 'Yes, and what did she say?'

'I knocked on the door,' Richard informed her. 'Several times, but there was no answer. The woman there said she thought Adisa wasn't in. Otherwise she would have heard my loud knocking and opened the door.'

Queen thought for a while. 'Okay then,' she said. 'Go there first thing tomorrow morning and give her the message. As for now, you can go downstairs and tell the head waiter to close up in thirty minutes' time. I don't want to be disturbed. I am going to sleep.'

But she didn't stand up. She heard Richard going downstairs and she sat back in her chair. She was satisfied sitting there in the quiet of the deepening night. That was what she wanted most, quiet. This was what she treasured most, quiet, this contentment, this sitting down, this peace within herself and with the external outer world. During the day, she was another person. She had to do things, whether she liked it or not. Things happened and involved her, destroyed her peace. She had to scheme and calculate and plan to outwit other players in the field. And by scheming, she too made things happen. It was action and counter-action, the meeting point was the melting pot ...

The lights broke upon the city like an explosion. One moment there had been utter darkness, the next moment there was revealing white light. The streets were flooded with light, those that were wired. Television sets became alive. Voices that had been dormant were stirred.

The darkness was broken up into fragments; where there was light there could be no darkness.

Unconsciously, Queen smiled. Her own peace of mind was gone. The light made it impossible for her to think easily, to concentrate. In the darkness she could sit and think and concentrate because before her there was nothing but an amorphous black void, the end of which she could not see. The light made her see and reminded her of her surroundings, of herself. She stood up, dragged the chair against the wall and went into the house, to her bedroom.

She was sitting down on the bed when Lilian came in. 'There was a man here this afternoon,' Lilian told her.

Queen looked sideways at her daughter. 'What man?'

'He left a card with me,' Lilian said and handed it to her.

Queen took it and then glanced sharply at her daughter. 'Did he tell you anything else?'

Lilian tried to remember. 'Oh yes,' she said. 'He said I had become a big girl.'

'And what else? Didn't he tell you whether he would be coming back?'

Lilian thought for a while. 'Yes,' she said. 'He said he would be waiting for you tomorrow at the Samson and Delilah as you wanted. He said he came here for a drink and felt like seeing you personally.'

Queen was thoughtful. Should she go? Going would mean conceding, agreeing, giving herself to him. And when she had agreed once, she would have established a precedent. The man would want to come back. And coming back invariably meant other times.

'You can go now,' she said to her daughter.

'Won't you come and watch television, Ma?' Lilian asked.

'No thank you,' Queen said, and Lilian went out of the room.

'Should I go?' she asked herself. And if she went, could the man avert disaster? She had telephoned to him simply on an impulse. The letter the government had written to her was so threatening that she felt she had to do something about it. Perhaps the man could help. But what if he couldn't? What then? 'I must take on more people,' she said to herself. 'I must take on more people, but I must keep the wages down.'

Then she thought about her husband. Surely, they were strangers to each other now. There was nothing she could do about it. But telling her if she wanted to take Idemudia was an insult. Yes, an insult, she told herself. Then she shook her head. Perhaps it wasn't an insult after all. If her husband could sleep with the man's wife, why shouldn't she sleep with the woman's husband? 'Not that it will ever happen anyway,' she said to herself. 'But Obofun certainly knows how to throw mud at other people. Oh yes, throw mud from a safe distance. But he isn't getting away with it,' she decided. 'If he doesn't care whether or not I drown, then I will not care about him either. From now on, I am going to do whatever I like whenever I like and wherever I like.'

She went to her cupboard, drew out a bottle of whisky and a glass.

Chapter 17

Her sleep was deep and peaceful, like one who hadn't slept for a long, long time and when she woke up suddenly at about four o'clock, she couldn't remember where she was. The light in the room was pale, half darkness, half light.

Underneath her head, the pillow was wet with the sweat. Then, it must have been the sweat that had woken her up, the heat and the sweat. But the sleep had been deep, deep as a pit that has no bottom. She sat up on the bed, one hand supporting her. She tried to remember. What had happened? And gradually it seeped back, her memory. Her husband, Obofun and everything else. She felt weak, so weak that her hand gave way on the bed and she fell back on the pillow with a groan.

Somebody had tried to wake her up, she couldn't remember how long ago that was but she remembered hearing repeated knocking on her door. Her mind went again to Idemudia and to Obofun. She bit her lip and wiped the sweat off her face. If there was some place she could have hidden her face, she could have hidden it there. Nervously she glanced at the table. The big brown envelope was still there. She smiled in the half darkness. Judas had sold his master for thirty pieces of silver. She had sold herself for one hundred naira!

What if Idemudia found out! The thoughts ran through her head as water through a pipe. 'I'll find out and I'll kill you! I'll tear it out, I'll throw it to the dogs ... ! So I am no better than a harlot,' she told herself. 'A prostitute for one hundred naira anyway.'

She smiled and closed her eyes. 'I am a prostitute! A cheap woman! But I had to do it. I had to. It wasn't my fault. I didn't want to. Yes, I had no other way out. It was the only chance I had! He may kill me but I did it for him. Only for him.'

She opened her eyes, turned sideways and looked at the room, walls, windows, table, the cooking pots and the kerosene stove. The food cupboard and the water pot, the glasses broken at the edges. But they still used them. Used them even more than newer ones.

'If they hold water, they should be used,' Idemudia always said.

'And if they cut your lips?'

'You are not blind, are you?'

'You are not supposed to look when you are drinking.'

Idemudia laughed. 'How would you know whether you have worms or poison in the water? No, you have to look. Always better.'

'But can't you see? The glasses are broken all over the edges. They are no good any more. They should be thrown away.'

'Well, let's end the matter. Don't drink with them if you do not want to. I will anyway. Nice tall glasses. What if they have small cracks? Nothing, nothing at all.'

The glasses stood there now. She didn't see the broken edges but she remembered that they were there, seeing that the glasses stood there.

The glasses, the broom, too short now for comfort and getting shorter because the rough floor cut them, sliced through them. Brooms do not last on this floor. Maybe sometime I would have had to sweep with my fingers. But that won't be necessary now. We have one hundred naira. One hundred naira!

She turned again on her back. She still hadn't counted the money. Perhaps Obofun had placed nothing there. And ... Oh God! What if she had given herself for nothing? Holy mother of God, that would be terrible. A tragedy.

She jumped up from the bed and pounced on the envelope. It was heavy. She carried it back to the bed and opened it. Sure enough the money was there, in one naira notes. She sighed and fell back again on the bed. What would she tell her husband?

'I will tell him the truth. I will explain,' she promised herself. 'He will understand. He has to. And if he doesn't? If he gets angry? If he makes a scandal? If he kills me?' She shuddered. 'But then how will I explain the money if I do not mention Obofun? And the whisky? And if he finds out for himself?' She shook her head. 'I have to tell him the truth,' she concluded. 'I have to tell him what I have done. I will explain. I will tell him how it happened. And how can he be angry anyway? His illness drove me to it! God knows I didn't want to have anything to do with Obofun. In the morning I will go to the hospital. I will go there and see him. How can he kill me for it? How can he be angry with me for doing something I shall forever hate myself for only because of him? God knows how ashamed I am now. But He knows too it was a sacrifice I had to make for my husband's sake. Greater love hath no man than the man who laid down his life for the life of his friend. I have done that. Committed adultery for his sake. Surely, I shouldn't be punished for that.'

She felt the money in her hands. One hundred naira. This was money. She had never seen or had so much money before. What would she do with the balance after she had paid off Idemudia's hospital fees? She would give it to Idemudia. They would move to a better place and open up a small kiosk of a shop. There she would distribute the whisky. She had no illusions about the whisky. It was all part of her sacrifice. She would accept it. Obofun was mad anyway to think that there could be a second time. That first time, that once, was for all time.

In the morning she would go out to buy some meat and other materials for soup. She would eat well from now on, she would make sure that she never fell hungry any more. It was bad to be hungry, it was worse to know that you could do nothing about your hunger, yes, it was terrible, horrible.

She tried to take her mind of what had happened between her and Obofun. 'I mustn't think of it!' she told herself. 'I must forget about it.' Thinking about it made her scared, ashamed.

The old man who had married them had read out the commandments in a solemn voice. 'You must not poison your husband's food in order that he may not look at another woman. You must not flirt, you must not commit adultery. You must not ...'

She held her head with her hands. The punishment was too severe, too harsh. 'It's your children's health and lives that your obedience buys, your own progress. If you disobey, then the punishment will fall on you and on your children.'

Perhaps Idemudia would not find out if she chose not to tell him, but what if Ogbodu fell ill? How would she account for it? 'I must confess everything to Idemudia,' she told herself a thousand times. 'He must know that it wasn't my fault, that I was driven to it by my consideration for him, for my hunger, by our general poverty.'

She bit her lips. 'If only we had enough! If only he hadn't been ill!'

Then she quietened herself. 'It's only my conscience,' she said to herself. 'My conscience torments me. Things will never be the same again. What I have done will always stand between us. He will not trust me any more. He will always doubt me! But he ought to understand. He will understand.'

The money lay on top of her like a heavy iron. She sat up on the bed and very quickly shuffled the notes back into the envelope. Then she threw the envelope on the floor.

All the effects of her sleep were gone, her eyes were hollow and haunted and by the time she stood up in the morning to take her bath, her head ached. She was shaky on her feet, she was shaky in her body, she was shaky in her head. The room seemed to revolve around her.

When she had lain down the evening before, she had not even thought of sleep. Her mind was confused, she had been unable to think. So she had slept and sleep had seemed to heal her, to rearrange her thoughts. But not now. The strong morning light reminded her too strongly of the evening before. And as she stood on her feet, she shook, her body trembled. She stood before the door and was afraid to open it. Perhaps whoever was outside would immediately discern in her eyes that she had slept with Obofun the evening before. And that would be terrible, shameful. How could she bear it, stand the knowing condemning eyes of the world? How could she alone? She stood there, her hand on the key but powerless to open it. She knew that Mama Jimoh usually woke up early. She would be outside. What did they normally say to each other in the morning? She couldn't remember.

She leaned against the door now, sapped of all energy. The envelope was still on the floor. She went and picked it up and then tucked it under the pillow. The pillow had been patched in many places but there were fresh holes on it now and the pieces of foam came out, fell out through them. She brushed the pillow softly, softly with her hand and then sat down on the bed.

'But I have to go out,' she told herself. 'I have to go out.' And then she murmured, 'Oh yes, it is only my conscience.'

She made up her mind. The moment of her irresolution was not completely gone but she was decided she would go out. She went to the corner of the room and picked up the bucket. It made a noise which surprisingly quietened and reassured her. She picked up the grey towel and flung it across her shoulders and marched resolutely back to the door. She put her hand on the key, turned the lock. The door was open.

Mama Jimoh was outside sweeping her door, with her back to Adisa. 'Good morning, Mama Jimoh!' Adisa called.

Mama Jimoh turned round. 'Good morning, Adisa. Ah, you are awake early again today. You wake early these days.'

Adisa still held the bucket. 'Yes,' she replied. 'It's my husband.'

Mama Jimoh laid her broom against the wall. 'Oh, yes. I forgot to ask you about him. How is he?'

Adisa dropped the bucket to the floor. 'He is better.'

'And when will they discharge him?'

'Today,' Adisa said. 'Idemudia says they will discharge him today.'

'Let it be today then,' Mama Jimoh prayed.

'I hope so, too.'

She picked up the bucket and proceeded to the side of the house, on the right, where the tap and the bathroom were.

'Oh wait!' Mama Jimoh called after her.

Adisa stopped and waited.

Mama Jimoh held her chewing stick in her hand. 'There was a man here last night,' she told Adisa. 'I nearly forgot to tell you.'

'What did he want?' Adisa asked, her heart beating wildly. She hoped it wasn't Obofun. He couldn't dare to come to her house to torment her.

'He said he was sent to give you a message from Queen. You know, the same man who was here the last time.'

Adisa waited for her to continue. Perhaps Queen had come to warn her to desist from seeing her husband. But how could she have known?

'We knocked at your door,' Mama Jimoh continued, 'but there was no answer. We thought you still hadn't come back from the hospital so he said he would come back early this morning. You'd better wait for him.'

'He didn't leave any other message?'

Mama Jimoh shook her head. 'No, he didn't.'

'Well, thank you. I hope he comes in time because I am going to the hospital as soon as I finish bathing.'

The man was waiting outside when she left the bathroom. 'Good morning, madam,' he said in greeting to Adisa.

'Good morning,' Adisa returned his greeting and passed by him. She stood in front of the door. 'Yes?'

'My name is Richard and madam has sent me after you.'

Adisa frowned. 'What for?'

'I don't know,' Richard answered. 'She said she would like to see you.'

'When?'

'As soon as you can. She is waiting even now. Madam of the Freedom Motel.'

Adisa thought it over slowly. 'Okay, I will come,' she answered at last.

Richard left.

She went into her room and dressed up slowly. She heard Mama Jimoh's voice outside. She was rebuking her son Jimoh.

'Didn't I tell you to bring the water here?'

Jimoh grumbled a reply back.

'Come here!'

There was a shuffling of feet.

'All you know is how to eat! Fetch some water and you can't. Come here! Do you understand me?'

Adisa heard quick and stinging slaps. Instantly Jimoh cried out.

'Shut up!' Mama Jimoh threatened him further.

'Mama-o! Mama-o!!' rose the plaintive voice of Jimoh.

'I said shut up!' There were more mean and painful slaps. And Jimoh's shrill cry registered the painfulness of the slaps.

Adisa was already fully dressed. She came out of her room and stood in the doorway, the key in her hand. There were plates in front of Mama Jimoh and Jimoh was writhing with the pain against the wall. Mama Jimoh's hand was raised to strike again.

'Mama Jimoh!' Adisa cried out. 'Mama Jimoh, please forgive him.'

'I have never seen a more useless child in my life!' Mama Jimoh complained. 'Only to get a bucket-full of water and he can't! His mates in the village sleep in the farms.'

'Please forgive him,' Adisa pleaded.

Papa Jimoh came out then. He was angry. 'I have never been where they do not let a man sleep,' he cried. 'If you are going to the market why don't you leave the rest of us who are not going in peace?'

'And if I left you in peace, how would you eat?' Mama Jimoh replied.

'I don't want to eat,' Papa Jimoh said. 'I am going

out to a meeting very soon. I wanted to sleep.'

'And will you feed the children when I am gone to the market?'

Papa Jimoh snorted. 'Haven't I told you to stop going to the market on Sundays? Must you always go to the market every ...'

Adisa did not wait to hear more but moved away very quietly.

Obofun woke up in the morning and his head felt heavier than twenty blocks of cement put together. His mouth was bitter and sour, as if it did not belong to him. His head ached. It seemed as if hundreds of blacksmiths were hammering metal in his head. He groaned and rolled from side to side on the bed like a small boat on a violent river.

'What is it?' he thought he heard somebody ask.

His eyes were closed to minimise the effect of the pain, so unconsciously he groped with his hand in the direction of the voice.

'Oi! Ai!'

'What is it?'

He opened his eyes and attempted to focus them on the person who stood by the edge of the bed.

'Richard?'

Queen was exasperated. '*I* am here,' she said coldly, 'not Richard.'

Obofun fell silent to let the words sink in. He closed his eyes again.

'You need some hot black coffee,' Queen advised him, and Obofun groaned. 'And a cold, cold bath,' she added. 'That will clear your head. In fact I think you should have a bath first.'

Obofun did not move for a long time. He was trying to remember a lot of things. Had Queen slept in the same room and in the same bed with him? It was difficult for him to think because of the hammering, tinkering and soldering in his head.

He struggled up from the bed to a sitting position. He felt a little better. Sitting down helped. He felt that at once and struggled up farther until he had his back directly against the wall, his legs spread out across the bed.

Queen threw the Sunday papers at him. Her hands were trembling. 'Look,' she cried. 'See what they have done!'

The frantic and urgent note in her voice registered sharply on his consciousness. He took up the papers and glanced quickly at the front page.

'They've dismissed all of them!' she cried. 'All of them! What am I going to do?'

Obofun saw what she was referring to. And seeing it jarred his consciousness. 'But how could they do it? Christ!' he thought

'I am finished,' she cried.

'It is terrible,' he admitted.

All their connections in the ministries where they had easily won contracts were either dismissed or retired from the service. He had got contracts by giving out up to twenty per cent of the value of the contracts to these same people. They demanded it. When he had been in the service, he had also demanded and received the percentages. But everything had been easy because they had always had their share of the contract money afterwards. Now all that was destroyed because the men, the majority of them involved, had been dismissed from the service. That was what the Sunday papers said.

'Nearly one thousand of them!' he breathed harshly.

'Why don't you look at the back of that one?' his wife asked him.

He turned the paper over and saw it. He whispered, 'Oseka!'

'Her contract has been taken away from her,' Queen burst out in a panic-stricken voice. 'You remember that only two of us were given the contracts to build the low-cost houses. The paper say she has now lost the contract because according to the government, the houses she was building were substandard and of low quality.' She spoke rapidly. The fear was evident in her eyes and voice.

'And she is to refund nearly three hundred thousand naira to the government!' Obofun read out.

Queen stood up wearily from the side of the bed to which she had sunk. She was filled with despair.

'And how much was her contract worth?'

'Nearly six hundred thousand,' Queen said. 'Mine was for less, four hundred thousand.'

'And that letter?'

Queen couldn't bear it any more. She fled from the room.

When Queen had received the letter from the Ministry the day before, she had not taken it seriously, not really. Letters often came like that which were soon forgotten and in any case she had not only decided to employ Idemudia, but she had also phoned to the Chief Architect and asked him to meet her at the Samson and Delilah. She felt that the Chief Architect would help her. But here was his name, the third on the list on the front page of the Sunday papers. But then how could they give her to the end of the month to complete the building? The end of the month was less than twenty days away and many of the houses were still in their foundation-laying stage. She had also consumed a considerable amount of the money on her hotel at Sakponba Road, near the church. She had imagined that she could complete the buildings in her own time with the profits she would make from the hotel. Now all that was gone.

Oseka, her friend and rival, had already suffered the fate with which she was now threatened. Where would she get the money if she had to refund it?

She had to act quickly. The work on the site had to be speeded up. She would deal severely with all those men whom the site engineer had reported were making trouble, asking for more money when they ought to be working! She told herself that she had to keep the wages down. That way, she could also save money and God knew she would need every kobo now.

Obofun read the papers several times and he simply could not believe his eyes. He put the papers down and then went into the bathroom and turned on the shower and began rubbing the soap on his body slowly. He would go to Lagos on Thursday or Friday to see a friend there who would advise him on how he could fully take over the Samson and Delilah before the other men knew what was happening. 'But Christ, one thousand men!' he whispered. 'How many are left?'

He knew of course that there were still many men of doubtful and suspicious character in the various places who so far had not been detected. He had seen that after going through the list several times. Morphi was not there and Morphi he knew had attempted to steal some eighty thousand naira two years ago. Then there was Bodigie. Surely events had caught up with a few of them, but the majority of them still remained. But it hurt him most because the few that were touched had been closest to him.

He was immensely glad about one thing anyway – that he was out of the service before all these things had happened. However, it was a serious handicap, his connections or most of them were broken and Queen was in trouble. And if Queen was in trouble, then his own business empire could be in trouble.

He left the bathroom meditatively. It was when he was getting dressed that he realised that he had slept the night before in his clothes. I must have been very tired, he said to himself and he had already placed one of his legs in the trousers when he heard voices in the sitting room. Very quickly, he drew up the other trouser leg and when he was dressed, he went close to the door and listened intently. That must be Queen's voice, and the other? Adisa? He wasn't sure. And why should she be here? His wife ... ? He opened his door and stood in the doorway. Adisa stood there, directly facing him. She looked so weak and yet so enticing this morning that all his resolves of the night before about her were now swept aside by the hurricane of throbbing in his groin. Very quickly, he went back into his room, but he left the door ajar and stood away from it so that he could hear what they were discussing.

'You will tell your husband that I have a job for him,' Queen was saying, and then Adisa replied, 'Thank you very much,' and then she was out of the room, Queen crowding her back towards the door.

Richard came in and placed the tray that contained the coffee things on the table.

Obofun slowly poured himself a cup of coffee and raised it absent-mindedly to his lips. He had forgotten everything about the news in the Sunday papers. He told himself that whatever happened he would have Adisa, if only once more. Then he smiled as he compared Queen with Adisa. 'So entirely different and yet so alike!' he cried in his heart. He almost spilled the coffee on himself because it was so hot on his tongue and he hadn't noticed it.

Now it was nearly eleven o'clock and Obofun's men had brought the cartons of whisky and gone. There were five of them. Adisa didn't bother to ask the men what had happened to the other five. Hadn't Obofun promised her ten of the cartons? And then, just as the men had been about to go, their leader had called her aside and given her Obofun's message. He would be waiting for her as soon as she could come but he hoped she would come that very evening or the next day.

She had said nothing because she knew she wasn't going. Again, her mind went to her husband. How would she account for the whisky and the money? Idemudia would never believe that her aunt had given her one hundred naira. That is, she told herself, if she chose to explain the drinks and the money away another way. She must think of alternatives. She took out the brown khaki envelope which contained the money and she opened the envelope and counted out twenty-five naira slowly.

Yes, Idemundia would believe that her aunt could give her twenty-five naira. 'He also knows that my aunt distributes the whisky,' she said to herself. 'But what if he wants to go and thank her? What if he says, "I must go and thank her at once"?'

She put the other seventy-five naira back into the envelope and dropping her handbag on the table, she drew out her old box where she kept her one Christmas dress. Then she opened the box and very carefully, placed the envelope between the folds of her dress. Then she looked at the dress and she saw that it was all right. At least Idemudia had never opened her box. 'He's not likely to now,' she said to herself and shut the box and pushed it back under the table and stood up.

She picked up her handbag and looked at the cartons of whisky piled one on top of the other beside the pot from which they drew their drinking water. Suddenly, the tears welled up in her eyes but she fought the tears back. She had to take the difficulties as they came. 'But, God,' she prayed to herself, 'please do not let Obofun send anybody after me. Please make Obofun keep away from me.'

The words of her aunt came back to her again. 'Leave him. Pack your things and leave him. There are other alternatives . . .' Resolutely, she shook her head. She could never leave him to take a room in the city. 'And become like my aunt,' she said to herself. 'No never!' Very slowly, she crossed the room and closing her door, went outside.

The sky was a pale grey, the sun was bright and strong, and it stroked the faces that were out carelessly. The breeze was cool but not cold. Later, as the sun climbed higher and stood in the centre of the sky so that a man lost his shadow, it would get hot, oppressively hot.

Now, however, it was still morning and it was different. The church crowds were many on the streets. They were all brightly dressed as the sun was. There was a certain urgency in their steps, mothers dragging their children along noisily as though they were sacrificial lambs. They dragged them along and scolded them.

'Peter!' And the motherly hand descended with Godly violence on the head of the child.

They were all in a hurry, they had to get to the church, they had sins to confess. They were cold inside, not warm as this morning was with the sun. They hurried along the streets in their brightly coloured dresses, dragging their reluctant children along with them.

And some of them went to the church in their big spacious cars. They drove unhurriedly, they pressed their horns for the others who were on foot to scatter so that they could pass. And they were brightly and expensively dressed, in fine agbada made of lace or brocade or georgette material. They talked and laughed as they drove along easily, on the rough hard road.

There were many who stood at the side of the road, their hands outstretched or walked along the road, their faces dry, their clothes rough and ugly and torn. They were thin mostly, dry like their faces. Their cheekbones stood out, their eyes were set deeply in their faces, the hunger had eaten out the flesh and dried up the fat. They did not think of the church, they did not think of God. They thought only of their stomachs, of the ants in their brains, the red ants that moved about in their heads eating them up slowly and gradually.

And there were children too, two of them this time who on this Sunday, were leading their blind father along the street, the empty plates in their hands, begging. The pus came from the man's eyes, his hand held a stick. One of the children, the elder one, led his father by the hand, the younger one lingered behind and stared at the women dragging their fat and well-dressed children like fattened calves to the altar for slaughter.

And the two children did not think about God. They were children of the world, not created by God. They led their blind father on, the pus dripped from his eyes, his teeth were brown and rotten, his bare feet were torn and dry, and his children held plates open, empty plates and went before the church crowds.

The church crowds hurried to the church. They held their coins, gripped them more tightly as they passed before the blind man and his children. They did not look at the man, their eyes were far away, searching out the cross that stood high above the roof of the church. The children could not understand, they stood now bewildered around their blind father and held the empty plates open for the church crowds to see. The hunger was in their eyes, flaming as the morning was with the sun.

Then, the truck pushers came, their bodies wet with the sweat like people drenched in a heavy rain. Their trucks moved slowly, they were piled high with firewood. They stood before the main body of their trucks, their stomachs flattened against the crossbars of their trucks, their chests flung out heaving, their whole bodies trembling and almost breaking with the efforts of pushing. The sweat covered their bare backs and poured out in front of them from their heaving and breaking chest muscles, like men in a tug of war. Their breathing came out in small harsh strangulated gasps. Still they pushed and the trucks went up with them slowly like the shells of tortoises, ambling. These too did not think of the church. Their truck was their church and their labour was their God.

Adisa came behind the truck pushers. Her mind was taken up by what Queen had told her. It was surprising, she thought that Queen should think of offering a job to her husband. But perhaps there was nothing unusual about it after all. Idemudia had worked for her and she had been impressed. Her husband was lucky, that was all. And then Obofun had come in, briefly. How impassive his face had seemed! So unconcerned and yet after she had left the house, he had sent Richard after her to remind her that the cartons of whisky would be delivered at ten o'clock.

She smiled cynically to herself as she walked slowly behind the truck pushers. Yes, need could drive a human being to anything. It could drive a person insane. It could kill a person, it could make her commit adultery with a man she had scarcely ever looked at. She had decided she wasn't going to cry over it any more. She had been forced to do it. She would explain to Idemudia and he would understand.

The truck pushers that were in front of her stopped to rest their limbs. She passed by them, scarcely looking at them. The songs from the church filtered slowly to her. She saw the man holding the stick and the children standing around him holding their plates, empty. She heard a man remark something as he passed by them. She heard his friends laugh as they passed into the temple of Almighty God.

Now that the hospital wasn't far away, a nervousness gripped her. She had felt so calm but now, near panic replaced her equanimity. Her throat felt dry, her head grew hot, her hands trembled. She was like a thief who had stolen for the first time and is afraid he will be found out. It wasn't going to be as easy as she had thought. It was nice and simple thinking things out in the darkness alone. But the daylight has a queer way of shattering the resolves one makes to oneself in the darkness. A man lies on his back and thinks out the things that he will do at dawn. But dawn reveals the weaknesses of this back-to-bed and eyes-closed scheming. A man sees that things are not as easy as he thought.

Idemudia was standing outside, his hands folded across his chest when she arrived. He moved towards her at once, motioning her towards a bench that stood against a tree outside. Seeing the dark look in his eyes the resolve melted away in her.

They sat on the bench, away from the ward and from the other patients. She glanced at him and she saw that the dark look had become bright as his anger deepened and suddenly she was afraid, and very, very nervous.

'What happened?' he demanded, his voice rough and harsh, his breathing uneven. 'I waited and waited.'

She avoided looking at him in the eyes and looked down at the grass instead. Surely, she couldn't tell him

the truth now? 'Nothing happened,' she said, and her
fingers were knotted into tight hard fists as they rested
on her lap so that the veins showed, dark blue.

'Then why didn't ...?'

'Idemudia!'

Idemudia turned his head round quickly to see
who had shouted out his name and he saw Osaro and
Omoifo walking towards them, from the side. He
waved his hands and half stood up, turning back to
Adisa at the same time.

'So what happened?' he demanded again, and this
time his voice was low but cold.

'You said ...'

'Adisa!'

'Good morning,' Adisa said to Osaro and to Omoifo
and she stood up to make place for them on the bench,
but they wouldn't sit down. They remained standing.

'So they will not release you unless you pay them
their money?' Osaro said and patted Idemudia on
his shoulder lightly.

'They will not,' Idemudia said.

'That's very bad,' Omoifo said. 'Very, very bad. Not
every man can be rich in this country.'

'But what do they care?' Osaro asked. 'And to think
that this is a government hospital!'

'They only care for their stomachs,' Omoifo said.
'Their stomachs and the stomachs of their dogs. See
how rich the ministers are!' And he spat on the grass,
away from them.

'Well, we have managed to put something together
now,' Osaro said.

'You have?' Idemudia asked and stood up.

'Yes. Nothing much but at least something. When
Adisa came round to see us last night, we honestly
had nothing on us but this morning we went to see
Osayi.'

'And he lent us fifteen naira!' Omoifo said.

'Fifteen naira!' Idemudia exclaimed, scarcely able to believe his ears.

'Yes, fifteen naira,' Osaro said. 'It has to be paid back in two weeks' time. So we promised.'

'Oh, how can I thank you!' Idemudia said, and the gratitude showed through his voice. 'I can never really thank you enough. You don't know what you have done for me. You have saved my life.'

'Oh nonsense!' Omoifo said. 'Nonsense. You would have done even more for us.'

'Then we can go and pay up their charges then?' Idemudia said and looked at Adisa.

'Yes, we can,' Osaro said. 'Here, take the money.' He brought out the money in carefully folded notes and gave them to Idemudia. 'They had no right to keep you here because you couldn't pay their bill.'

Adisa walked slowly behind them and her feet felt dead beneath her. The thoughts raced through her mind, each chain of thought chasing the other, swiftly, like the dance of shadows. How could she have given herself to Obofun only to hear this morning that she needn't have done it, that it had all been useless, that she had been a fool? She felt near to tears.

Now, they were standing by the gates of the hospital and Adisa held the small bundle of Idemudia's belongings in her hands.

'Must they keep patients on the floor?' Osaro asked and looked at Idemudia.

Idemudia shrugged his shoulders. 'It is terrible,' he said. 'The ward is divided into two parts and between two doctors. On one side of it, my side, the patients share the beds or sleep on the floor. On the other side, things are different.'

'But why? Isn't it ...?'

'Ah yes, it is the same ward, but you know these doctors. The one who runs my part of it demands that patients must come and see him at home before they can have a bed to themselves.'

'See him at home?'

'Yes, pay him some money. He takes money privately from the patients he treats in the hospital and if yours is a bad disease and you must have an operation, then you must pay him the money before he will perform an operation.'

'And if you cannot pay?'

'You die there on your bed or on the floor. Wasn't I kept there because I couldn't pay the bill?'

'It is a tragedy,' Osaro said. 'A real tragedy. You have to bribe first to be treated.' He shook his head vigorously. 'And that patient on the floor?'

'Which one?' Idemudia asked.

'The one who has his head severely bandaged. By the door, as you enter the ward. What happened to him? He was moaning when we went into the ward.'

'You mean the one who has his head cut into two?'

'Yes.'

'He was brought into the ward late last night. We had returned from the play and were just about to sleep when they brought him. You should have seen the blood.' He shook his head from side to side, slowly. 'I never thought a single man could have so much blood in him.'

'What happened?' Osaro asked. 'Was there a fight?'

Idemudia was silent for a while, then he looked directly at Adisa and in a very quiet voice said, 'No, it wasn't a fight. He was found in bed with the wife of another man.'

'My God!' Osaro cried. 'Holy mother of God!'

'The husband of the woman is a farmer. He had gone to the farm but yesterday he returned very early. And he found his wife in bed with this man ...'

'So, he drew out ...'

'Yes,' Idemudia said. 'He drew out his matchet.'

'It is horrible,' Osaro exclaimed. 'Horrible and ugly.'

'And the woman?' Omoifo asked. 'What happened to her? Did she raise the alarm?'

Idemudia shook his head sadly. 'She raised no alarm ...'

'You mean she let him ...'

'No, no, no,' Idemudia said, and his voice trembled. 'I understand her body is in the mortuary at Ubese. That is where it happened. Ubese, near Ughelli. He killed her before he set on the man.'

They were all silent for a while, then Osaro said, 'It is terrible. The man is a butcher.'

'You mean you wouldn't have done the same?' Omoifo asked.

'How could I?' Osaro said. 'There must be other ways to punish a woman for such things besides killing her,' he said.

'I think they got what they deserved,' Omoifo said. 'The cheats.'

'And the man? The farmer?' Osaro asked.

'Ah. He ran off into the bush. You know how the police treat cases of this kind. When they catch up with him, they will tell him he has nothing to fear. Then, they will take all his money and promise to help him but in the end they will hang him.'

'I am sorry for him,' Omoifo said.

'Oh, come on,' Osaro said angrily. 'How can you be sorry for such a man?'

'You mean you have no sympathy for him? You imagine it. A man goes to the farm and while he is cutting the trees and planting the yams, his wife cheats. This other man comes and takes his wife ...'

'Perhaps the farmer is ...'

'Oh, don't say that,' Omoifo said angrily. 'Please don't say that.'

226

'Or perhaps this other man tempted his wife with money.'

'And she should accept?'

'Well, Idemudia, what do you think?' Osaro asked. 'Should a man murder his wife for . . . ?'

'Committing adultery, cheating?' Omoifo cut in.

'I don't know,' Idemudia said. 'I agree that the way it is done matters. But I don't suppose my wife will ever commit adultery,' and he glanced at Adisa. 'So the question would never arise.'

'And if she did?'

'What?'

'Why, that's a very foolish question,' Osaro said. 'How can you say that in the presence of Adisa?'

Idemudia smiled and his breathing became a shade faster. 'Well, I will answer it,' he said. 'I know she would never do it but if she did and I found out, I would kill her. Just as the farmer has done.'

Chapter 18

Now they were back home and Adisa opened the door and stepped out of the way so that Idemudia could go in first. Then she went in after him and placed the little bundle she had been carrying on the table. Idemudia inhaled the air in the room deeply and then, seating himself on the bed, he raised one of his legs and was about to remove his sandals when he saw the cartons piled up against the wall and frowned.

During the walk from the hospital to the house, he had kept ahead of his wife, silent, his mind busy as he thought about what he would do to her as soon as they got home. And Adisa had walked behind him, also silent, her face set, her heart beating unevenly and much more rapidly as they got nearer their home.

Idemudia dropped his foot back to the floor and pointing, asked, 'What are those?'

Adisa drew out the chair away from the table and sat on it so that she directly faced the door and he could not see her face except in profile.

'They are cartons of whisky,' she said, without looking at him.

'Cartons of whisky?' Idemudia's frown deepened.

Adisa did not answer him.

Idemudia raised his foot and bending forward at the same time to remove the sandal asked, 'Where did they come from?'

'From my aunt,' Adisa said, and she shut her eyes.

'From Aunt Salome?'

'Yes.'

'Why the whisky and why didn't you tell me?' He dropped the sandal on the floor.

'You didn't ask me,' Adisa said.

Idemudia was silent for a while. Then he lay back on the bed and staring at the ceiling asked, 'Why didn't you come yesterday?'

'I went to look for some money.'

'And you found some?'

'Yes.'

Idemudia sat up now, surprised, the frown still on his face. 'And how much did you find?' he asked.

'Twenty-five naira,' Adisa said, and suddenly she didn't care any more but was relaxed and the pounding of her heart in her chest was gone.

'Twenty-five naira!' Idemudia exclaimed. 'You mean your aunt lent you twenty-five for my sake?'

Adisa did not answer him.

'And why didn't you tell me?'

Adisa shrugged her shoulders. 'How could I tell you?' she asked. 'You paid no more attention to me than you would pay to a fly that you have crushed. What did you expect me to do?'

Again, Idemudia was silent. Then he asked, 'And where is the money?'

Adisa looked at him now directly in the eye. 'You do not need it any more,' she said. 'I am going to return it.'

Idemudia sprang up from the bed and grabbed her handbag from where it lay on the table. 'You will do nothing of the kind,' he cried, searching the inside of the handbag. 'Are you crazy? Don't you know we have to eat?'

He drew out the money and throwing the handbag back on the table, he began to count the money. Then he went back and sat on the bed, holding the money in his hand. Holding the money and looking at her,

Idemudia realised how much Adisa had suffered on his account during the days of his illness. She had grown considerably thinner and her eyes were still bloodshot from the sleepless nights he had caused her. Knowing Aunt Salome, he knew how much canvassing it must have taken Adisa to have got twenty-five naira out of her. Then there was the whisky.

'Well, why are you sitting on the chair there?' he asked her now. 'Why don't you come here? Come and sit near me here, on the bed.'

'I am all right here,' Adisa said, and the wild pounding in her chest was back but very briefly.

'Well, I am back at home,' Idemudia said, and stood up. 'Are you not happy that I should be back at home after all these days?'

She did not answer him, because the tears welled up in her eyes and she began to cry.

Idemudia began to pace about the room in front of her, surprised. 'Why are you crying?' he asked. 'All right, I made mistakes. I did not treat you properly and I know you have suffered much, but you must understand that I too have many reasons to be bitter and angry ...'

He stopped in front of her now and looked down at her. Then he went back to the bed and again sat on it. Adisa wiped her face with the back of her hand and said to him, 'The woman of the hotel wants to see you.'

Idemudia looked at her quickly. 'You mean Queen, Obofun's wife?'

Adisa nodded.

'What does she want me for?'

'It appears she has a job for you.'

'A job?' Idemudia laughed. 'To offload cement in the rain perhaps.' Then his voice became serious. 'Did she not tell you what type of job it was?'

Adisa shook her head.

'When did she send the message?'

'This morning,' Adisa said. 'She sent for me. She wants you to bring Osaro and Omoifo and Patrick.'

'Did she tell you when we could call on her?'

'Any time.'

'Then I'd better go straightaway,' Idemudia said and stood up. 'And you mustn't think I am ungrateful. I am going to see your aunt to thank her for the money and the whisky.'

Again, that violent pounding in her chest was back. 'I have already thanked her enough,' she said quickly. 'The proper time to thank her will be when we return the money.'

'Well, I've got to see her anyway,' Idemudia insisted. 'She must not think we do not appreciate what she has done for us.'

'She is leaving for Badagry anyway,' Adisa said, and this time it was as if her heart was going to burst with the pounding.

'When?'

'With the newspaper van this evening. That is where she buys the whisky. You know that.' She stood up and tried to open the window so that she stood with her back to him.

Idemudia stood and thought for some time. 'Then you must let me know when she comes back,' he said. 'We must show our gratitude in the most proper way.' And he left the room.

It was not until the evening that Idemudia returned. For the first time ever, he was slightly drunk, and he smelt slightly of palm wine.

'Everything is all right,' he said in answer to the enquiring look in Adisa's eyes. 'Osaro and the others have gone home but tomorrow morning we start at the woman's building site at Ugbowo. This is the job she has for us.'

He washed his hands and quickly ate the food that she placed before him on the table.

'Queen was drinking when we got there,' he told Adisa. 'She was still drinking when we left her.'

Adisa sat on the bed. She did not speak.

'I wonder why a woman like her has to drink so much. She was sitting down and drinking. The whisky was in front of her, the tall glass beside it. She swallowed her drink after each pause.'

Adisa still did not utter a word.

'What are you thinking about?' he asked her.

'Nothing,' she answered slowly, standing up at the same time to switch on the light. She came back and sat on the chair which he had vacated because now he was sitting on the bed.

'Why are you sitting so far away?' he asked her. 'Come, sit nearer. On the bed.' He tapped the bed.

She stood up slowly and went and sat beside him on the bed. How would she react to his advances now after so much water had passed under the bridge? He put his arm round her and drew her closer to him. He did not understand. She seemed to freeze up, to resist him. 'What is happening?' he asked himself. 'Why is she so cold?'

He left her for a moment while he stood up and and went to turn off the light. Then he came back and in the yellow light of the night that wasn't yet completely dark, he wanted to undress her, but again, she resisted him.

He ceased his efforts and lay beside her.

'Why are you so nervous?' he asked her.

'How am I nervous?' she asked.

'It is there,' he said. 'The way you are behaving. It has never been like this.'

'And that is being nervous?'

'Well, what should I call it? You struggle and your hands tremble.'

'I do not want anything,' she said.

He laughed and his teeth flashed in the yellowish darkness. 'Why not?'

'I am not well,' she said.

He tried to caress her on the flat side of her stomach, but she moved away from him.

He was silent. He was angry and sullen, and he could not understand.

Inside her, Adisa was frightened. How could she sleep with her husband without giving herself away? Yes. She didn't want to sleep with him, at least not this night. She was too conscious of herself. The memory of Obofun hung about her like a shroud.

They didn't say anything to each other until the following morning when Idemudia got up and began to dress up. His eyes were lowered and angry like those of a wounded hound.

'I don't think I will need that money you borrowed from your aunt,' he said to her slowly.

She hadn't expected that. She was warming up the soup on the stove and her back was towards him.

'I have already used part of it in buying some food. I thought I told you about that yesterday evening. As a matter of fact,' she added, 'our supper yesterday was from there.'

He would have said more but Osaro, Patrick and Omoifo were already waiting.

'We will settle that when I come back,' he hissed, and left.

It was an open truck that took them to the building site. The four of them sat at the back of the truck, on the floor. The truck rode on the rough road noisily, as if its joints of metals and rubber were all loosely bound together.

There were many unfinished houses at the site

where the truck stopped. Queen, who had driven in her car behind them, got out of her car as Idemudia and his friends were climbing down from the back of the truck. The other workers were already there and they gathered as soon as they saw Queen.

Queen faced them. 'I understand that some of you want more money,' she said quietly.

Idemudia was surprised at the hardness in her voice.

'You there,' and Queen pointed to a tall, shirtless man. 'You have always made trouble, ever since you came here.' She drew an envelope. 'Here is your money,' she spat at him. 'You will find twenty-three naira, seventy-seven kobo inside the envelope. Not one kobo more, not one kobo less.'

She threw the envelope at the man but it was another man who caught it.

'And you,' she pointed again at a small man, thin and ragged like the edges of a precipice. 'You came here to sit down and complain, not to work. Yet you want more money.' She threw another envelope at him. 'There are eighteen naira and forty kobo inside that envelope. You too can go.'

The man silently took the envelope. In another three minutes, Queen had dispensed with two more men. The men she had asked to go stood together, their faces black with their anger and frustration.

'You just can't treat us like this,' one of them threatened, but Queen ignored him.

'Come,' she said to Idemudia and his friends. They fell in behind her.

The site engineer was a thin Greek. He had a pencil moustache on which each hair stood out like the quill of a porcupine. He was standing outside the wooden shed where he had his office and smoking a cigarette.

'I have told those four you spoke about to go,' Queen said to the Greek, putting her handbag back under her arm. 'And I have brought you these four to replace them.'

The Greek spoke bad English. His fingers, the sides of them, were brown from smoking cigarettes, his teeth also.

'Good,' he replied. 'Very good. And the others, they have gone away?'

'They will go,' Queen assured him.

'And these ones? What rate?'

It's one naira fifty kobo a day.'

'You have told them?'

'Well, they are hearing it now.' She looked at them. She seemed to be making up her mind about something.

'Wait,' she said to the Greek who had already taken out a pencil and a pocket notbook. The pencil was thin and slim as if it had been plucked from his moustache.

'This one,' she pointed at Idemudia. 'He will be paid one naira eighty kobo a day. But make him work for it.'

The Greek laughed. The wrinkles on his face relaxed. 'Sure, Madam Queen. They will all work for it.' Then he turned to Idemudia. 'Go to that machine there and wait.' He pointed to a concrete mixer. 'I will come now, just now. I give you work to do.'

Queen followed the Greek into the wooden ramshackle hut that was the office.

'You heard what she said?' Idemudia asked as they walked up to the concrete mixer.

'What?' Omoifo asked.

'We have come to replace the four she has just sacked. I don't like it.'

They stood by the mixer. The cement and the sand

235

were there by the heaps of stones all ready to be fed in. The crushing machine stood by the mixer. They were all old.

'I guess she does that all the time. Tomorrow it might be our turn. I don't like it either,' Osaro said.

'If you don't like it you can go away.' Patrick was sarcastic.

There were planks and logs lying about, and many broken blocks of cement. The earth was rough like a battlefield where the buildings struggled to rise above it.

Idemudia looked round. He saw that one of the deckings had caved in. It had broken into two in the middle.

He pointed. 'That is dangerous.'

'We won't work there.'

'We will in time. Just you watch.'

'For one naira and fifty kobo it's not worth it.'

They were silent for a while.

They saw Queen re-emerge and go down towards her car. Soon afterward the thin Greek came towards them.

'You heard what madam said,' he explained to them. 'No laziness and no agitation. If you work hard, you stay. If not, you go.'

He paused, then said to Idemudia and Osaro. 'You will both feed the materials into the machine here. One will feed them in, the other will use the shovel to fill the basins and containers as the other labourers come. You other two, follow me.'

On his way back, the thin Greek came to them. 'You will wait until a man comes,' he instructed Idemudia and Osaro. 'He will show you how to do it.'

Idemudia and Osaro had worked on building sites before and they knew exactly what to do. But they had taken an instant dislike for the Greek so they kept quiet until the man he spoke of came.

'How long have you been here?' Idemudia asked the man. He was wearing a footballer's cap. His face was thin, his eyes were deep in his face and closely set together like the headlamps of a Land Rover.

The man was slow to reply. 'One month,' he grumbled.

'One month? Then you are new here.'

That seemed to have unlocked the man. He laughed and the wrinkles and lines on his face were deeper than eroded hillsides.

'I am one of the oldest here,' he boasted.

'How come?'

The man dropped the small shovel on the gravel. 'How come? New ones come and the old ones go.'

Idemudia pretended not to know. 'Why?'

The man laughed again and his ribs jumped out vividly on his body from the effort of laughing. He was so lean. 'You have just come,' the man reminded him, 'and because of you another four were told to go. That's what the woman does all the time. You can't ask for higher wages. Go to the site nearby. It is also bad there but at least the labourers there get better paid and better treated. And they still complain, but not us.'

'So if we complain we get kicked out?' Osaro asked.

The man picked up the shovel again, 'The best thing to do is to keep your mouths shut. Personally I have children to feed and jobs don't come easy.' He brushed the sweat off his face and smiled bitterly. 'The day she came for us at Iyaro I remember that two people fell off the truck. I nearly broke my arm. Such was the rush!'

Idemudia nodded. He understood. 'We are from there,' he said, 'but she lives on our street. That's how she picked us up.'

The man began explaining to them. 'You must feed in the cement, gravel and sand simultaneously. One load of gravel, one load of sand, half a load of cement. After some time you add water. Some other men will come here with wheelbarrows and buckets. Sometimes we use headpans.' He paused, then said in a low voice. 'Everything here is borrowed, mixer, wheelbarrows and buckets. Only the headpans are ours.'

'Who is the foreman or headman?' Osaro asked.

'Headman? The engineer has not named him this morning.'

Idemudia whistled. 'You mean they are changed every day?'

The man dropped the shovel on the rough coarse soil. 'I was foreman yesterday. That's why he called me to show you this. Today, why, one of you could be foreman!' And he walked away, leaving them with their mouths wide open.

Idemudia bent down and took up the shovel. He couldn't speak.

'You pour in the cement and the water,' Osaro said. 'I'll feed in the gravel and the sand.'

'This is certainly a place!' Idemudia exclaimed. 'You may be foreman today!' He flung his shovel on the ground and both men laughed uneasily.

The cold weather began to change slowly. The sun long hidden behind the mists came out of the shrouds gradually. The sky changed from grey to an orange red.

'Open the mouth of the machine,' Idemudia said to Osaro.

'What do you want to do?'

'Feed in the gravel.'

'We need more men.'

'They will come when they see us feeding in the

gravel. You can put the bags of cement on your right. Let me shovel the sand nearer.'

'What about the water?'

Idemudia looked round. 'There ought to be a hose around, straight from the tap.'

He took in the place slowly. There was no hose.

'This isn't good,' he continued. 'Looks as if I am going to have to walk backwards and forwards to get the water.'

Osaro grunted a reply back and began shifting the bags of cement. He straightened up and wiped his forehead with the back of his hand.

'It is going to be hot,' he observed. 'I am already sweating. Idemudia, look.'

Idemudia turned and looked. Understanding came into his eyes.

'The bags we unloaded,' he nodded.

'The very same bags,' Osaro said.

More men came in with wheelbarrows, buckets and headpans. Not far away a welder was welding rods together. The bright halo of flames and sparks were blinding to the eyes.

Three days later the Greek came out of the shed, holding a paper in his hands. When he got to the group on the concrete mixer, he stopped and put one hand in the pocket of his shorts. 'We have to work quickly today,' he urged the group. 'Very important.'

The group ignored him, but they listened.

'These houses must go up faster. No standing about. Break reduced by thirty minutes. If you are not satisfied, you go, and we hire somebody else.'

His eyes were hard, his face impassive, but the sweat was breaking out across the carefully oiled wrinkles. 'There will be Sunday work too,' he continued. 'Sunday is overtime but everyone must come.'

He watched them to catch any effect that his speech might have produced. He couldn't discern any. The men stood massed together, their hands folded across their chests. Idemudia put one foot down on the spade and the shovel bit deeper into the earth.

'How much is overtime pay?' he asked, just as the Greek was about to go.

The Greek's hard face went harder. He looked at the men and tried to see who had spoken.

'What did you ask?' he asked, just so as to place the speaker more properly.

Idemudia removed his foot from the shovel but continued to lean on it. 'I wanted to know how much the overtime pay is,' he repeated.

The Greek thought for a while. 'We will decide that when we know how many of you are coming to work,' he answered, a thin smile on his lips.

'We have to know before we can come,' Osaro insisted.

The thin smile disappeared from the Greek's face. His face became mean and beastly. 'You will know well in advance,' he promised. 'That is, those of you who are lucky enough to be here by Saturday morning. Now you must work. No more talk.'

The Greek left them, his hand still in his pocket.

Idemudia turned to the man who stood next to him, 'What kind of place is this?' he frowned.

The man avoided Idemudia's eyes. 'We want to work,' he said. 'I was out of a steady paying job for a whole year.'

'And so what?'

'If you want to work, you must keep your lips sealed.'

'Even if you are being fried alive? Even if you are being worked like slaves?'

'I mind my own business,' the man advised Idemudia, and as he walked away the conversation broke up.

It was the lunch break now, and it was only fifteen minutes because the Greek had reduced it by thirty minutes.

Idemudia and his friends came together, the sweat on their foreheads, the cement dust on their hair and face and eyebrows.

'It's a rotten place,' Idemudia said, wiping the sweat off his face.

The others were silent.

'Something ought to be done,' he said again.

'Like we did at Uke Construction? No, no, no,' and Osaro shook his head in disagreement.

'What do you want us to do then?'

'When a hen gets to a new place, it rests on one leg first,' Patrick advised.

'Exactly, exactly,' Omoifo agreed.

Not far away, the labourers crowded around the woman who sold them rice and *dodo* on the site. After buying the food, the men carried their plates to the wooden benches that stood against the wooden shed. Some of them sat on the moulded blocks while two others went out to the buildings that were still struggling to get up.

'You will come to work on Sunday?' one of these asked of the other.

'If I am lucky to be here by then, by Saturday.'

'You will be here if you keep quiet.'

'And what have I got to say anyway?'

The men fell silent as they spooned up the rice into their mouths, throwing the rice far inside their mouths, into the deep of their gullets just as they threw the gravel into the concrete mixer. Then they chewed silently for some time before one of them said, 'The rice is becoming smaller and smaller.'

'Oh yes,' the other agreed. 'Last week it was more.'

'They say the woman who sells rice on that other site is not as mean.'

'Ah, Bernard! So you've been to all the sites!' There was laughter, then quiet.

'We are underpaid. We ought to do something about it.'

The other man laughed. 'The only thing we can do about it is to leave.'

'And what is wrong with that?'

'A lot. I have kids to feed. Six of them and a wife. Then there are my mother, my brothers and my sisters. I couldn't give up this job. You are lucky. You are not yet married.'

'Who says I am not married?' was the proud reply. 'A wife and three children!'

The other man laughed instantly, 'Ah you see, still much less than I have to cater for.'

'We could go on strike!' Bernard said stubbornly.

The other man dropped his spoon into the plate and it rattled against its emptiness. He looked sharply at Bernard. 'Don't say that a second time!' he warned him, glancing suspiciously from side to side. 'If somebody else hears you, you won't be here by Saturday.'

He stood up and took his plate while the man Bernard sat, his chin on his hands, his plate on the rough ground, his eyes bitter and helpless and frustrated.

'Something ought to be done,' Idemudia said again, and he spat into the dust. 'We should stand together here.'

He received no encouragement, so he went back, a little way away from his friends and sat on the pile of gravel.

'You have only just got this job,' one mind told him. 'Do not risk it.' He shrugged and hunched his shoulders more. The sun came down fiercely. It burned and scathed, any movement produced heat and sweat. The air was hot and dry as if a lighted match could ignite the whole air.

He hunched his shoulders and stared at the loose gravel at his feet. 'What kind of life is this?' he asked himself a hundred times. A man gets a job and he cannot protest. He cannot ask for higher wages, the period of his leisure is cut down arbitrarily and he must come out to work when he is told. This was slavery, this was … yes, he remembered, it came to him slowly, this was violence. And now that his mind had established an essential link, found an apt description of the conditions of his life, he began to fill in the actual content of that violence, what it consisted of.

He picked up a stick that was lying beside the gravel and began to prod among the gravel at his feet. His unfinished education, his joblessness, his hunger, his poverty, all these he found out were different forms of violence. It consisted not of physical, brutal assault but of a slow and gradual debasement of himself, his pride as a man.

With his stick he drew figures on the ground and as he sketched with his stick, his mind went on endlessly reviewing the circumstances of his life. It had all been so unfair. So unfair. And now?

A gong sounded and startled him out of his thoughts. He did not stand up immediately but looked around at the other workers. He saw them all, one after the other, dusting the seat of their shorts or trousers. He saw them standing up. The break was over. He stood up from the heap of gravel and went towards the mixer. Patrick and Omoifo were already gone.

Osaro confronted him at once. 'What are you thinking about?' he demanded.

'It is bad,' he answered. 'The pay, the work, the site, everything.'

'You are not forced to stay on,' Osaro chided him.

'How can you say that?' Idemudia asked. 'Why do you say I am not forced to stay on? If I went away, how would I eat? How would I pay my rent? How would I survive? I stay because I have nowhere better to go.'

Osaro dropped the stone he was holding in his hands. 'I was only joking,' he admitted. 'I have never been in a place like this before. The labourers do not talk, they whisper. They are afraid. Remember that other place where we had that strike? It wasn't half as bad as here.'

They fell silent as they fed the concrete mixer. The men came again and again and each time they brought the wheelbarrows, and headpans and the buckets. Their chests glistened with sweat, their faces glistened with sweat, their backs were bathed in sweat. They worked in subdued silence like prisoners, coming and going in the intense light of the sun.

It was another two days later, during the afternoon, that the first signs of a crack came. The men were restless. Even the appearance of the site engineer did not spur them to more work. They stood about talking in small groups.

Idemudia was back at his favourite place, the pile of gravel. His body was bathed in sweat. He was tired, completely worn out. Luckily the other men had stopped coming for the mixed concrete and it was no use feeding the mixer with fresh sand and gravel. So both he and Osaro scrambled to the pile of gravel and sat on it, their backs to the rest of the workers.

'Something is coming,' Osaro observed.

'What?'

'You can see it. You can smell it.'

'You don't think the men will go on strike?'

'Sure, they will. They are not working now. They are just standing about. And Idemudia, what is wrong with Patrick?'

Idemudia picked up a round stone and nursed it in his hands. 'Patrick? Patrick doesn't want a strike, he is afraid of it,' Idemudia said.

'But why should he be?'

'He thinks that the woman will take the jobs away. His wife is pregnant. Can you blame him?'

'Perhaps you can't, but we ought to speak to him. Call him and talk to him.'

'I tried it yesterday. After work. He only laughed it off. Said a strike was unnecessary. I could even feel he had something against me. I don't know why. Let us leave him.'

'And Omoifo?'

'They always go together.'

Idemudia could hear some of the men coming towards the mixer with their wheelbarrows. If they had decided to come to pick up the mixed solution, he would again stand up to feed the mixer. He looked behind him. There was a line of men coming.

'Let's get going.'

'What do you think the site engineer will do?' Osaro asked, as they stood by the mixer and waited for the first man to come up.

Idemudia shrugged his shoulders. 'I don't know. He could inform the woman that there is trouble on the way.'

'And Queen?'

Idemudia laughed. 'There will be more sackings. More people will go.'

The first group of men were already standing around the mixer.

Osaro picked up the shovel. 'We ought to do something,' he said generally. 'It is time something was done.'

Idemudia wiped the sweat off his face with the back of his hand that was covered with cement and sand and gravel. 'I think we ought to organise a strike,' he said recklessly.

The assembled men looked quickly at each other. One of them let go the handle of the wheelbarrow and rubbed his hands together. 'Isn't that what we have been saying?' he asked, and his face was serious, earnest. 'Isn't that what we have discussed these past three weeks? And here is a man who has just come saying exactly the same thing!'

He came and stood beside Idemudia. 'You are new here,' he repeated, 'but one could have said you have been here for months. I have tried to make them understand. We need to work together. This woman, if she sacks one man wrongly, then we all say no. And we show we mean it by putting down the head-pans, shovels and buckets, not individually but together.'

'Things are so bad!' another man spat out, in utter disgust.

'We earn so little and yet we are worked harder than slaves.'

'When you point it out, she dismisses you.'

'How then do we stop it?' the first man asked. 'By standing together. By showing her that we can stand together,' he pointed out. 'Those four men she dismissed this week should be brought back.'

'And how do you tell her that?'

Idemudia dropped the bag of cement he had dragged up. He wiped the sweat off his face. 'I know where she lives,' he offered. 'We can meet today after the work is done and decide on what to do. I don't

246

even think we have to go to her. We can talk to the site engineer.'

'That man is poison,' one of the men warned.

'Well, we can still talk to him. Let him inform the woman about our decisions.'

'Can I pass the word then?' Bernard asked, looking from one man to the other.

The others nodded their heads silently and he left. He was seen going from one group of workers to another, explaining.

The sun continued to bear down mercilessly. And one after another, the men removed their shirts until their backs glistened with the sweat from labouring. The mixer turned round slowly, insatiable as the men fed the gravel, the cement and the other materials. The wheelbarrow drivers came and went, then came back for more and not far off, the vibrator worked noisily as the men tried to keep the cement from sinking to the bottom in the several pits.

Where the houses were struggling up was like a scene of battle. The land was upturned, hoisted and flung in several directions. The bush was held back by the piles of gravel and sand but here and there some green grasses had taken root and now boasted flowers with yellow petals, small tongues of yellow fever which dangled, danced, shivered and sliced through the wind.

Not far off were the houses which sweat and labour had already erected. The property-owners lived in them already. Life there was ablaze where labour had left its positive mark, the labour of hundreds of thousands of workers, working either in the intense sunlight or in the biting cold or in the blinding rain, piling the blocks higher and higher and wiping the salt and the sweat from their eyes and their foreheads with the backs of their hands, and all underpaid, underfed and treated no better than slaves – the highest form of violence maintained and jealousy guarded by a greedy, unfeeling class of exploiters, greedy moneymakers, conservative and reactionary public officials who in the end took all the credit for the achievements of labour, just as the slave drivers took all the credit for the achievements of the slaves.

Chapter 19

The Greek, Papiros Clerides, was normally a cold and hard man but as he rushed his big powerful car along the dirty, dusty streets, excitement surged through him. When he finally arrived at the Freedom Motel, he rushed up the stairs, two steps at a time, and having arrived at the top, pressed the bell button nervously. Now he was as nervous as he was excited.

Richard opened the door for him.

'Where is madam?' he asked excitedly. 'Call madam quickly. This is important. Quick!' he commanded Richard, forcing himself to hold the story back from Richard.

He was sitting down when Queen came out of her room but the news he had blew him from the seat and he burst out in his unusually thin and harsh voice, 'They are going on strike!'

Queen stood dazed for a time, then she quickly recovered herself and laughed, 'Mr Clerides, Mr Clerides! Sit down please and tell me the story.'

Papiros Clerides sat down but on the edge of the chair. He waved his hand wildly in the air like a drowning man and Queen had to turn on the ceiling fan before she took her seat opposite him.

'I come back this afternoon,' Mr Clerides began, 'and there are three men waiting for me.'

Queen smiled, 'Only three men?'

The dark excitement in the man Clerides slowly ebbed out. It was replaced by anger against Queen for smiling too light-heartedly at the very important things he had to tell her.

'Oh yes, three men,' he repeated now, without heat.

'Three men sent by the others. And among them two of those from the last four you brought.' He was happy to see the rapid change of countenance in the woman.

'Two of them now? What did they want?'

Papiros Clerides delayed his story. He fished for a cigarette in one of his pockets, doing it so slowly that he had Queen leaning forward.

'What did they want?' Queen demanded impatiently.

Papiros Clerides smoothed out the cigarette, took out the matchbox, extracted one matchstick and scratched it against the rough dark side of the matchbox.

Queen waited, her nerves stretched to breaking point. The man Clerides stuck the cigarette in his mouth. 'They want to go on strike,' he said from the corner of his mouth, and eyed Queen from the corner of his eyes. 'Beautiful black bitch,' the man Clerides thought viciously.

Queen called to Richard to bring her the whisky while she studied the cold calculating Greek. He was hard, brutal and mean. She knew that and it was because of these very reasons that she had employed him to use her own people.

'What are their reasons?' she asked. 'Why do they want to go on strike?'

The Greek scoffed as he puffed at his cigarette. 'That new man you brought ... What is his name? I forget.'

'Idemudia?'

'Yes, yes, Idemudia. He is the one to speak. He works very hard. I see that from the very first day, but he organises. He knows. He is an organiser.'

'What did he say?'

The Greek leaned back in his chair, relaxed. 'He says what they send him to say. That they work very hard for too little pay. Too many hours of work and

250

too many sackings. Every day. Every hour. He says,' and the Greek paused, 'he puts it grandly,' the Greek continued, 'He says it is violence!'

'Violence?'

'Yes, violence.' The excitement began to build up in the Greek again. 'The first educated man you bring to the site,' he said. 'The first one and he speaks out. He says, "It is violence. It must stop!" I am curious and I ask, what violence?' The Greek smiled thinly. 'That Idemudia is clever,' he added.

'Experienced,' Queen substituted bitterly.

'Poor wages and too much work he says is violence. Too much work, too many hours and the firing of men. Two days ago, four men, he says. They want more money but they do not say how much.'

Queen inhaled deeply. She had always sensed something in that man, Idemudia. Something unspoken, dangerous, like a grudge, and a grudge as deep as an ulcer. He had to be handled carefully and that was why she had decided to pay him more than the others. Papiros Clerides had called him an organiser but she guessed he had succeeded because the other labourers had been waiting for somebody like him, ready to be organised. And that was why she had fired any of them who had started any organising or campaigning. But she had taken on Idemudia because he was ...'

'I could fire the three of them,' Clerides suggested

'And what would happen?'

'The other men would go to work, at once.'

Queen shook her head. 'No,' she said firmly. 'I have only eleven days left. I cannot afford any strike action now. I will come down tomorrow morning to address them. That man Idemudia, as you say, is a hard worker. I have never seen anybody like him. You should have seen him and his friends offloading the cement from the trailers.'

'When will you come?'

'As always. In the morning.' She gulped down part of her whisky, tossed the rest of it against the back of her throat and coughed. 'Times are hard,' she thought. 'Very hard.' She took up the bottle and filled the glass again. She had to do something about this Greek too. He was becoming unbearable. She looked at his eyes, shifty like a snake's.

The Greek rose to go and Queen stood up with him. She watched him going down the stairs, his neck dark brown from the sun as his teeth were brown from smoking.

She came back and sat by the glass and the whisky. She decided she would send for Idemudia. 'Every man has a price,' she told herself. She would buy him over now. In the future, she could do away with him, discard him as rubbish into the dustbin. But she was bitter that Idemudia should have turned against her after she had extended a helping hand to him. She shrugged her shoulders. 'Perhaps,' and suddenly she smiled, 'perhaps there is a way to get him. Perhaps Obofun is not wrong after all.'

Idemudia bought a loaf of bread and a tin of sardines on his way home and when he got home, he put both of them on the table. Adisa was in the backyard. She came in to find him cutting through the tin of sardines. The bread was unwrapped and already on the table. She was silent for a while. Then she said, 'You don't mean you are not going to eat again?'

Idemudia did not answer her but continued to cut through the tin of sardines. She went and sat on the bed, her wrappa tied high above her breasts.

'I cannot continue to cook if you will not eat,' she broke out again. 'I have already cooked for five days and wasted the food.'

During the past five days, Adisa had thought a great deal, particularly after she had gone to her aunt and told her everything.

She sat on the bed now, and as she watched Idemudia cutting through the bread, her mind went back to her aunt. She remembered the smile on her aunt's face and she trembled, involuntarily. Why was Idemudia so determined to destroy her and their marriage after all the advice she had rejected? 'So you are no longer blind,' her aunt had said to her. 'I am glad you are beginning to see reason.'

She saw the light of approval in her aunt's eyes now and she heard herself saying, 'But I am ashamed of what I have done, Aunt Salome. I am ashamed, and frightened. If he finds out he will kill me!'

'He will kill you if you do not leave him,' her aunt said, and patted Adisa on her shoulder. 'This is the time to leave him. If you do not now, then surely, you are doomed. As doomed as the obstinate child who closed his eyes to his mother's advice and got drowned.'

'But Aunt Salome,' Adisa said and the tears were back in her eyes, 'How can I leave a man who has sacrificed so much for me and whom I have sacrificed so much for? A man who sold his blood to feed me. Not that he told me, but I always found out afterwards.'

'He sold his blood to feed you?'

'Yes. At the University Hospital. Not once, but many times. And each time they paid him fifteen naira for a pint of his blood.'

Her aunt had kept quiet then. 'So what do you want me to do?'

Adisa stood up then. 'Sooner or later, he is bound to come here to thank you for the money and the whisky.'

'And so, I accept his gratitude. I show no surprise. Is that it?'

'Yes, Aunt Salome. I want you to confirm that the whisky and the money came from you.'

'And if he finds out in some other way?'

'But how can he?'

'Perhaps ...' and her aunt fell silent.

'Perhaps somebody else saw you.'

But Adisa shook her head then. 'Oh no, Aunt Salome. I looked round several times. There was nobody. I was quite safe.'

'Very well then, and may God help you, my dear child,' Aunt Salome said. 'I really want you to be happy. You must not think I want to break your marriage. I have found men to be selfish and ugly. They want a woman, they get a woman, and they use her and then they ditch her in the gutters. Our mother used to tell us that life is beautiful when put to good use, but I found nothing but ugliness and hardship. My husband made my life a misery. So I learned to distrust all men. But a man who sells his blood so that his wife can eat is another matter. Do not be afraid. I will help you and God help us all. What you must do ...'

Her aunt's voice died away in her mind and she came back and saw that now Idemudia was opening the tin of sardines and because he used a knife, it made a lot of noise.

'So why do you not want to eat my food?' she asked again and looked at him.

Still Idemudia ignored her. The sardines were open now and he drew the plate towards him and emptied the fish into it. He drew the chair backwards and sat on it. His back was against the light and his head threw a long shadow across the table, up against the wall. He ate silently, chewing carefully and occasionally sipping some water. As he ate, he thought about the site, about Osaro, Patrick. Yes, Patrick. What was wrong with him? Why had he suddenly turned yellow? Osaro was still all right but Patrick was far gone.

Almost finished. He sighed as he rinsed his mouth with some water.

This was something Adisa couldn't stand, her husband ignoring her. 'You must be patient,' her aunt had said, but how long could they remain like this? 'He will get over his anger. You must be patient.' But her aunt had been mistaken. He was harder now two days later than he had ever been before.

She said to him from the bed where she was sitting, 'What have I done that you should refuse to eat my food?'

He made no reply.

'At least you offend somebody before he can get angry. I haven't done anything. What are you angry with me about? Have I killed your child?'

At that Idemudia grumbled deeply in his throat, and Adisa instantly seized upon it.

'Well, speak out. Speak out. Tell me what I have done!'

He looked at her sideways and his eyes flashed. 'Tell you what you have done?'

'Is it because of what happened five nights ago?'

Idemudia shifted his eyes and Adisa knew she had to proceed cautiously now. 'Can you never imagine that I should be tired, that I should be ... ?' and her voice trailed off.

Idemudia looked at her sideways again, 'That you should be what?' he demanded.

Adisa hesitated, then she said, 'For nearly a whole week you were sick and I had to fend for myself. God knows the things I have borne—the things I have done just to keep alive, just to get us this money so that you could pay the debt to the hospital people. And what do I get in return? If you had come in and said, "Oh Adisa, how did you survive?" I shouldn't have been worried. The first thing you want is to satisfy yourself, and when I cannot respond because . . . because . . .' and she stopped and buried her head in her hands.

Idemudia looked blankly in front of him. Was he as selfish as she had portrayed him? Did he think only of himself? Hadn't he done everything he possibly could for her? Hadn't he even sold his blood just so as to get money? For the past year or more, he hadn't bought a single shirt for himself. All the money he got he had spent on buying her a few clothes, so she wouldn't go naked as he went naked, on feeding her so that she wouldn't look outside. How had he been selfish? Well, five days ago he had been unable to hold himself back. He had been glad to be back at home with her and he had expected her to be equally happy. But she hadn't been happy. She had been sad and withdrawn as if regretting that he should have returned home, alive.

And in the hospital he had thought about her, how he would change this little room, how he would bring Ogbodu from his village to come and live with them, how he would visit home with her, if only he had the money. He looked round at the room again, the rough walls, badly plastered and bent, all their belongings piled up in a corner, the eight spring bed, narrow and always screaming. He intended to move into a room and a parlour, just because of Adisa. Alone he could have stayed on here indefinitely. How then was he selfish? Why was she now throwing accusations against him? Anyway, nothing serious had happened, he finally concluded. Nothing that couldn't be mended.

'How much have we spent from that money?' he grumbled.

But Adisa made no reply.

'I want to know so that we can plan how to repay it,' he said. And it was evident that he was now trying to make amends, no longer angry, relaxed, a great weight lifted off his soul. 'We will pay the money back at the end of the month,' he said again.

Adisa took the headtie from the bed where it lay beside her and fidgeted with it. 'It is less than twenty naira,' she said, and her voice was low and unhappy.

'Twenty naira,' Idemudia repeated, standing up, and still with his back against the yellow electric bulb hanging from the ceiling. 'Twenty ...' His speech was broken into by rapid knockings on the door. Idemudia turned and called, 'Yes?'

Adisa half stood up and then sat down again as a hand cautiously parted the curtain.

Richard stood there. 'My madam has sent me out for you,' he said.

'Who?' Idemudia asked, frowning, and Adisa's heart missed a beat.

'You, sir.'

'Is that why you cannot offer any greetings?' Idemudia asked.

Richard paused, embarrassed.

'What does she want from me?'

'She just said to call you. She didn't say anything else.'

Idemudia looked across at Adisa, then shrugged. 'Tell her I am coming, just now.'

'Goodnight then,' Richard said and he left.

'Goodnight,' Idemudia called after him.

'Is anything wrong?' Adisa asked.

Idemudia debated whether or not to tell her. In the end he asked himself, 'Why not?'

'We are going on strike on the site,' he told her.

And she looked up quickly, 'So soon?'

'They were ready to go on it when we came. We just had to join in. There was nothing else we could do.'

257

Adisa was silent for a considerable time. Her mind went back over so many things. 'That is what you said last time,' she reminded him at last.

He looked away from her. 'It is not my fault if each time I arrive at a place, there is something already in the wind. What can I do? If I refuse to join in, it is bad. It is cowardice. We have to fight for everything, everything we want.'

She didn't say anything to that. But she asked him, 'I guess you will come back in time?'

'I don't know.'

'You still haven't eaten. That bread and the water are nothing. They cannot fill the stomach.'

Idemudia laughed. 'I am not hungry,' he said. 'I am all right.'

He remembered what his father had always said, 'When a man refuses to eat his wife's pounded yam, he removes his eyes from it.' Funny, he told himself, that Adisa should now remind him of his father. 'You can leave the door open,' he told her as he struggled into a shirt. 'When I come in, I will lock up.'

Adisa breathed a sigh of relief after he had gone. In spite of everything her aunt had told her, she had had great moments of doubt when she thought that what had happened would never leave them. Now, however, she told herself that what had happened could never really separate them. Idemudia would never know about it and she would never give him any cause to doubt her. But what had happened between her and Obofun was her secret. Alone, she would always have to live with it but she would never allow it to haunt her. She would bury it in her womb and leave it in peace there, never waking it.

She thought about Obofun who had sent a message to her that she must see him at the hotel on Sunday morning to tell him about her progress with the whisky. She told herself that she would have to return the whisky. If she returned it, Obofun would have no reason to send for her. But she couldn't do it immediately. She would have to wait at least another week and then she would return the whisky after her husband had gone to work. But then she would have the seventy-five naira to show to him as the profits she had made on the whisky. Then she would open a small kiosk and sell provisions there. Idemudia would never find out and Obofun would have no cause to worry her again.

Yes, Idemudia would be convinced. She could always say that her aunt had changed her mind and was not giving her any more of the whisky. Monday week, she told herself, would be the beginning of a new life. The old life,would be behind her, forgotten, tucked in her womb, away. She stood up and went to turn off the light. Then she came back, stretched herself out on the bed and drifted into sleep.

Idemudia came into the room much later, silently. He did not turn on the lights. He stood in centre of the room until his eyes grew accustomed to the darkness. Then he drew the chair away from the table and sat on it, heavily. He removed his clothes slowly as he turned over in his mind what had happened between Queen and himself.

'What does she take me for?' he asked himself. 'I am poor but I can tell my right from my left.'

He was about to lie down when he remembered that he still hadn't locked the door. He went back to the door and began to grope for the key. The key was not in the keyhole. He came to the table and felt its top with his hands. The key wasn't there. Reluctantly, he went to the switch and turned on the light. The key was there at his feet where it had fallen from the keyhole with the banging of the door. He picked it up, put it back into the keyhole and switched off the light before turning the lock in.

He walked back to the bed cautiously. The coming and the going of the light had temporarily blinded him. He felt the edge of the bed and was about to turn in when Adisa asked, 'So you are back!'

He flattened himself out on the bed before he answered her.

'You were so long coming,' she said, passing her hand over her face in the darkness. 'I have been asleep for a long time.'

He couldn't see her face but her voice was warm. 'She kept me,' he replied. 'I didn't want to wake you.'

They were silent for a while during which only the sounds of their heartbeats filled the small room.

'Was it about the strike that she sent for you?' She brought out her hand like the head of a tortoise, cautiously, and passed it over his bare chest.

His voice choked and he coughed. 'Yes.'

'What does she want now?'

'She doesn't want the strike.' He paused and then smiled in the darkness. 'She thinks I can make them call it off.'

She stroked the hairs of his chest and he lifted himself up, nearer her.

'And can you make them call it off?'

Idemudia covered her hand with his own and held it. 'I cannot make them call it off, but she can, if she wants to.'

'Oh, how?'

'Well, we want more money. We are underpaid. If she pays us a little bit more, we will not be so angry.'

'But she is not prepared to pay?'

Idemudia rolled his head on the pillow from side to side. The bed creaked when he moved his body.

'She is not prepared to pay and yet she does not want

a strike.' His voice became serious. 'She even offered me money!'

Adisa almost stopped breathing. 'Offered you money?'

'Yes, she did.'

'How much?'

'One hundred naira!'

'And you accepted it?' Her voice was laden with despair and hope, suddenly.

He turned his head and stared at her in the darkness. 'Accept the money? How could I? I remembered the thirty pieces of silver in the story of Judas. I refused. I couldn't sell my friends for one hundred naira.'

There was sad relief in her voice and again the change was swift. 'You did well!'

Idemudia laughed. 'You didn't think I would accept her money? I never could. I told her I would never accept her money but that I would try to speak to the workers.'

'And you will?'

'We want more money. It is true that I have been there for only five days, but I have been on so many of these building sites that it doesn't make much difference when I started there. We understand each other. We want more money and she has to pay. The work is long, hard and difficult. Why, we are supposed to report again for work on Sunday although the site engineer refused to tell us how much he would pay us as overtime! It is bad, terribly bad, just like everywhere else, and we will go on strike.'

She pressed herself closer to him. Their bodies were warm. 'You will lose this job again,' she reflected sadly.

'I can't help it. It is not my fault. What can I do?'

She rubbed her cheek against his, while her hand

remained in his hand, warm and soft the way he held it. 'So she offered you a hundred naira!' She sighed aloud. 'And you refused it!'

Idemudia pressed her hand gently and made no reply for some time. Then he asked, 'Do you think I should have accepted it?'

'No, no, no. I have said you did well,' she answered. 'Only ...'

'Only what?'

'It's ... a lot of money.'

'Yes, I suppose it is.'

He was pressed hard against her now, her breasts were against his chest and they were hard, and suddenly he was very, very hot. He drew her upwards because he was taller than she so that they lay against each other, level, her breasts rubbing against his throat, their hearts throbbing violently, almost painfully, every fibre and vein of their bodies engaged in an exchange of fire.

A long, long time passed before they fell apart as two logs of fire separate after burning for a while. Then they glowed darkly, burned quietly even in the dark. It was better than Adisa could ever have dared to hope, yes better, even beautiful. She remembered the words of her aunt: 'Life is beautiful when put to good use.' Yes, she told herself, and, smiling in the darkness, she fell asleep.

But Idemudia did not fall asleep immediately. He put his head back on the pillow and his mind was blank for a while before it went back to Queen, to the site, to Patrick. Of all, Patrick angered him most, his attitude was one thing he could not understand. He would see what would happen tomorrow. Perhaps Queen would have an answer ready. If she dismissed them, the workers would all go on strike. Perhaps she would find it easy to employ new hands but he doubted that very much. New people would have new problems, they would have to understand the place.

However, was it worth it? What if the workers deserted the three of them? It had happened the last time at the Uke Construction Company. They had all planned to go on strike, only to discover that a small section of the workers had broken the vow. As a consequence the strike action had failed and he and four others had been dismissed. Osaro had been one of the four dismissed. He told himself now that the circumstances had been different then. And that was a long time ago.

'And she drinks so much!' he told himself. 'Drinks so much! Always drinking ...'

He drifted into sleep.

Chapter 20

In the morning he woke up early. The cocks crowed loudly and boldly. It was cold also and the morning light, weak at this time, filtered slowly into the room. He placed his head on his two hands and stared at the ceiling. Today was going to be an important day. The workers would go on strike if Queen refused to meet their demands. 'She has to,' he told himself. 'She must. We are not slaves.'

He sensed Adisa also coming alive fully. Her hand went over his chest.

'You are awake?' she asked.

'Yes.'

'Why so early? What are you thinking about?'

Idemudia half closed his eyes. 'Nothing,' he replied. 'It is so cold!'

'It is the harmattan.'

'Yes,' he agreed. 'It is the harmattan but it is early. It will go no doubt. There will be more rain.'

'Do you think so?'

He thought for a while before he replied. 'It has always been like that. The harmattan comes a little. Then the rains drive it away before it comes again fully.'

'Was that why you woke so early?'

He laughed in a soft low voice and turned towards her. The bed immediately creaked. 'I have to go to work early. Today is important.'

She rolled over him. The bed creaked again. She sat on the edge of the bed for some time before going to the switch to turn on the light. Then she busied herself preparing the morning's meal while Idemudia got dressed, his chewing stick between his teeth. He chewed thoughtfully. He was absent-minded while he ate and on his way to work he wondered too about what would happen on the site.

He arrived to find the group of twenty-five or thirty already gathered around the concrete mixer. The majority of them were silent. They were tense and any moment they could become violent. They waited for the site engineer and for Queen.

'So the woman tried to bribe you?' Osaro asked, and grimaced after Idemudia had told him the story.

The news spread round quickly. 'Madam tried to bribe Idemudia!'

'Madam offered Idemudia money!'

By the time the whispering came back to Osaro's end again, absurd figures were being quoted.

'Madam offered Idemudia five hundred naira!'

'And he refused it?'

'So he claims.'

Idemudia and Osaro stood near the mixer. Patrick and Omoifo stood at the edge of the crowd.

'I do not support all this,' Patrick said quietly.

'We will probably all be sacked!' Omoifo speculated.

'You can bet on it. All thanks to him. Perhaps it is because he thinks we owe our employment here to him.'

'I don't owe anybody anything,' Omoifo spat out. 'I work here with my own hands.'

The man Bernard was standing next to Patrick and Omoifo. He looked darkly at Patrick.

'Everybody works with his hands. Tell me who doesn't.'

Patrick stared back resentfully. 'I got this job after a long search. I don't want to lose it just because some of you want some ten kobo more.'

265

'Then why don't you tell that to Queen when she arrives?' Bernard suggested.

Patrick drew circles on the dust with his toes. 'I intend to do just that,' he promised. He would perhaps have said more but Omoifo pinched him on his left arm and he fell silent.

Patrick had been out of any kind of work nearly six months. He didn't want to lose the job he had found, come what may. His wife was pregnant and failure to earn a few naira this month would be catastrophic. He needed money badly and a strike threatened the only source of hope he had.

The site engineer and Queen came together, in Queen's car. She wore a buba and wrappa of lace material, deep blue, and round her neck were white coral beads.

'I will speak to them first,' the Greek offered, as they walked towards the gathered group of labourers.

But Queen immediately disagreed. 'What is the point?' she argued. 'They want money and I am going to have to give it to them. The only question is how much?'

'Give them a block increase.'

'I thought so too. About how much?'

'Ten naira.'

'That will cost me nearly three hundred naira!'

'But the work goes on.'

She was now face to face with the workers, Papiros Clerides beside her.

'I understand you want more money,' she addressed the gathered labourers. 'I think you will only deserve it after you have worked for it. Look,' and she pointed at the buildings. 'They are all waiting to be completed. Other sites have completed their buildings but not you here. The work drags on.'

The group murmured disapproval. Just before Queen arrived, Bernard and Idemudia had got together to plan strategy. They now stood together, ahead of the group.

Queen continued with her speech. 'I am prepared to give you, I mean each one of you, five naira extra each month.'

The crowd was silent before a gradual murmuring started. Idemudia put up his hand, and Queen quickly looked from Mr Clerides to Idemudia. Papiros Clerides understood. It was time for him to come in. He stepped forward.

'We have decided that a foreman each day is no good. You have already chosen three men to ask for more money. From these three, we take one. He becomes the site foreman. Permanent.' He pointed at Idemudia. 'He is the new foreman. As from today. Mr Idemudia is foreman forever.'

Queen looked pleased, as if she expected the crowd to clap their hands in appreciation.

'And, if you have more complaints,' she raised her voice again, 'you can speak with the engineer or with,' and she paused, 'with Mr Idemudia, your new foreman.'

Stunned by the sudden announcement, Idemudia's upraised hand wavered and gradually fell back to his side. He was conscious of the stony silence behind him, and his immediate thought was to step forward and declare his rejection of the appointment. But when he heard a low voice asking behind him, 'And you said he rejected the money?' he wasn't quite sure what to do.

'But madam!' he cried out as Queen and Clerides were about to leave for the shed. 'Madam!'

Queen stopped and turned back to face him as if to say, 'Are you not happy with your appointment?'

'Madam!' Idemudia's voice rasped with inner panic. 'We cannot accept the money. We want an increase on a daily basis!'

'One naira a day,' Bernard said, coming to his rescue.

'We want one naira more every day, not five naira a month,' Osaro shouted from his position inside the crowd.

It was Queen's turn to be surprised. She hadn't expected that. 'Give me time to think about it!' she suggested her voice thin and sharp.

'We want the answer now,' Bernard demanded.

'One naira, nothing more, nothing less,' Osaro called out again.

'I want more ...' Queen began, but some twenty voices shouted her down.

'Now! Now!' they cried. 'We want the money now!'

The labourers surged forward towards Queen. 'Our money!' they cried.

'Now! Now!'

Queen stood rooted to the ground terrified. She looked wildly out for Mr Clerides but the Greek himself was already shrinking backwards. In another moment, there would be violence.

Idemudia raised his hands above his head – and waved wildly. 'Wait!' he cried. 'Wait!' He seized upon Bernard. 'We do not want any violence!' he rasped. 'Stop them!'

Bernard immediately responded. 'Wait!' he too began to shout. 'Wait!'

The word caught on. Other voices seized on it and shouted, 'Wait!'

In two minutes, the storm subsided, but Queen still stood there, terror clearly written in her eyes. Mr Clerides was out of sight.

Idemudia shouted again. 'Osaro, Bernard and I will go to them,' he said quickly. 'We will discuss the affair just like yesterday.'

The angry voices died down. Quickly, Queen scampered away towards the shed. She was sweating.

Idemudia was angry too. 'Either you let us discuss this with her or you go yourself!' he said angrily. 'We must be organised or we fail.'

The other labourers fell silent.

Then somebody said, 'But you are foreman now. You are one of them.'

Bernard stepped in quickly. 'That's just what the woman wants, to divide us. Idemudia is with us unless ... unless of course you want another person in his place.'

He kept quiet and waited for their reaction. The labourers shifted on their legs and stared vacantly in front of them.

Osaro said, 'Let us not deceive ourselves. We know that only this man can speak for us anyway. He goes with us unless,' and he eyed Idemudia, 'unless he decides to remain as foreman.'

'Well?' Bernard prompted Idemudia.

'I am going along with you as before,' Idemudia said, large drops of sweat standing out on his face. He looked round at everybody. Nobody protested. 'And what do we tell them?' he asked.

'We want one naira a day more.'

'And if she refuses?'

'We go on strike. Tomorrow morning.'

'Are we all agreed on this then?' Osaro asked.

The burning look in the eyes of the men showed that they were agreed.

The men were restless as they watched the trio going into the shed where Queen and Mr Clerides were already waiting uneasily.

'You should have brought the police,' Mr Clerides reflected sadly.

'They wouldn't have dared to touch me,' Queen

boasted, but without conviction. Her voice still trembled as if she had just escaped a fatal accident.

Mr Clerides smiled. 'They could have done anything to you,' he said. 'You have never seen a mob. In my country they are many. They go wild, they throw stones and they kill.'

'So that was why you ran away,' she thought contemptuously. 'But you shouldn't have left me there alone,' she said, and Mr Clerides flinched.

'I didn't leave you there alone,' he cried out in self-defence. 'What's the use? Only two of us. They kill us and no evidence. I went away because I thought of the police. A mob is dangerous, very, very dangerous.'

Mrs Obofun shrugged her shoulders. What was past was past but she was still sweating. 'Well, what do I tell them?'

'What to tell them? Easy,' Mr Clerides said. 'Say that you will pay.'

'But I cannot,' Queen disagreed. 'Where do I get an extra nine hundred naira a month from?'

The crafty eyes of the Greek shifted. 'No, madam. You do not understand me,' he said. 'You promise everything now but you pay nothing later. Why man, you want them to work. We need time. We don't want a strike.'

Queen thought about that. Then slowly she shook her head. 'I couldn't do that. They would expect the money.'

'Let them expect it!' the Greek cursed. 'But they get nothing. Why, they are overpaid as it is.'

'No, no no,' Queen disagreed again. 'It is true that I need time but I do not want my houses destroyed. I have seen it before.'

'Then what are you going to do?' the Greek asked.

'That man Idemudia ...'

'Yes?'

'He is the most important.'

'Yes. And he is the ringleader.'

'I must get him over or out at all costs,' Queen said. 'When you announced he was foreman, it nearly broke them up. You saw that?'

'Oh yes. Why, man, that was clever. They were ready to fight each other after that.'

'Well, I think ...' She hesitated because there were demanding knocks on the door.

'Yes?' she called out.

The door was pushed open and Idemudia, Osaro and Bernard entered the room.

There was open hostility in the Greek's voice as he rasped, 'So you have come? What do you want?'

The silence that greeted this question was more hostile than any speech. Queen noticed it and drew her chair back from the table so that she could face the men properly.

The negotiations did not last more than twenty minutes and when the three of them emerged from the shed, the group of workers were gathered at the door. They made way at once for the committee members who led them back towards the buildings, away from the wooden shed and out of earshot.

'What happened?' Omoifo asked.

Idemudia waved his hands and motioned to them to listen to him. 'We gave her until Monday,' he announced quietly. 'If by Monday nothing happens, then we lay down the buckets, the shovels and the wheelbarrows.'

'That's good talk,' one of the men said. 'We lay down the buckets.'

'We go on strike,' another man said.

'Yes, we go on strike. We gave her enough time.'

'But she has said she would like to see the three of us again on Sunday evening at her place before she finally tells us all on Monday morning whether or not she will pay,' Osaro informed them.

One man at the edge of the crowd shook his head. 'Eh, eh, what she has to say, she better say at once to all. There will be no need for you to meet her again in her house.'

'No need to meet her again! We have given her enough time,' another man cried out. 'She wants to bribe you.'

Idemudia raised his hands. 'I think we should see her,' he said.

'No, no need,' the first man insisted.

Idemudia raised his voice. 'I think we should,' he insisted.

'Why?'

'I think we must try to resolve the conflict at all costs by trying peaceful negotiation first,' he began.

'Hear, hear!' the first man interrupted him bitterly. 'Because you are now her foreman ...'

'I am not her foreman.'

'You are. Why didn't you reject it when the man announced it? You have divided interests.'

Idemudia was angry at the accusation. 'Watch your tongue,' he cried out angrily. 'Once the strike starts, nobody knows when it will end. We have ...'

The other man came back. 'What did I say?' he said to the group. 'He wants to discourage us now. He sympathises.'

'With whom?' Idemudia asked angrily.

'With her. Yesterday she offered you money. You said so yourself. Nobody knows the arrangement you made thereafter.'

Idemudia glared at the man and his heart was black with hatred. 'I began organising this thing ...'

'And now you are foreman,' the man said insinuatingly.

'Comrades! Comrades!' Bernard's voice called. 'Let's stop this quarrel. It leads us nowhere.'

The other man disagreed. 'It does lead us somewhere,' he insisted. 'I am proposing that we drop him from the team.'

'And who do you propose to replace him with?' Osaro asked scornfully.

The man laughed. 'There should be no difficulty about that,' he said. 'If it comes to it, I am prepared to serve on the committee myself.'

'Then I will not serve on that committee,' Osaro said.

The man ignored Osaro's statement. 'I am old here,' he said. 'So are the others here. You two are new. I propose that Bernard should stay on the new committee. He should lead it. Then we choose two others, two others who have been working here.'

There was silence.

Then another man said, 'I think Anyam is speaking the truth. We need people on the committee, people who have been here all the time.'

Anyam immediately seized upon that. 'So you see, I am talking sense,' he declared. 'Ifeanyi has also seen the truth in what I am saying. A foreman cannot serve on the committee.'

The other members of the group shuffled their feet, silent. Even Bernard kept quiet.

'So who do we elect?' Anyam asked.

A tall man resting his weight on a shovel cleared his throat. 'I do not think we should rush the matter,' he said quietly. 'Idemudia has done a good job and ...'

'Agreed,' Patrick called out, and Idemudia stared at him with surprise. 'We are being unfair and unreasonable,' he said. 'Idemudia wants us all to have our jobs. If you force a confrontation with the woman, we all lose. She has nothing to lose.'

'I still think we should drop him,' the man Anyam said.

'No, that would be foolish,' Bernard said now. 'We will not go to see the woman and if by Monday nothing happens, then we lay down our buckets.'

'Or form another committee,' the man Anyam said. 'If on Monday nothing happens, we drop him from the committee and form ...'

'We lay down the buckets,' Bernard said. 'That's what we will do.'

'Anybody who reaches a private agreement with the woman will be publicly shamed and disowned,' the man Anyam insisted.

'Yes, disowned and done away with. We cannot afford any treachery,' the other men agreed. 'We cannot ...'

Now Idemudia and Osaro were walking down the road and they were past the signboard that bore the name of the company when Queen's car drew up ahead of them. She beckoned to Idemudia and he went to speak to her through the car's window which she had rolled down. They talked briefly, then the car drew away.

Osaro walked up to him where he stood by the side of the road.

'What did she want? Osaro asked.

'She says I should see her this evening in her house.'

'And you will go?'

'Well, I don't know. I may.'

They were silent as they walked down the road. Both men felt bitter towards the man Anyam and exasperated with the other workers in general.

Idemudia was extremely depressed by the time he got home, depressed and moody. And Adisa noticed it at once.

She hovered around him, her face serious and quiet

and apprehensive. 'What have they done to you again?' she cried.

He did not answer her but removed his sweat-soaked shirt. 'Hang it outside, so it will dry a little with the blowing of the wind,' he said to her.

She took it from him and went outside. He could hear her dusting the shirt by blowing it.

Later she came inside and saw him, head bowed, sitting on the chair, his hair rough and blown and red and white from the cement and the sand. His ribs stood out, the bones on his neck and cheeks were also sticking out like the old indicators of old cars. His neck and throat were wiry, askew and twisted like the neck of a tortoise. So much had hard labour and poor eating and selling his blood done to him.

She saw that he did not want to talk, so she said to him instead, 'The water is outside. You can bathe, then you must eat. Go and have a bath.'

He obeyed her dumbly and stood up from the chair. 'You need hot water to get that cement and sand off your hair and body,' she said. 'So I boiled the water. Go quickly before it cools down.'

He smiled when she said that. That was the first ray of sunlight thrown into his soul since morning, that statement, that caring about his well-being by Adisa. It was the first ray of the sun but because he was depressed and his heart was misty wtih hatred and bitterness against what he regarded as a show of ingratitude from his fellow workers, the ray could not dispel all the mist. He went outside and thought about Adisa. Surely he loved her. She was the only person in the world who cared about him, the only person apart from his mother. One day, he would show her how grateful he was, how happy he was to have her. Thinking of Adisa brought more sunlight into his soul. The mist in his heart began to clear slowly.

He bathed and as he bathed he thought about work, about the strike, about the attitude of his fellow workers. He bathed slowly because he thought about many things. His mind as he bathed and thought was like an immense empire stretching backwards and forwards. He thought about Iyaro, about the East Circular and again he saw cars stopping, it did not matter which cars. He saw himself and the other jobless workers rushing towards the cars every morning, leaning into the windows towards the drivers and owners of the cars. 'You want labourers, sir? You want workers, sir?' Again he saw himself there each morning, heard himself asking the usual question. 'You want labourers, sir?' Always he was rushing towards a car or a lorry. Always he had to smile before he asked, 'You want labourers, sir? You want workers, sir?' And most of the time, the faces that were in the cars, turned away and they were either shy and embarrassed or amused and completely indifferent as they thought briefly about these people who were asking them if they had any jobs to offer, if they wanted labourers.

Yes, his life had always been like that, hard and hard, harder than iron or stone, hard and difficult, the hunger always there, the disease always there, the hollowness and the despair always there. And now, when he had organised the labourers to fight for their rights, they had threatened to have him thrown out. If Queen heard about that, she would laugh at him, she would be merciless, she would throw him out at once.

He scooped the warm water on to his body, and the vast empire of his mind turned to Adisa. Good Adisa! How dearly he loved her now. And yet to think that during the past few days, their marriage had been threatened, that he had hated her, completely misunderstood her. How she must have suffered on his account! Was it right that he should have married? Yes, was it right? What right had he over a woman whom he couldn't feed, provide for? And yet more often than not, he was angry with her. 'But I shouldn't be,' he said to himself. 'No, I shouldn't. At least not from now on. I will respect and love her. I will try to make her happy. Try, try harder and harder ...'

Later, when he had eaten and broken a piece of wood off the broomstick with which to pick his teeth, he pushed the chair back from the table so that Adisa could clear the plates away. Adisa got up from the bed and approached the table.

He said to her, after looking at the corner of the room where the cartons stood, 'What about the whisky?'

She had already lifted a plate clear from the table. She held it in the air. 'What about it?' she asked and took the plate and dropped it into the bucket he had just used for bathing.

He looked a her as he probed in his teeth for small chunks of stockfish that were lodged there. They were lodged in between two of his back teeth. He prodded the strands of the stockfish with the thin edge of the broomstick that he had broken, his mouth open, his left eye half closed, his chin raised the better to pick his teeth.

He looked at Adisa as she bent down to place the plate inside the bucket and asked, 'Well, how is it going? How are you selling it?'

Adisa straightened up. 'It is good,' she said. 'It goes quickly.' She put her hands on her hips.

'But you still have many left?'

'Yes, I have some left but not many.'

'How many?'

'I did not count them.' Adisa walked round to the table and began cleaning it with a dirty torn, yellow, old rag, her heart beating faster.

He drew his chair farther backwards to give her more room for her cleaning. There were still threads of stockfish clinging round the base of his back teeth, one part deep in his gum between the two teeth. He picked the threads of stockfish, spinning the piece of broomstick round quickly in the gap between his teeth. He gasped as the stick bit into the meat of his gum. His eyes watered from the sharp and sudden pain. He drew out the piece of broomstick. The tip was red with his blood. He felt his gum with his tongue, gingerly. He could feel the salty taste of the blood. He stood up, went to the window and spat out the blood into the evening outside.

Adisa had finished cleaning the table and now she was sitting on the bed.

Idemudia went back to his chair, the broomstick still in his hand. He had no other alternative as the threads of stockfish were still clinging to the base of his teeth. His head ached from the wound in his gum.

He said to her, 'Can't we open one?'

She smiled slowly, her nervousness gone. 'Open what?'

'The whisky,' he said. 'One of the bottles of whisky.' He held the broomstick in his hand, afraid to send it back to dig for the strands and threads of stockfish.

She thought about what he had said. She was reluctant. 'If you open one now,' she said, 'you will open another one later.'

Idemudia smiled. 'You have had it here for nearly a week,' he reminded her.

'Well, you were bound to ask for it sooner or later. I have been expecting it.'

He laughed broadly now. 'I don't drink,' he said.

'I am not a drunkard. You know that.'

She shrugged her shoulders. 'The cartons are there. You can drink them up. But for every one you drink, you must pay the price.'

He laughed again, his eyes gleamed. He forgot about the pain in his gum. 'What price?' he asked.

'The prices that others pay. Four naira, fifty kobo.'

'And you will accept the money?'

'Why not? It is not my whisky.'

'Ah, it's okay then,' he said gently. 'I was only joking. I hate drinking. I do not want to drink.'

But Adisa did not believe him. She laughed. 'The price has frightened you,' she said.

'Hear, hear!' he laughed excitedly. 'The price! I could drink it and refuse to pay. If I drink it and refuse to pay, what will you do?'

She thought about that. 'Perhaps there is nothing I could do to you,' she said, 'but you would never feel comfortable with whisky you haven't paid for in your belly.'

He jumped up from the chair as the laughter hit him in his heart. His chest heaved with laughter and he rushed upon her and flung her out on the bed. He pushed the pillow against her face while she struggled and thought, 'What is happening to him? What has entered into him? Listen to him laughing and screaming like an irresponsible child!'

She began to choke under the pillow and cried out, 'You are choking me! Please remove the pillow!'

He removed it and released her from the bed to which he had pinned her. She sat up on the bed gasping and smiling.

'You nearly strangled me,' she said, breathing heavily, her eyes laughing and happy.

'How could I?' he asked, also breathing heavily for it had been an effort to hold her back on the bed as both of them were struggling and kicking like wild cats, and laughing.

They stared at each other and he told himself in his heart that he had never been more in love with Adisa than at that moment. She looked so beautiful, so weak and yet so powerful!

'Adisa!'

'Yes!'

He said nothing. She looked at him again and again, through and through. She was happy seeing him so happy. How she wished that things could remain like this always. How she wished it!

'Queen says I must see her this evening,' he said to her at last.

The sound of his voice dispelled her wishing.

'Queen?'

'Yes. I must be going.'

He stood up. 'I won't be long. Where did you hang my shirt?'

'On the line against the wall,' she said. 'Where it always hangs.'

'I will take it from there then.'

'But it is dirty.'

'Ah,' he said carelessly. 'I never wear it when I'm working. So it is good enough. Leave the door open. I won't be long.'

He lingered in the room for a moment, then resolutely went outside and picked up his shirt from the line where it hung against the wall.

Chapter 21

It was the deep of the evening now, deep because the evening was far gone and soon it would be actual darkness, night. The air was fresh as it blew down from the great vaults but as it swept across the rotting and decaying gutters, across the sewage and rubbish dumps, across the thatched houses and the bungalows set inside hibiscus and whistling pine groves, the air became coloured with several odours. It stank, it smelled, it was never sweet.

The air blew down Owode Street, around the Freedom Motel, and because of the cooking, the drinking and the pines, the air here smelled too and the smell wasn't sweet.

Inside the Freedom Motel, cutlery and teeth clattered as they bit and chewed, tongues wagged as the beer and the palm wine were swallowed and gulped down. In one corner a group of customers talked about the prices, prices higher than the tallest buildings in the city, frightful prices. They thought and talked about money, how to steal to make money, cheat to make money, work to make money, make money to make money. They talked and concluded that the best way to make money was to steal it from the government. Steal a huge sum, put most of it in some foreign bank, make business with the government's money, steal goods and equipment ordered by the government, steal government cement on the high seas, steal land and buildings from the people in the name of the government. Yes, steal, cheat, dupe and even murder in the name of the government. They talked and concluded that the government encouraged stealing, applauded and rewarded it. What was retirement with full benefits, they asked? Steal. Steal huge, gigantic sums, hundreds of thousands, hundreds of millions of naira of government money and be retired with full applause. Steal and be retired and then enter business.

They talked and plotted ways of stealing. Then they laughed and kept quiet and listened to the loud music coming from a player in another corner of the motel. The music was sharp and flat but these customers listened and tapped their fingers on their knees and shuffled their feet on the floor in response to the sharp shrilling and flat music that came from the corner of the motel.

In the upper part of the Freedom Motel, Queen sat, the whisky and the tall whisky glass beside her. Sitting opposite, Idemudia watched her, thinking, 'What will she say next?'

'You say you don't want any whisky then?' Queen asked again.

Idemudia avoided looking her in the eyes. 'No,' he replied again. 'I do not want any.'

Queen laughed. 'But whisky is good. It makes half a man a full man. Don't you think so?'

He looked at his hands and smiled. He remembered his conversation with Adisa. 'I have used whisky but only a little,' he replied. 'It burns your throat and brings tears to your eyes. Then again there is the smell in a man's nose.'

Queen smiled at him. 'How little you know,' she said. 'You can see. Can't you? I am not weeping, am I? True, it burns a little, but that's what makes it whisky.'

The events of the day were behind her now. As soon as she had got home she had opened the bottle of whisky and now with half the contents of the bottle

282

already in the pit of her stomach she was in a buoyant, carefree mood.

'So?' Queen prompted. 'You refuse my whisky?'

Idemudia shook his head. 'No, madam,' he said. 'I do not refuse your whisky. Only I do not want it, at least not now. My wife even sells whisky but I have never used it.'

'You will drink something else then? Beer?'

'Oh yes,' he said, 'I do not mind beer. I think I would like some beer.' He was getting nervous with this woman trying to please him when he knew there was nothing he could really do for her.

'But beer smells stronger than whisky,' Queen said. 'And you are lucky not to have ruined your stomach so far with beer.' She thought of her husband's large, heavy stomach, like a pregnant woman's. She shook her head. 'No, I prefer whisky to any other drink.'

She called out to Richard to bring the beer and a glass.

The house was empty now, empty and quiet. Obofun had gone to Lagos and would not be returning until Sunday morning. Then the children had gone to meet her own parents in the village to spend part of their holidays there. It was the village she had left many years ago after completing her primary schooling to marry Obofun. The marriage had been arranged by their parents. Now, she was considered educated after living in the world her husband had carved out for her. Of course, she had struggled on her own, taught herself many things. Today, she was respected in the village. They called her 'Mama'. And any time she went home and saw the old and haggard faces of the women in her own age group, their thin legs and large collar bones from the work on the farm, planting melon, garri and cocoyams, she was glad, immensely glad, that she had left the village. But then she had been one of the most beautiful girls in the village. Yes, one of the most beautiful, matured and knowledgeable about the ways of the world.

But now all that was behind her. She would be called 'Mama' when she went there again on Sunday afternoon to bring the children home so that the house would be full again in the evening. Obofun would be back, the children would be back and so would all the noise, some of it very unpleasant and bitter, which comes from living together. Now the house was quiet, the music and talking and clatter of cutlery in the lower part of the house did not reach up here. It was quiet and peaceful and the whisky had helped to loosen her mind and her nerves so that they hung loose and relaxed like the strings of a guitar, unstrung.

But then there was also the nervousness which comes from drinking too much and from knowing that on Monday, there would be a strike and at the end of the month perhaps the loss of her contract and the refund of hundreds of thousands of naira. This nervousness came from knowledge which half a bottle of whisky could not submerge. And knowing, she was prepared to prevent the strike and so save her contract at all costs. Yes, at all costs. After all, what did Obofun care? Had he not gone to Lagos to save his own business while leaving her to lose everything?

Richard brought the beer and set it on the stool beside Idemudia. Next he placed the glass on the stool. He brought out the opener from a side pocket and opened the bottle of beer. Then he filled the glass with some of the beer.

Idemudia murmured 'Thank you' as he picked up the cold hard glass. Then he swallowed half of the brownish-yellow cold bitter beer in a single gulp. The cold beer tasted so good that unconsciously, he licked his lips. He sighed. It was good to be treated like a human being, decently, he thought.

It was good, this sitting down in the cool and quiet of the evening drinking this cold bitter beer served in a tall beer glass. It was good sitting on this heavy soft chair, his legs flung out on the deep soft reddish-blue rug just drinking from the cold hard glass. It was good to have the hard labour, the sun and the sweat behind him, yes it was ... ah, but it was not so good after all, this sitting and watching and waiting for what Queen would say. It was like eating with the Devil, this watching and waiting and knowing that nothing could ever make him compromise his position. Yes, not even the attitude of his fellow workers. Unconsciously, he dragged up his feet from the rug until he had them squared up against the front of the big heavy chair.

Queen tossed the rest of the drink in her glass into the back of her throat and swallowed. Then she set the glass down.

After the whisky had settled in the pit of her stomach and she seemed to have come out of her reverie, she refilled her glass and said to him, 'I don't want a strike. You are my foreman. You should know that.'

Idemudia had been expecting that statement all evening. He set down his own glass and looked at his hands cold from the coldness of the beer.

'I don't want a strike,' Queen continued. 'Just as I told you the last time that you were here, I do not and cannot afford any strike now. I am prepared to do anything for you to make your friends call off the strike. That was why I asked you to see me this evening. You can do it if you want.'

'But, madam!'

Queen waved his protest aside. 'What do you want?'

she asked harshly. 'Tell me, what do you want?'

For the first time, Idemudia raised his eyes to Queen's face. How could he make her understand that there was nothing he could do for her? 'It is not me,' he said earnestly and sincerely. 'I am nothing.'

Queen's voice was accusing, 'I gave you a job to help you and the first thing you do is to organise the workers against me! That is ingratitude.'

'But madam!' Idemudia tried again.

'It is ingratitude,' Queen insisted. 'You have paid me back with ingratitude, biting the hand that fed you. But I don't mind. I only ask you now to tell me what you want. I want you to persuade your friends to call off the strike.'

Idemudia was angry because the woman had called him ungrateful. She had given him a job, true. But had she not milked him and the other workers? What about the long hours of work? The poor pay, the treatment of workers as if they were lower than dirt, scum. He was angry but he said quietly, 'It is not me, madam. It is not me.'

Queen did not understand him. 'Just tell me what you want,' she said placatingly. 'Remember you are my foreman now. You should work with me.'

Idemudia became more and more nervous. 'I do not want anything from you, madam,' he said.

Queen laughed. 'You are a man,' she said. You need money. You need many other things I could give to you. Things you have never had before.'

Idemudia was silent.

'Well?'

He held his head in his hands now, his head which throbbed with the beer she had given him and from the pain of thinking. 'I need time to think,' he said. 'Give me some time.' He didn't want to displease her by an outright refusal. He had to be careful. Yes, very careful. And perhaps he shouldn't have come. He ought to have stayed away.

But Queen immediately seized upon what he had said. 'Time? What will you say then that you can-not say now? I will give you two hundred naira, even three hundred, perhaps more later.'

Again he was quiet as he thought fiercely in his heart. Could he accept her money and let her down? No, that would be dishonest. But what if he accepted it and stood by her. Surely the workers would find out. They would find out and ostracise him. The story would follow him everywhere, even if he chose to go elsewhere. No, he didn't want anything from this woman. Three hundred naira was a lot of money. He wanted money very badly. But it would be like blood money. He couldn't accept it even if he really wanted to help her. He didn't want any money, any bribe, from her. He had many, many more years ahead of him. A single mistake and the word would go round. And then he would be finished. Really finished.

Queen stood up and came to stand behind him. She put her hand on his shoulders, her hand that was soft and warm like her eyes. 'Three hundred naira!' she breathed down at him. 'I'll give you anything you want, anything that you ask, for now.' And she squeezed his shoulder blade like a comrade's. 'Well?'

He had to say something. What should he say to her? That he couldn't accept it because this was sweat money, almost like blood money, that his conscience would never give him peace of mind if he accepted it? He shook his head. And again, not to give himself away and not to offend her, he said, 'I am not alone, we are ...'

'I know,' she broke in readily. 'I know. There are these other two, Osaro and Bernard. But I want to know about you first. Once you have assured me, you can persuade your friends to come here tomorrow.'

He pretended to think this over. Then he said, 'As a matter of fact, I want nothing for myself. I want nothing from you.'

Queen lifted her hand off his shoulder, angered by his refusal. She had never imagined that a man could be so stubborn. 'Aren't you being foolish?' she asked.

He shrugged his shoulders. He was a man. He could never accept sweat money no matter what happened.

'Yes,' he agreed. 'I know I am foolish but I want nothing, honestly.'

'But you will speak to the others?'

He nodded. 'Yes. I will try if you want me to. But I cannot guarantee that they will follow me.'

'They will,' Queen said from where she still stood behind him. 'They will if you can speak to them, if you try to persuade them. But the funny thing is that I do not believe you will persuade them if you accept nothing from me.'

'Oh my God!' he cried in his heart. 'Why can't she leave that alone? Why must she continue to tempt me? I should never have come at all! I was a fool to come!' He said to her in a firm voice, 'You just have to believe me, madam. There is nothing that I want from you.'

She paused from behind him. Then she said, 'I do not believe you. You will deceive me. I will not trust you if you refuse to accept something from me.'

Idemudia searched in his mind. 'What should I accept from you?'

'What should you accept from me?'

'Yes. What?'

'You could still have the three hundred naira. Money.'

He shook his head, 'I do not want the money. True,

I need it and I am poor. But I could never accept such money. I am a man.'

'But a man has to eat, survive.'

'Yes, but not on blood, on sweat money.'

'Sweat money? What is that?'

Idemudia smiled. 'Ah, it is nothing. Just nothing.'

She looked at the nape of his neck. He was uncomfortable with her behind him. She could stick a knife in his back. But he resisted the temptation to turn round and look to see if she had a knife in her hand.

He shivered.

'You will not accept the money then? Because you are a man?'

'Well, yes. That and other things. I do not want it.'

'You are a rare kind of poor man,' she said. 'But you are foolish. Extremely foolish and stubborn.'

Idemudia tightened his lips.

'Will you accept something else from me then?'

He made no reply.

She said, 'You are silent? You don't answer?'

Idemudia cleared his throat. A fog from the cold beer had formed there. 'What else should I accept from you?'

'What else you should accept from me?'

'Yes. What?' The circle again, he thought.

She was silent where she stood behind him. Then she said, 'Wait! Wait and I will show you what you must accept from me.'

She had bent down to speak close to Idemudia's ears. The smell of whisky was strong in her voice and on her breath.

He turned round quickly, half expecting the thrust of a knife in his back. But he saw her walking into a room directly behind him. He was becoming increasingly uncomfortable. What was it that he must accept from her? He released his legs like arrows from a bow, flung them out on the soft rug so that they could be relaxed. Then he took the beer and sipped it. The beer tasted flat in his mouth now from standing so long. He put it back on the stool and felt his teeth with his tongue. His tongue felt slimy, like a living snail's meat, out of the shell but not yet cleaned with the lemon.

He heard steps coming up from the inside stairs. But before the person appeared, Queen called to him. He hesitated before answering because the person had appeared. He was wearing the uniform of a waiter. He greeted Idemudia and then he asked for 'Madam'.

'Queen?' Idemudia asked.

'Yes,' the waiter repeated. 'Where is madam?'

'Idemudia!' Queen's voice was demanding, like a clarion call.

'Wait,' he said to the waiter and went towards the door behind where Queen was calling. The open door was sealed only by the heavy yellow door blind.

He parted the curtain hesitantly. He saw that Queen was sitting on the bed.

'Shut the door,' Queen said to him from where she sat on the large bed in her nightdress, a small short blouse thrown over the long nightdress.

Idemudia continued to stand in the doorway, part of the door blind gathered in his hand. 'There is a man outside,' he said. 'He wants you.'

Queen frowned. 'What does he want?'

'I do not know. He did not say.'

'Find out and then come back and tell me.'

Idemudia let the curtain fall back on the door. He went back to the waiter. 'She says I should find out what you want,' he told the man.

The waiter eyed Idemudia. 'There's a man downstairs.'

'What does he want?'

'He didn't say but he said to call madam.'

'He gave you his name?'

'Yes. Iriso. Mr Iriso.'

'Wait then,' Idemudia said. 'I will tell the woman all that you have said.'

He went back into the room. Queen was still sitting on the bed. She looked at him expectantly.

'I heard you talking. What does he want?'

'He is one of the waiters. Somebody else sent him. Mr Iriso. He is downstairs and he sent for you.'

Queen frowned. 'I don't want to see any Mr Iriso.'

'Should I tell the waiter that?'

'No! Tell the waiter to say I am not in. That I have gone out, that I will return late, perhaps in the dead of night. I do not want to see him.'

Idemudia crossed the door again and went back to the waiter.

'She will return in the dead of night. She is not at home.'

The waiter took the message and went downstairs.

Idemudia stood in the centre of the room, undecided, and was about to resume his seat by his stale glass of beer when again Queen called out to him.

'Please, shut the door,' Queen said to him. She was now lying on the bed. 'Shut the door,' she repeated. 'Then come here and sit beside me. Here on this chair beside the bed.'

Idemudia shut the door while the blood throbbed in his head. 'What does this woman want with me?' he asked himself as he turned round and faced her.

'Come and sit here on the chair beside the bed,' Queen said again. 'There is at least one thing which you cannot refuse from me.'

Idemudia wondered what the thing was as he sat on the easy chair beside her bed. She was wearing a see-through nightdress, soft and light blue. He saw the dark outlines of her body in the pale nightdress and quickly turned away.

His heart beat against his chest, violently. Surely, she must hear this thunderous pounding of his heart? Surely she must hear!

The bed was large as the room was large, big and wide and low. There was the big dressing table beside which the dressing mirror stood. To the right of the mirror were the big, tall built-in wardrobes. Half the dressing table was taken up by cosmetics. On the left of the dressing table were some wooden figures, moulds of human heads, six or seven of them, on which black and dark brown wigs were placed. Against the walls and further to the left of the wigs were the trunk boxes, iron and wooden trunk boxes, large and heavy.

The shoes were arranged under the bed but in such a way that any visitor could see and count them easily. There was another basket that held the old pairs of shoes. It stood full, against the wall. The bed was soft. It sank where Queen lay on it. The bedclothes were also soft and blue like the clouds against a clear evening sky.

Again, Idemudia's eyes wandered back to the woman on the bed. He was sure that but for the dark blue bulbs hanging at the head of the bed, he would have been able to see everything clearly of this woman.

'Help me off with this,' Queen said to Idemudia, turning so that she lay flat on the soft of her belly on the bed.

It was the small short blouse that she wore over her nightdress that she wanted Idemudia to peel off her. Idemudia swallowed and his hands trembled as he bent down to obey her.

'You can sit on the bed now, beside me. Come.

Sit so,' she said and wriggled and crawled away from the edge of the bed deeper inside.

Mechanically and automatically, Idemudia obeyed her.

'Your hands are harsh, almost brutal,' she observed. 'Perhaps that comes from the rough work?'

Idemudia could not trust himself to speak. He grumbled deeply in his throat, as he unfastened one of the buttons at the back of her blouse.

When the blouse had been removed and she was lying no longer on the soft of her belly but on the fine ridges of her back she said to him, 'Come, bring that hand of yours. It is rough, almost like the carpenter's paper, Bring it. Let me feel it.'

Idemudia was sweating from the mere effort of trying not to look at her. The curve of her breasts, the sharp ridges at the top were still unbroken. The breasts still held together at the top. Later, they would fall apart, the breasts would become heavy and sprawl all the way, deflated and formless except when she was standing and they were gathered together inside a brassiere. Now the breasts still held tight and out against time. All the lines of her body were unbroken; childbirth had not destroyed the line of her stomach, lower down. Perhaps it would sag later on, just as her breasts would, just as all of her would. But now, it was still flat and unbroken, the line that was her stomach, hazy now as her legs were under the soft blue nightdress and dark blue lights.

Her eyes sparkled darkly in the half-darkness. She seemed to be toying with him as she lay back on the bed on the straight lines that were her back, her buttocks pressing through the hazy nightdress and boring holes into the soft mattress that was the bed. Her luminous eyes were up against the white of the ceiling, her hair loose and wavy, everything black and dark and sensuous. Then there were her legs thrown carelessly apart, softly calling, the nightdress throwing its haze upon them. Then the waistline, swelling and swelling and swelling like a time bomb that is ticking away to explode any moment and yet intact, held together under the general logic of its tight structuring.

She lay and she said to Idemudia who was sweating and staring at her now, 'Come, bring that hand of yours. Offer it and let me feel it. I know it is rough and harsh but ...'

'It is not my fault ...' Idemudia said, offering her the palm of his hand, the sweat standing out in beads on his forehead.

She took it and felt it with the softness of her own palm. 'I am not laughing at you,' she said. 'In fact, it is wonderful. Wonderful, because it is so rough and manly. Very manly and masculine. I like the palm of your hand, rough as it is.'

He did not know what to say but he let her feel the palm of his hand. His blood was up, he was stirred.

'You will not go on strike against me, Idemudia,' she said, and he made a noise in his throat as of someone choking.

Queen laughed. 'You will not go on strike against me,' she said again and she weaved her body away from the edge of the bed as a weaver bends the straw to weave the basket or as the sky weaves the colours to make the rainbow. 'You will not go on strike against me but will come and lie down here beside me. Come here and lie down beside me. But take your shirt off first. It smells so strongly of sweat, now that you are so close. Take it off and come here and lie down. Here, beside me.' She patted the bed with her hand. 'But take your shirt off first.'

Idemudia hesitated and withdrew his hand from where she held it.

'Come in quickly,' Queen said. 'Come in quickly and lie here.' She took his hand again. 'Your hand is so warm,' she said. The blood was up in her face almost choking her.

'What are you waiting for?' she asked again, turning on the soft of her belly, her buttocks up, dark hills of flesh and blood rising about the flatness of the bed and above the straight elegant line that was her back. 'Come in quickly, now.' She released his hand and rested her chin on her cupped hands. Her eyes looked up at him.

Idemudia stared beyond her, his heart pounded and thundered within him more than ever before. He could feel and hear the blood crashing through his veins, as the windstorm crashes through the trees. Was this a trap? Would the woman's husband not come in any moment? He wanted to turn and run blindly for the door but something held him, prevented him.

Queen was getting impatient. 'What are you waiting for? Take off your shirt and come here and lie down beside me. Your shirt smells of sweat and the sweat smells strongly of salt. Is it ever washed? Do you ever wash it? Take it off and come in, but quickly.'

Idemudia found his voice at last. It was a small voice. He too was almost choking, seeing and hearing the blood of Queen crashing through her veins and body and voice. The temptation was great, greater than any amount of money she ever could have offered him.

'Can I have some of the whisky?' he asked.

'Some whisky?' Queen rolled over on her side and the silhouette of her flesh was softer than the moonlight outside now.

He saw how the curve that was her ribs merged with the swelling curve that was her swelling waistline and he could see the heaving but compact breast, the lower one, rubbing against the bed.

He swallowed. 'I would like some whisky. I need some whisky.'

She raised herself up on the bed with one hand. 'What for? I thought you said the whisky smelled stronger than swine.

She saw that he was at a loss for what to say, so she said, 'It is still there in the sitting room where I left it. You can have it. You can go and take it.'

Idemudia stood up and was about to cross the room when she stopped him. 'No, wait,' she said. 'I have some bottles here, not opened yet. They are in that carton. Bring one out.'

He saw the carton and went to fetch the bottle of whisky. There were twelve bottles in the carton. He took one out and carried it back with him towards the bed. He set the bottle on the floor, beside the bed.

'The glasses are there, in the wardrobe. Bring two of the tall ones.'

Again he crossed the room to obey her.

Now he was sitting again on the chair beside the bed and she was watching him intently. 'Break the cork by unscrewing it,' she told him. 'To the right. Twist it to the right. The strap breaks and the cork comes free.'

He twisted the cork to the right and the strap snapped and the cork came free.

'You wanted a drink. Now help yourself,' she said to him. He poured out the drink until the tall glass was almost half filled.

'Mind, you are not drinking water,' she said to him. 'I don't want you to get drunk here.'

'I won't get drunk,' he retorted. 'I am a man.'

She laughed immediately. 'What a man! A man who has to drink whisky before he has the courage to lie down beside a woman? A man indeed!'

The first sip of the whisky was like mentholatum on his tongue. He tried it again by sipping it, then he threw the rest of the drink into the back of his throat and closed his eyes as he swallowed and he felt the sharp burning flames of the whisky going down his throat, all the way to his belly.

Again she laughed at him. 'You will choke yourself like that. You may not get enough wind to carry it.'

When he opened his eyes, the tears ran down both his cheeks and he began to cough.

'Didn't I tell you? Pass the bottle here and I will show you how to drink whisky.'

He passed the bottle silently to her and watched her through tearful eyes. She poured the drink into her glass and began to sip rapidly.

'It's the same thing,' he said. 'You sip it. I knocked it back just once.' He wiped the tears off his cheeks with the back of his hand.

'But I do not weep or cough as you do.'

'With practice. I guess that comes with practice.'

She handed the bottle and her glass back to him. He set both of them on the floor, beside the bed.

'Well, now that you have had your wish, you can come here and lie down. But take off that shirt.'

Again she patted the bed for him to lie down beside her.

The whisky reached his head, quickly. He felt slightly dazed. She was lying back again on the bed, he could see the two swellings that her pelvis made and desire was robust within him. And seeing her the way she was, his mind went to Adisa, to their last night, to that moment when before he had come out to this woman's house, he had struggled with Adisa on the bed and they had eyed each other and laughed afterwards. How he had loved Adisa then, how he had felt things returning to normal between them, even better than they had ever been before ...

He shook his head now, unconsciously, impercept-ibly. And she saw it.

'What are you shaking your head for?' she asked.

A foolish drunken smile appeared on his face. 'I can't,' he said. 'I can't. No, no, no. I can't.'

Queen sat bolt upright and all the soft loose lines that were her body immediately became taut. The nightdress fell away from her legs, her parted legs that were brown and straight and fair, her parted legs that were soft and warm and dark and mysterious. Now they were parted but tight, flexed.

'What can't you do?'

Idemudia stared in front of him and although he did not think of Adisa now, another thought occurred to him. And remembering that he had thought about it before, he became afraid of the woman. How was he sure that she wasn't pretending, that she wouldn't begin to scream for help the moment he got into bed with her? How could he be sure that Obofun was not somewhere in the house waiting for some sort of signal? Most rich people were dangerous, extremely dangerous and mean. Perhaps the whole plan was to discredit him in the eyes of his fellow ...

'What can't you do?' Queen asked again, break-ing into his thoughts.

'I cannot do what you want me to do,' he said.

She made him look like a coward. 'What do I want you to do?' she asked, ton-loads of scorn in her voice.

Idemudia looked her back in the eye. 'Lie down with you. I can't.'

Queen laughed. There was a lump of pain swell-ing in her heart. To be rejected, turned down by an ordinary labourer!

'I am asking you to come in,' she said command-ingly. 'Can't you forget who you are? You don't have to be afraid!'

He avoided her eyes. 'It's not that,' he said, and again his mind went to Adisa.

'What is it then?' she asked. 'Why can't you lie down with me?'

He looked her straight in the eyes. 'You have a husband and I have a wife,' he said. 'It would be adultery.'

Instantly Queen sent up a hurricane of laughter. 'It would be *what*?'

Idemudia's mind was clearer now. The fog that the first fumes of the whisky had sent to his head was gone, what remained was the momentary determination, the false courage that the whisky left in the blood. He did not want this woman. Having her would bind him to her as no other thing could. He would follow her thereafter anywhere, a complete stooge. It would be even worse than accepting the money. And it would be unfair to Adisa if he had this woman now. How could he go home afterwards and lie down on the same bed with her, pretending that nothing had happened? How could he go home with the smell of the woman upon him? He had never thought about this and he would never do it. No, never. It was wrong.

'It would be adultery,' he repeated, the foolish-sheepish-drunken smile in his eyes and lips. 'It is wrong.'

Queen had been surprised before but now she was completely stunned. 'What do you know about adultery?' she asked harshly. 'What do you know about right and wrong?'

The peevish drunken smile broadened on his face as he thought about the woman on the bed. She might be 'madam', but essentially, she was a woman, nothing else. She might own houses and the Building Company, but she was far inferior to the woman he kept in his house as his wife. Adisa would never behave in this way.

'I know what is wrong,' he said to her. 'I am not a child.'

She spat out scornfully. 'You are no better than a child.'

But there was despair, hatred and bitterness in her heart. If she had a knife then, she would have killed him, stuck it in his throat.

'You are married,' he said again, as if he had not heard her. 'You are married and I am married. That is what makes it adultery, it is wrong.'

Queen cupped her soft palms into round frantic fists. 'I told you before that you were a fool,' she said. 'Now I am doubly sure.'

Idemudia shrugged his shoulders and stood up. He towered above her, lying as she did on the bed, head raised, like a snake.

'I am going home,' he said to her.

'Do you really know what adultery means? Are you sure you know what you are doing?' she asked, a malicious look in her eyes.

Idemudia continued to smile peevishly at her.

'And you have never slept with another woman? Apart from your wife?'

He swayed lightly on his feet, the smile on his face like a lamp. 'Of course, I never have,' he said.

Queen smiled as she thought about Adisa. She had even meant to use the woman but only it never occurred to her that it would be this way. She had thought of calling her and telling her to persuade her husband to call off the strike or else ... But she hadn't done it because she knew how little influence the women usually had over their husbands, she knew that the men ...

Idemudia moved to the door.

'So you have never slept with another woman?' Queen asked again, and Idemudia stopped and looked at her and said nothing. Again Queen smiled, but there was venom in her tongue when she asked, 'And her?'

The question caught him like a blow. He looked at her searchingly. 'What do you mean?'

'I mean what I asked. I mean Adisa, your wife.'

Suddenly his heart was like a thatched roof on fire with the dry harmattan wind blowing. He had got the message for this job through Adisa. Queen had sent Adisa to tell him. What did she know about Adisa to make her look so triumphant?

'Well?'

'Well, what?'

'I asked you a question.'

She sat now on the bed. 'I asked you if your wife Adisa had never slept with another man.'

Something made him answer the questions as she asked them. 'My wife has never slept with another man,' he said slowly, the sudden fear evident in his voice.

'Are you sure? Have you ever asked her?' The smile smoked on her face like a dirty paraffin lamp.

He tried to answer her with all the dignity he could muster. 'We are poor, madam, yes, very poor, but my wife does not sell herself.'

Queen fell back on the bed. Now she was laughing. It was a bitter laugh, insinuating, damaging. 'If I were you, I would go home and ask her, not take things for granted.'

She sat up suddenly to see the expression on his face: a hurt, doubtful look, from the swelling lump of pain in his heart. And she was glad, immensely happy that she had been able to reach him where it hurt him. The bastard, she thought. The cheap stupid bastard!

'Oh yes, I would rush home and ask her, if I were

you,' she laughed again from the bed, all her body writhing with her laughter. 'Ask her about last Saturday evening at the the Samson and Delilah. With my own husband. My own husband! Now you can get out of my house! Get out of my house and do not appear any more on my site. The police will be waiting for you there. Clear out! Get out!' Her voice had risen and she was shouting.

Chapter 22

There was a hollowness in the pit of his stomach and murder in his heart as he fled down the steps of Queen's house. He rushed along the street cursing in his heart and head.

'I will kill her for this!' he swore hoarsely. 'Prostitute! Harlot!' he cursed. 'I will kill her!' His voice trembled and he tightened his hands, flexed all his muscles, like one man strangling another.

Now everything fell into place, her absence from the play on that Saturday evening, her behaviour at home, her nervousness. He understood everything clearly. She was guilty. There was no need to ask her. And he hurried, ran, breathing heavily and swearing.

The night was already far gone and the moon hung to the edges of the sky now, precariously, a dirty, old warped half-piece of lemon. Soon it would die out altogether, this candlelight of the sky. The sky would blacken, then grey. And as the sky greyed, the cocks would wait restlessly around the houses, on top of the thatched roofs, picking their feathers, waiting for the first incense of dawny brightness. Then they would crow all over the city, all over the land, as the grey sky gradually lifted the sun for the day from the womb of the earth and hoisted it like a flag above the earth.

Now, at this time of night, Owode Street was quiet and deserted except for him and his thoughts, rushing along the dirty-red quiet street making a great noise and swearing to kill his wife.

He entered their room with the same great noise, he banged the door before probing for the light switch against the rough plaster and flatness of the wall. He pressed the switch down and the electric bulb that always burned like the yellow of traffic lights broke light upon the room in a small explosion.

He saw her. She was sleeping, far gone in a deep sleep that was fully dreamy. She lay on the bed, her long slim body stretched out like a bright red ribbon, her hand, the right one also flung out across the full breadth of the bed and because the bed was narrow, the hand suspended on the outside. Adisa did not turn on the bed even with the violent banging of the door, the burning of the yellow light, not even with the noisy violence of his breathing.

She lay still, sleeping.

He crossed straight to the bed and stood above her. He wanted to wake her by slapping her face repeatedly. His dark shadow eclipsed her from her body upwards. All he had to do was grip her by the throat, tightly, strongly and choke the confession out of her. Yes, grip her by the throat and strangle her.

He hesitated because he thought he heard the noise of feet just outside the window. He listened intently, stalling even his own breathing. There were no footsteps, all was quiet but for his own resumed belaboured breathing. He stood there and thought briefly, quickly. The night was too quiet for what he wanted to do. He would wait until the early hours of the morning when the dawn brought its first noises. Yes, he would wait.

Now, however, he must drink more whisky. The one he had taken in Queen's place was still strong in his blood; he had a dull ache in his head and heart. But he must drink some more now to kill those pains. He must drink. He went to the corner of the room and ripped one of the cartons open. The bottles were all lined up there, like those in Queen's bedroom. He carried one of the bottles to the bed and broke the cork, still standing. Then he threw his head backwards and let the jet of the bright golden yellow whisky spurt into the back of his throat. He felt the sharp burning taste of the whisky flaming down his gullet. He stopped and threw his head forward again, holding the bottle towards the bulb hanging from the ceiling. More than one quarter of the bottle was gone.

He smiled darkly and sat on the edge of the bed, putting the bottle on the floor. Then again, he reached for the bottle, but this time he saw that there were two of them, not one. He missed it and his hand knocked the bottle sideways. The golden whisky spurted out of the bottle on to the floor. Cursing, he grabbed the bottle at the bottom, held it up again, his head thrown backwards, the yellow, sharp, burning whisky running down in a steady flame into the pit of his stomach.

He set the bottle down again and smiled. He felt tired and worn out. He must sleep now to wake early in the morning for what he had to do.

He leaned heavily on the bed and the bed creaked and groaned. He looked back at Adisa on the bed. He smiled as he saw the tiny movement that her eyelids made as they fluttered, briefly, preparatory to her coming wakefulness. He growled in his throat. She lifted her hand up and covered her eyes to shade the harsh glare of the light.

'So you are back!' she yawned.

He grumbled deeply in his throat and averted his face because his eyes ran with the tears from the whisky.

'You were away so long!' she said.

He looked at her now through his tears. He looked at her on the bed and his voice was soft—harsh—hoarse and cracked. 'I had to. Obofun kept me!'

'Obofun?' she asked quickly, still keeping her hand on her eyes.

'Yes,' he said. 'Obofun, the man you slept with, last Saturday evening at the Samson . . .'

She caught her breath quickly, frowned and made to get up from the bed. But he pushed her back. She lay still, trembling.

'She is silent!' he cried in his heart. 'Silent! She is guilty! Oh God, how come? How?'

He leaned over her, his teeth set, his eyes half-shut and drunken, his breathing laboured, heavy and sharp. His heart beat violently and his hands trembled as he rested the sharp edge of his elbow against her, on the tender flesh of her throat.

Adisa opened her eyes now, widely, and they were dilated and wild with the deep terror that was clearly written there. 'What is it?' she coughed and choked and struggled to lift his elbow away from where it rested on the bones of her throat. 'Idemudia!' she cried and choked. 'Idemudia! Wait! Please! Idemu . . . !'

He did not answer her but stared at her face that was beginning to bead with sweat and her eyes that were wild with her terror and anguish and suddenly, something in him gave way and it was as if a bucketful of cold, icy water had been thrown on his face and the tears started to his eyes.

'Why didn't you tell me?' he cried, and lifted the sharp ridge of his elbow away from her throat. 'Why? Oh God, why didn't you tell me?'

Adisa moved away from him and struggled up the bed until she had her back against the rough wall. Her face was wet now with her tears as she felt her throat with both her hands and her face still had some of the shock and terror and anguish plainly written there.

Idemudia would not look at her but buried his face in the bowl of his hands. 'Oh my God!' he cried to himself. 'Why didn't she tell me? Why? He would not ask why she had done it because he understood very clearly now. And because he understood, he realised how utterly rash and foolish and unreasonable he had been in his anger.

Hadn't he sold his own blood so that they would not starve? And wasn't that a sacrifice, this frequent selling of pints of his own blood? Yes, he said to himself, a sacrifice as great or perhaps even less than the one Adisa had made on his behalf. And how could he have been so blind as not to have seen that if she had done it, then she would have done it only for his sake? Only for my sake, he thought, and that makes it a sacrifice more than anything else.

But then, he reasoned within himself, she would have told me, confessed to me instead of ... He stopped because again, he understood. He hadn't told her about the times he went out to sell his blood. He had always felt ashamed about it afterwards and yet he knew that Adisa had known about it although she never discussed it. 'Yes,' he said to himself. 'She couldn't have told me. No, she really couldn't have. And to think that ...' No, he must not think about it. He had been wrong to have attacked her, still more wrong to have thought of ... No! He didn't want to remember this, ever. It had been a fever just as the illness that had taken him to the hospital had been a fever. And they were both over. What remained now was for him to show her that he understood, that he would hold no malice against her.

He lifted his face from the bowl of his hands and looked at her and seeing the streamlets that the tears made on her face, he wanted to stretch out his hands to wipe them out. But he was afraid that he would perhaps frighten her, so instead, he leaned back towards her and buried his head against the warmth that was her bosom.

Also in Longman African Classics

Fools and other stories

Njabulo Ndebele

Winner of the Noma Award 1983

'And when victims spit upon victims should they not be called fools? Fools of darkness.'

A taut, lyrical and compelling collection of stories, vividly bringing to life the black urban locations of apartheid South Africa.

These are rich and enchanting stories told with the warmth of childhood memory: of the adulation of a child for his trumpet-playing uncle; a teenager's trial of endurance to prove himself worthy of his street-gang; a child's rebellion against his parents snobbish aspirations.

And the title story, *Fools*, tells with painful intensity of events sparked by a meeting between a disgraced teacher, haunted by the impotence of his present life, and a student activist railing against those those who do not share his sense of urgency.

The author believes 'we have given away too much of our real and imaginative lives to the oppressor'. These beautiful award-winning stories of township life in all its complexity are his answer.

'Njabulo Ndebele's first book represents the kind of beginning in fiction that will prove to have altered the contours of our literature ... His storytelling is full-fleshed and elegant ... of thrilling significance'.

Lionel Abrahams *Sesame*

'Brings with it an exhilarating current of fresh air ... solid, vibrant prose'.

E'skia Mphahlele *The Sowetan*

ISBN 0 582 78621 5

Hungry Flames and other Black South African Short Stories

Edited by Mbulelo Mzamane

From the bare concrete of the crowded prisons to the carpeted drawing rooms of the new African middle class, these fifteen short stories by South Africa's finest Black writers paint an urgent and vital picture of contemporary South Africa.

These stories rank with those of Steinbeck and Hemingway in their honest portraits of working men and women in all their strengths and in all their weaknesses — all of them living in the shadow of the apartheid state.

Ove fifty years of Black South African writing in English is represented in this collection. A critical introduction describes the evolution of writing from the pioneers, such as R.R.R. Dhlomo and Sol Plaatje, through the urban 'jazz' style of the fifties to the more politicised Black Consciousness writers of the Sharpeville and Soweto eras.

The editor, Mbulelo Mzamane, is himself a distinguished writer of short stories and is the author of *My Cousin Comes to Jo'burg* (1982) and of *The Children of Soweto* (1982). He now teaches in the Department of English, Ahmadu Bello University, Zaria in Nigeria.

ISBN 0 582 78590 1

The Last Duty

Isidore Okpewho

Winner of the African Arts Prize for Literature

Against the backcloth of a violent and murderous civil war six individuals linked by conflicting ties of honour, greed, lust, fear and love play out a drama of their own that is no less bloody than the war itself. The resolution of the drama has the cathartic force of classical tragedy as the individuals recognise their final duty to reclaim their self-respect from the quagmire of corruption and betrayal into which they have all been led.

'*The Last Duty* is a highly sophisticated and successfully achieved piece of work ... an imaginative reconstruction of the experience of the Nigerian Civil War. In its deep moral concern and in its technical accomplishment, *The Last Duty* has earned an honourable place in the development of African literature'.

British Book News

'C'est un beau livre'　　　　　*Afrique Contemporaine*

'A strong and original voice in Nigerian literature'
Books Abroad

ISBN 0 582 78535 9

Scarlet Song

Mariama Ba

Translated by Dorothy S. Blair

Mariama Ba's first novel So Long a Letter was the winner of the Noma Award in 1980. In this her second and, tragically, last novel she displays all the same virtues of warmth and crusading zeal for women's rights that won her so many admirers for her earlier work.

Mireille, daughter of a French diplomat and Ousmane, son of a poor Muslim family in Senegal, are two childhood sweethearts forced to share their love in secret. Their marriage shocks and dismays both sets of parents, but it soon becomes clear that their youthful optimism and love offer a poor defence against the pressures of society. As Ousmane is lured back to his roots, Mireille is left humiliated, isolated and alone.

The tyranny of tradition and chauvinism is brilliantly exposed in this passionate plea for human understanding. The author's sympathetic insights into the condition of women deserve recognition throughout the world.

ISBN 0 582 78595 2

Tales of Amadou Koumba

Birago Diop

Translated by Dorothy S. Blair

Retold with wit and charm, this classic collection of folk tales by the 'poet of the African bush' stands comparison with the fables of Aesop and La Fontaine. Originally told to Diop by his family's *griot,* these tales take us back and forth between the surreal world of the miraculous and the profound reality of African daily life.

'The poetic nature of Birago Diop's writing, in its primitive majesty, is in direct line from the Griots and the oral tradition'.

Jean-Paul Sartre

'Everything in this subtle and perceptive work is a delight'. *Présence Africaine*

'This show of African wisdom, constitutes, without a shadow of doubt, the finest prose work in our African literature'.

Afrique en Marche

ISBN 0 582 78587 1